Secrets

OF A

Viscount

ROSE GORDON

D1569056

SECRETS OF A VISCOUNT

Copyright © 2013 C. Rose Gordon

Cover image copyright Lily Smith

All rights reserved.

Parchment & Plume, LLC

www.parchmentandplume.com

Chapter One

June 1812
Gateshead, England

A sharp, scraping sound rent the chilly night's air, jolting Isabelle Knight awake from her dreamless sleep.

Isabelle's green eyes sprang open and her fingers clutched the bed sheets.

Another loud screech from the direction of her only bedroom window broke the deafening silence that had once again fallen over the room.

Her heart hammering wildly in her chest, she forced her eyes to the window. A billowed curtain of cream and lace and the tops of a pair of black leather boots was all she could see through the dim moonlight. The blood in her veins sped up, but her body was still paralyzed. Someone was breaking into her room and she was too frightened to do a single thing about it except remain still with her eyes locked in terror at the curtains.

"Are you ready?" a male voice whispered in the dark.

Relief flooded Isabelle's body. She knew that voice. It belonged to her neighbor Sebastian Gentry, Viscount Belgrave. Isabelle and her sister Rachel had known Sebastian since they were children. However, just because she'd known him nearly all her life and trusted him entirely, did not explain why he was in her room, nor why was he asking if she were ready.

"Ready?" she queried, sitting up in bed and instinctively putting her hand over her chest to keep him from seeing any part of her that he shouldn't.

Sebastian heaved a heavy sigh. "Have you changed your mind?"

"Changed my mind about what?"

"The elopement," he burst out.

Shock, followed by anger, filled Isabelle. Rachel and Sebastian had made plans for an elopement? And they hadn't told her. Of course they hadn't told her. It was an elopement. That was the point. Elopements were about sneaking off and getting married without telling anyone.

She gazed at the outline of Sebastian's broad form by her window; she had only a second to make a decision that would alter both of their lives in more ways than she could even comprehend at the moment. But the truth was, she was the daughter of a country squire in the most unpopulated part of England. Her prospects were slim at best. If she didn't wish to become a spinster, or worse, marry a man thrice her age, there was no need to question the good fortune that had just befallen her.

"I've not changed my mind," she whispered, hoping he hadn't yet realized he'd entered the wrong room. "Why don't you go wait on the balcony? I need to grab something, then I'll be ready."

"Very well," he said crisply. He stepped through the open window to wait for her on the balcony.

Isabelle sat still for a minute. Did he not want to marry Rachel, either? His tone would suggest as much. With a shrug, she pushed to her stocking-clad feet and slid them into a pair of black slippers she kept under the edge of the bed, then grabbed her biggest hooded cloak and put it on. Though her room had been so dark all she could see of him was his outline, and she doubted he could see any more of her than that, too, she had no doubt that outside where the moon was illuminating the hillside, he'd be able to see her and know right away he'd fetched the wrong sister. That was the last thing she wanted to have happen.

Satisfied she could both walk and conceal her identity at the same time, Isabelle made her way to the window and tentatively allowed Sebastian to help her through.

"How do we get down?" she asked, scowling at the trellis. Not that she was scared to climb down it, mind you. She'd climb to the top of the Great Pyramids on her hands and knees if it meant she could have someone as young, virile, honest and sincere as Sebastian for her husband. The problem was more of how she'd climb down the trellis without having to remove her cloak and expose her identity.

"Not to worry," he said, breaking into her thoughts. He pointed to the far end of the balcony. "To my good fortune I passed a ladder as I came through the garden."

Isabelle nodded. A ladder would be much easier to navigate with her cloak than the trellis. "All right, then. I'll just be on my way and wait for you at the bottom."

Sebastian's large, tanned hand covered hers just as her fingers closed around the top of the ladder. "I think not. I'll go down first, that way I can hold the ladder steady for you as you come down."

Pursing her lips and biting her tongue so not to make the retort that was waiting on the tip of her tongue, thus giving away her identity, she politely nodded her head and stepped away from the ladder. The exact thing Rachel would do.

As soon as Isabelle was far enough away from the ladder to give Sebastian ample room to climb down, he swung his leg over and descended the ladder so quickly she'd have missed it had she blinked. "All right, Rachel," he called. He grabbed onto the sides of the ladder to keep it from moving. "Come on down. Nice and slow."

Isabelle walked up to the ladder and halted. "Can you turn around, please?"

"Why?"

"Because if you're standing beneath the ladder you'll see right up my nightrail," she stated primly.

He snorted. "In a matter of hours I'll be seeing everything you have under that nightrail anyway. And more."

Her face grew hot. She'd forgotten that little detail. If they were about to elope, they were also about to have marital relations. Unfortunately, her mother had never actually informed her of all the details, but she'd surmised from whispers she'd overheard between the servants that it involved both parties removing their clothes. She shivered. She was only sixteen and regarded Sebastian as nothing more than a friend, for her father wouldn't allow it any other way, often reminding her of her place in this world—which was not at the side of a titled gentleman, for he would never return her love and affection. Therefore, there was no love or affection between them, perhaps a measure of adoration that she went to great pains to conceal. Instead they had friendship. And friendship would be a very acceptable foundation for a marriage, in her opinion. But still, the idea of *him* seeing up her nightrail—both now and then again in a few hours—made her face burn like it had caught fire.

"Are you having second thoughts?" Sebastian asked from the bottom of the ladder.

Did he want her to have second thoughts? Or more specifically, did he want Rachel to be having second thoughts and cry off? Perhaps that's why he wanted to go down first. It made sense to her. He could have held the ladder still from the top. He'd wanted to go down first in order to find one more way to scare her out of going through with this.

Steeling her spine, she carelessly threw her leg over the edge of the balcony railing (clutching the top of the ladder for dear life at the same time), and in the most disgraceful and unladylike way possible, descended the ladder, stopping only briefly three rungs from the bottom to make sure her hood still covered her face adequately.

Chapter Two

Sebastian was shocked. Absolutely shocked. First, he was in shock that he'd allowed Rachel Knight to talk him into stealing her away in the night to avoid marrying her father's senile second cousin Lord Yourke, a match her father had somehow managed to arrange for her. But then when the shock wore off, he'd come up with a plan: he'd purposely frighten her into crying off. Not that he didn't like Rachel, he did. But only as a friend, and even that was questionable at times. However, for as temperamental as his feelings were for her as a friend, he liked her far better than her younger sister: Belle.

At sixteen, Belle was three years his junior and had grown up following him like a second shadow when he was a boy. Rachel had too, but her presence didn't bother him nearly as much. At least Rachel knew her place most of the time and acted like a lady. Belle was stubborn, willful, and so blunt she'd tell Prinny himself he needed to mind what he ate because he was in danger of growing as round as he was tall. Quite frankly, Belle lived up to the nickname he'd given her when she was only eight, and he eleven. She was stubborn, loud, and obnoxious. Decidedly not the kind of young lady a gentleman wanted to make his wife. Not if he didn't wish to be publicly embarrassed and ridiculed, that is.

When Rachel had so carelessly climbed onto the ladder and made her way down, Sebastian would have sworn it was Belle in all of her defiance on that ladder. If he'd not glimpsed the outline of her bosom while in her dimly lit room earlier, he'd have demanded she remove that cloak as soon as she reached the bottom to confirm he'd retrieved the right sister. But he hadn't because he knew he had the right sister. See, Rachel had plump, lush breasts, and Belle's were nearly nonexistent.

They were there of course, but not nearly as prominent as Rachel's. It hadn't been until a year or so ago that he'd even been

5

aware Belle *had* breasts. And the only reason he found out then was because he'd accompanied them to go see a traveling circus and some stumbling drunk knocked into her and Sebastian had reached out to right her and accidentally brushed her soft breast with his forearm. If not for that, he'd still think she was as flat as a chessboard due to the way her gowns hung off her in the front.

Shaking his head to dispel all thoughts of Belle and her blasted breasts, he helped Rachel into the carriage and plopped down on the seat across from her.

He hadn't planned to marry so young. But for some reason he still couldn't place, he'd softened to Rachel's chronic pleas and agreed to haul her off, and like any gentleman, he intended to keep his word—even if he didn't want to and had to drink half a barrel of whisky to force himself to go through with it. He closed his eyes for a moment to let his mind clear. He hadn't really consumed so much whisky before coming to collect her, but he'd consumed some. He had to. Any gentleman of only nineteen would have to be at least partially foxed in order to willingly hand over his freedom.

He took a deep breath, opened his eyes and gave the roof of the carriage a sharp tap. "Why don't you take your cloak off now?"

Rachel shook her head.

"Suit yourself," he said with a shrug. Leaning his head back, he closed his eyes again to take a little nap, not sure if he wanted it to sober him up a little more or just pass the time. He'd never cared one way or the other about living so far north. Sure the winters were bitter, but other than that, he saw no difference between living in the northern or southern part of the country. However, just now, he was rather glad he lived so far north because they were only an hour or two from Gretna Green.

Sebastian jolted awake what felt like only minutes later. He blinked his eyes and waited as Abrams, the coachman, came around to open the door for him.

He descended then reached up to help Rachel and nearly rolled his eyes. She still wore her blasted cloak wrapped around herself as if exposing one inch of her would bring her harm.

"Here we are," he said easily, leading Rachel up to the door of the smithy's shop. Frowning, he took out his pocket watch. It was five. The smithy should be out here waiting for him. As a precaution in the event that Rachel became as stubborn as Belle— and why wouldn't she be when faced with marriage to a man who had more wrinkles than a prune and breath more foul than the slums of London—he'd sent Fowler, his valet, to make arrangements with the smithy so he and Rachel wouldn't have to track one down at such an absurd hour.

"Milord," a stout man a few shops down the street called out.

"Yes?"

"I's to do ye's wed'in, milord," the man said with a large, nearly toothless grin.

Sebastian gave him a curt nod and nudged Rachel to walk in the man's direction, simultaneously suppressing a shudder at the man's scraggly appearance. He'd sent Fowler here with three pounds; surely he could have paid a nicer-looking man to officiate.

"Aye, the bride," the toothless man said, ushering Rachel inside his shop.

Walking behind Rachel as she crossed the threshold, Sebastian saw her tense. After a quick glance around the shop, he knew why. Dirt and filth was everywhere. The dirt floor had turned to mud from the water dripping from who knows what above the ceiling. Rusted anvils and hammers littered the makeshift unsteady worktables, as did an assortment of other broken and poorly cared for tools. The back window was covered in some sort of greasy sludge so thick that even if the sun had been up, there wouldn't have been a single ray coming through from back there.

Trying not to cringe himself, Sebastian fisted his hands and shoved them into his pockets, silently vowing not to remove them until they were safely out of this shop. Then he took his spot next to Rachel who still wore that blasted cloak, now drawn so tightly around her face he couldn't see a single facial feature. Not that he blamed her. He wanted as much of his skin covered as was possible, too. Had this been a serious wedding and a love match, he'd have marched her out of the room immediately. Instead, he nodded to her.

In less than twenty seconds the ceremony started.

Sebastian had always assumed these Scotland weddings were informal and lasted about two minutes. He was wrong. Apparently this toothless smithy missed his calling in life and would have preferred a life in the ministry.

Pulling out a Bible, the smithy started flapping his jaw about the sanctity of marriage and other such nonsense that Sebastian nearly snorted at. If this ministering smithy really knew the reason behind this marriage, he likely wouldn't be performing the ceremony, Sebastian thought wryly.

To take his mind off the sermonette he was hearing, Sebastian let his eyes wander around the dingy room again. A few minutes later, he mumbled something akin to "I do" when the smithy paused in his speech for a few seconds.

Vaguely listening to the smithy as he continued on with the ceremony, his mind started drifting to what would be happening *after* the ceremony. On the way to the smithy's shop he'd spotted an inn. It didn't look too terribly grand, but it would be suitable. Though he might not be overly fond of Rachel nor have given much thought to what she concealed under her clothes, only a blind man wouldn't find her at least mildly physically attractive with her small facial features, auburn hair and flawless skin. Besides, for a man of nineteen, who'd lived under strict orders from his father that hadn't allowed him much freedom to sample the wares of those in London, but kept him mostly secluded to the high country with no suitable options, he was certainly ready to begin his mastery of the female body.

Blinking to rid himself of those mental images the thought provoked so not to give himself away, he started listening to the smithy more carefully just in time to hear him announce they were now man and wife and he could kiss his bride.

Under any other circumstances, Sebastian would have pushed the hood of Rachel's cloak off her face in order to kiss her. However, his desire not to remove his hands from his pockets and touch anything in this dirty shop was so strong he couldn't force himself to unveil his bride, so to speak.

Leaning toward her, he gave her a quick peck on her surprisingly soft lips before turning back to the smithy and curling his fingers into the fabric lining of his pockets at the idea he was about to have to grab the man's grubby pen and sign the book he'd opened.

The smithy first held his blackened quill out to Rachel, and before her trembling fingers could close around the stem, Sebastian took it. "I'll go first," he murmured, scribbling down his name on the register. When he was finished signing, he held onto the quill and used his other hand to reach into his breast pocket and pull out his handkerchief. Wrapping the quill in his handkerchief, he handed it to Rachel.

She quickly nodded once and her shaking fingers took the quill from him, her eyes never meeting his. Or if they had, he couldn't tell because of the darkness that the cloak created around her face.

As soon as she had the quill and started scratching out her name, Sebastian grabbed his other handkerchief and wiped off the dirt the quill had left behind on his fingers. "Finished?" he asked inanely when Rachel had finished scratching out her name.

She nodded again without looking in his direction and extended the quill back to the smithy.

"Shall we?" he asked, offering her his arm.

Rachel's delicate fingers closed around his arm and she allowed him to escort her out of the shop.

"I don't know about you, but I feel I need a bath," Sebastian said lightly to his new bride a few minutes later after they'd entered the boarding house. They could have just gone home. But what was the rush? They were married now and going home would only lead to questions and uncomfortable conversations. No need to rush home to that when one could enjoy his new bride for a day or two first.

Sebastian arranged for a room and ordered a bath and breakfast tray brought up to their room while Rachel fidgeted next to him. He smiled. "Don't be so nervous," he teased, nudging her with his elbow. "It's not as bad as your mother explained it, I promise. But you will have to take that blasted cloak off."

"I know," she whispered, causing him to shake his head. They were married now; her reputation was not going to suffer by being seen with her own husband at an inn.

The innkeeper handed Sebastian a key and spouted off a few simple directions before the couple left the lobby in search of their room.

"Here we are." Sebastian slipped the brass key into the lock. He quickly unlocked the door and swung it open to reveal a spacious bedchamber. "Will you take that ugly cloak off now?" he asked as soon as they were both inside the room.

Rachel didn't have a chance to respond when a knock rattled the door.

A maid carrying an elaborate breakfast tray and two footmen carrying pails of water came in and set up a warm bath and nice breakfast. Tipping the trio handsomely, Sebastian dismissed them and stared at the steaming tub, then at the breakfast. "You've been awful silent today, Rachel," Sebastian mused. "How about you make the decision, eat first or bathe first."

"I'll bathe. You eat," she whispered.

He blinked. He'd only attended a dinner theater once in London a year ago and swore never to go again. But this kind of dinner theater he could do every day. "All right," he said huskily, then went over to the table and fixed himself a plate.

"What are you doing?" Rachel asked quietly when she realized he fully intended to watch her bathe while he breakfasted.

"Don't mind me. I'll not bother you. Just go on and bathe."

An unladylike noise formed somewhere in Rachel's throat and caused Sebastian to stiffen immediately. That was a sound very similar to the one Belle made when she was vexed. He shuddered. Perhaps his wife was more like her wretched sister than he'd originally thought. No matter. He could handle an occasional slip in private. At least Rachel would never make such a horrendous noise in public.

With a shrug and another half-growl, half-grunt, Rachel marched over to the far corner of the room and grabbed the edge of

SECRETS OF A VISCOUNT

what appeared to be a folded dressing screen and started dragging it across the floor.

"Oh, come now, you don't have to do that," he protested jovially as she settled the screen in front of the tub to block his view of her.

Rachel's only answer was tossing her cloak over the top of the screen in such a way it covered the crack in the screen between two of the panels. A second later, her nightrail came to rest on top of the other crack.

Sebastian chuckled at her gesture. "That's not going to keep me from peeking," he teased, quietly padding over to the screen. He grabbed the side of her cloak that was hanging on his side of the screen and pulled it off just in time to catch a small glimpse of one of her legs stepping into her steaming bathwater. He snatched down her nightrail and peeked again from that angle, being rewarded with a very generous view of one of her pert, pink-tipped breasts before she shifted in a way that no matter which crack he peeked through all he saw was her back or if he looked over her shoulder he could see her feet at the end of the tub.

Small amounts of water splashed over the side of the tub as his new bride scrubbed her body and washed her long cinnamon-colored hair. Sebastian stood entranced behind the screen as he watched her fingers work the lather into her silky hair. He had no idea she had so much of it. Perhaps tomorrow when she took her bath again she'd allow him to wash it for her.

"Can I bring you a towel?" He winced at how uneven his voice sounded to his own ears.

A wet hand reached out from behind the screen and waved in anticipation for him to hand her a towel.

Sebastian smiled and picked up the rolled up towel that rested on the stool right next to him. He extended it to her and just as her fingertips touched the end of the soft garment, he pulled it back, grinning at the way her empty fingers closed around nothing but air. Her hand flipped over with her palm facing up and she wiggled her fingers. "My towel, please," she said softly.

"Come and get it," he encouraged, bringing the towel up and

briefly touching the bottom of her hand with it.

"I don't want to play games, Sebastian," she whispered.

He frowned. Why was she still whispering? And more importantly, why didn't she want to play games and have fun? This was their honeymoon, after all. They may be married now, but they were both still young.

"Fine, you can have your precious towel," he said, tossing the towel over the screen.

"Ooof," she squealed when the towel flew over the screen and landed on her head.

"Not what you expected," he teased, poking his head completely around the screen and eliciting a little scream out of Belle. *Belle?* He blinked. "What the blazes are you doing here?" he demanded, reaching for her arm to guide her out from behind the screen.

"Trying to dry off," she replied smugly, bringing the towel up to cover the front of her body.

Sebastian closed his eyes again, more tightly this time. Surely he was mistaken. He had to be. He married Rachel, not Belle. He'd gone into Rachel's room, he was sure of it. This all just had to be a figment of his imagination. He'd barely slept last night, opting instead to drink to his final night of freedom. Then he'd gone to her house and fetched Rachel, then traveled to Scotland and been married in a dirty smithy shop. That was a lot for a man of nineteen. Perhaps his brain was so muddled from all of those activities, or the after effects of the whisky, he was seeing things. He opened one brown eye and looked at the creature in front of him. No he was not mistaken. Isabelle Knight with her dark red hair, emerald eyes, bow shaped lips and stubborn attitude stood before him glaring in his direction as if he were the one in the wrong.

"Once again, what are you doing here?" he asked tightly.

"I already told you. I'm drying off."

"I know that," he bit out. "Why are you here?"

"Because we just got married," she said as if he were a young lad and she his governess.

"Why?" he growled. "Why did you do this?"

"Do what?" she asked, blinking those sparkling green orbs at him.

Sebastian jammed his fisted hands into his pockets so not to give into the temptation to throttle her. "Get dressed. We're leaving."

"Leaving?" she echoed.

"We're going home."

"You mean to Cross Pointe?"

He shook his head. "No. Well, yes. *I'll* be going home to Cross Pointe. You'll be going back to your parents' estate."

Belle crossed her arms under her bare breasts in defiance, causing her towel to drop to the floor. "Absolutely not. I am your wife. I will not be living with my parents any longer."

Snorting, Sebastian took his hands out of his pockets and crossed his arms. "You're not my wife."

"I beg to differ," she said sternly, her eyes not straying from his. "I just said vows, and I do believe you repeated them, too."

"No. I said my vows to Rachel, not you."

Belle blanched and for a brief second Sebastian felt remorse for what he'd just said. But her next words washed all those feelings away and allowed irritation to take its place, making him harden his resolve not to keep her as his wife.

"Odd that, I don't seem to remember her being there," she countered, her tone full of typical Belle sarcasm. She cocked her head to the side and tapped one long, slender finger against her chin. "No. I was the one you said those vows to. Therefore, you are my husband, not hers. Which means I shall be spending my nights at Cross Pointe from now on."

"I wouldn't wager on it, were I you," he said harshly. "Get dressed."

"No," she said, not moving an inch.

Sebastian stepped forward. "Belle," he began with a calm he didn't feel, "we need to go. It's barely seven now. I can have you back to your estate before your parents even find out you were missing. Now let's go."

ROSE GORDON

She knit her brows. "Why would we do that?"

Blowing out a deep breath, Sebastian scooped up her nightrail and held it out for her. "Surely you know we're not really married."

"Yes, we are," she countered, refusing to take her nightrail from him.

A bitter laugh passed his lips. "No, we're not. As I told you earlier, I said those vows to Rachel. You're not Rachel. Therefore, *we're* not married."

"What are you talking about? I was there. You said the vows to *me*. You kissed *me*. I was your bride!" she burst out.

"I may have kissed you," he conceded softly. "And I may have said, 'I do,' in front of you. But not *to* you. Actually, now that I think about it, I'm not married to her, either." Relief flooded through him. Blessedly, he still had his freedom.

"No, you're not married to her," Belle agreed. "But you are married to me."

He shook his head, trying not to smile. "No, I'm not. I went into that ceremony with who I thought was Rachel and came out with you. I don't know what kind of scheme you two are devising, but it didn't work."

"How so?"

"Because I said my vows to who I thought was her, and turned out to be you. But you forget, even a proxy bride doesn't sign the register. Either her male representative does, or she does at another time. That's where you made your mistake. You signed the register in her stead and legally you can't."

A grin as big as the English Channel spread across Belle's face. "It is you who is mistaken, my lord."

"What are you talking about?" he asked, an eerie chill settling over him.

She shrugged. "Perhaps you were right. I should get dressed." She snatched her nightrail from his limp fingers and pulled it over her head then she walked to the other side of the screen and came back with her slippers and stockings. "I'm ready to go now, Sebastian." She grabbed her discarded cloak and tossed it over her arms. "However, while we're still here, I think we should run over to the smithy's together."

"Capital idea," he agreed, ignoring the dangerous gleam in her eyes. She was up to something, he could tell. Her eyes always told on her when she was up to mischief. They'd sparkle and the edges would crinkle ever-so-slightly.

Settling their bill and returning the key to the innkeeper, Sebastian caught a quick view of Belle getting into his carriage. What had she and her sister been thinking trapping him into marriage this way? He should have known something was off when she insisted on wearing that blasted cloak. Well, he'd play the fool no more. They'd go to the smithy's where he'd explain the situation and get their names scratched off the register. Then he'd take Belle home and never have anything to do with either of them ever again. He'd never expected Rachel capable of doing something so stupid. Belle, yes. But not Rachel. Now he knew differently. He now knew Rachel was just as undignified as her sister if she'd agreed to participate in this nonsense.

He ground his teeth. Those two had better pray nobody ever finds out about this. Not only would it bring scandal and embarrassment to his name, but it would absolutely ruin both of their reputations. Not that he thought for a second the pair didn't deserve such a thing.

"Back to the smithy's," he called to Abrams before climbing up into the coach.

"You shouldn't scowl so much, Sebastian. It's going to leave some unflattering marks on your handsome face."

Sebastian purposely deepened his scowl at her words. "Perhaps you shouldn't concern yourself with my looks. You'll not be around to see them as I age."

"We'll see," she said smugly, slipping a pin into her hair.

The coach jolted to a stop outside of the smithy's shop. Sebastian was half out of the coach before Abrams set the brake.

"Wait for me, please."

A moment of temporarily remembering his gentleman's honor, or perhaps insanity, led Sebastian to grant her wish and fall back onto the seat. He crossed his arms and leaned his head back against the squabs, waiting impatiently as Belle continued to haphazardly pin her mess of hair onto the top of her head. "You look fine," he lied when he could take it no longer.

Belle pursed her lips. "Well, if you don't mind taking your bride out when she looks affright, why should I?"

"Excellent. Let's go." He climbed out of the carriage and reached his hand up to help her down. He may not like her and he certainly didn't wish to be her husband, but he still could afford to show her the courtesy she deserved.

"Dinna 'spect ta see ye 'gain," the smithy said, waggling his eyebrows as Sebastian and Belle crossed the threshold.

"Yes, well, circumstances have changed," Sebastian said uneasily.

Belle waved her hand through the air. "What my husband is trying to say is that he'd like to have a peek at your registry, if he might."

Sebastian smiled thinly and waited for the smithy to get his grubby book from where it rested on the table in the corner.

"Still canna believe yer mar'ed?" the smithy jested as he brought the book over and opened it to the most recent page. His keen eyes followed his dirty finger down the page until he reached the last line. "Here it is. Seb'as'ten Gen'ry an' Is'belle Kni't."

"What?" Sebastian gasped, reaching for the offending book. His eyes read the words. Once. Twice. Thrice. It couldn't be. It was. Anger surged through him and his face flamed. "This can't be. It just can't."

Belle flashed him a triumphant smile. "It is."

"No, it's not," he growled. "It may be your name, but I said those vows to Rachel."

"No, you said them to me," she replied, her voice sugary sweet.

"I don't remember hearing your name," he snapped. "Trust me, if I had, I'd have run out of here faster than a man walking across a bed of hot coals."

"Wot's ta be de pro'lem?" the smithy asked, prying the book

from Sebastian's death-grip.

"She tricked me," Sebastian spat. "Scratch those names off. We're not married."

"Ah, but ye is," the smithy countered with a smile. "It says so righ' here."

"No," Sebastian argued. "I did not agree to marry her."

"Yes, ye did. I asked ye if ye took tis woman ta be yer bride. Ye sed ye did."

This woman? *This woman?* He racked his brain. The smithy was right, confound it all! He hadn't asked if he took Rachel or Belle to be his bride, he'd said *this woman.* Damn and blast! Lost in his lusty thoughts, he'd agreed to marry Belle. She'd even outwitted him by signing the register in her own name.

"Get into the carriage," he barked.

"As you wish, dear husband."

Chapter Three

May 1818
London

Isabelle sat still as Tilde, once a chamber maid, now acting as her lady's maid, ran a heavy brush through her long red hair. She hated sitting for hours while Tilde did her best to get her ready for another tedious ball almost as much as she hated going to the ball itself. It would seem her folly regarding Viscount Belgrave nearly six years ago still made her a laughingstock across London Society. She closed her eyes and willed herself not to think of him again. He was the past, and Lord Kenton was the future—provided she couldn't find another suitable match before the end of the Season.

After her very brief marriage she had little recollection of the disastrous year that followed it, her sister was to be married and her family had gone to London for the Season. However, the rumors that swirled about Isabelle and the viscount were vicious as was the scorn she'd faced for fraudulently trapping a lord into marriage. It was so much that her parents feared Lord Yourke wouldn't wish to marry Rachel and it was decided Isabelle would be packed off to Lincolnshire to be a companion to an older woman named Suellen Finch. During her time as a companion she met Mrs. Finch's nephew, Edmund Roth, Lord Kenton.

At forty-five upon their first meeting four years ago, Edmund was only three years shy of being three decades Isabelle's senior, but that hadn't stopped him from showing her undue attention when he'd come to visit his aunt. It wasn't exactly loving attention, more of that of a friend. All the same, it was unwelcome. At first Isabelle had tried to put him off, claiming the difference between their rank and her scandalous past would make it difficult for him if word were to get out that he was associating with her.

As the years passed, Edmund's persistence continued. He easily dismissed the rumors of her trapping a lord into marriage. He even went so far as to openly call Sebastian a fool for letting her go. And as always, he'd end his tirade by smiling the biggest, brightest smile his lips could stretch into and announce how glad he was that Sebastian was a fool, for now Isabelle could be his prize. Prize. Isabelle's lips twisted. She hated when Lord Kenton referred to her as his prize. He hadn't won her. Moreover, she wasn't an object to be claimed or won. She was a person—albeit a flawed one.

Unfortunately for her, Edmund was no longer the only one who thought she was a prize to be fought over and claimed.

A year and a half ago Lady Clearcreek, Sebastian's mother, passed away, and unbeknownst to Isabelle, Lady Clearcreek had left a sizable trust to her. Three months ago, the still grieving Lord Clearcreek, came to see her in Lincolnshire and informed her he would be carrying out his wife's wishes and arranged for the money to be put into an account in London for Isabelle.

Just as the earl finished informing her of the money, Lord Kenton entered the room and Isabelle nearly groaned in annoyance as he fished for details from Lord Clearcreek.

"Now we can marry," Edmund said jovially as soon as Lord Clearcreek was out the door.

Isabelle stared at him, dumbfounded. It was one thing to have him regard her as a close friend, but to want to marry her and worse yet, for him to have some belief that she returned the interest was absurd. "What are you talking about?"

Edmund plopped down in a brown leather chair and rubbed his hands together excitedly. "This provides the perfect solution. Now that you have money, nobody will care about the scandal in your past and we can marry."

"I see," she said softly. If one were interested in the truth, Isabelle would admit she had no real love for Edmund. She tolerated him well enough, and she enjoyed his company from time to time, but by no means did she love him. Nor did she think she could grow to have such an emotion for him—even as a friend.

She really wasn't sure why he thought the two had such a profound love for one another to begin with—or perhaps he knew they didn't but because of his age, just didn't care. She'd learned from spending the past few years in his company that his mind worked in ways she might never understand.

"Just think, you can go to balls, soirees, and musicales."

"Why would I wish to do that?"

"To reenter Society, of course," Edmund replied offhandedly. As if she'd ever wanted to enter Society in the first place. "You can go to London for the Season to flaunt your money and at the end, you can snag an earl." He winked at her to let her know which earl he had in mind for her to snag.

"Lord Kenton," she began softly, "I know you hold me in high esteem. But you do realize there's a significant age difference between us, do you not?"

He shrugged. "It's of no account. Men are supposed to be older than their wives. It's the perfect arrangement actually. See, we men get to have our bachelor freedom until we're ready to settle down and take a wife, then we find a beautiful young lady like yourself and marry her."

"And what does the young lady get from such a perfect arrangement?" Isabelle asked, cocking her head.

"A skillful lover," Edmund said automatically.

Isabelle dropped her head to her hands and tried not to laugh. The idea of going to bed with him was *not* what young ladies dreams were made of. He wasn't fat exactly, but he could stand to lose at least a stone or better. His hair was greying—or gone. It was easy to tell his face had been very handsome when he was young, but as he'd aged, time had left its stamp.

"You'd get a title, too."

"I don't care about titles, you should know that," Isabelle said flatly, all laughter gone from her voice.

Edmund's large hand rested on her shoulder. "I know," he said softly. "Are you worried you'll see him there? Is that what's holding you back?"

Lifting her head, she met his gaze. "I don't know," she

whispered. "I haven't seen him in so long."

"You're a strong woman, Isabelle. If he confronts you, just incline your chin, stiffen your spine and give him the cut direct. He doesn't deserve the right to even look at you after everything he put you through."

"You're right," Isabelle said with a confidence she didn't feel. "He probably won't be there anyway. Last I heard he was having a grand time cavorting around the continent."

Edmund nodded. "See, nothing to worry about." He pushed to his feet and shoved his hands in his pockets. "I'll see if my aunt can act as your chaperone."

"You'll have no trouble convincing her," Isabelle supplied, shaking her head ruefully. For the past four years Mrs. Finch had tried every trick she could to get Isabelle to go to London. Isabelle suspected it was more so that Mrs. Finch would have a reason to participate in the activities and entertain a lover or two before it was too late, not so that Isabelle could find a husband.

"I know I won't," Edmund agreed smugly. He walked to the door and turned around. "Isabelle, I want you to know something." He withdrew his right hand from his pocket and ran it through his thinning hair. "I know I've expressed interest in marrying you many times, but I don't expect you to make a promise to me yet."

Isabelle stared at him and licked her lips, thinking up a tactful reply. She'd never seriously considered marrying him before and hated feeling like she was going to tear his heart out by finding someone else.

"There will be other gentlemen—younger gentlemen," he continued, looking decidedly uncomfortable, "I'll not get in your way, Isabelle. If one of them strikes your fancy, I'll retreat."

Stunned, she stared at him. "Th—thank you, Edmund."

"You're welcome," he said simply, shrugging one shoulder as if to say he truly didn't care. Which was a lie. He did care. She knew he did.

As she expected, Mrs. Finch was more than willing to act as her chaperone and three months later, she now found herself being fawned over in an effort to make her beautiful for yet another suitor-slobbering, nerve-wracking, dreadfully uncomfortable ball.

"Lord Kenton has arrived," Mary, the only true housemaid still in Mrs. Finch's employ, said as she peeked her head inside Isabelle's bedchamber.

For a reason she couldn't explain, Isabelle breathed a sigh of relief. Lord Kenton may not be the most handsome or charming gentleman she'd ever encountered, but he was certainly someone who she'd consider a genuine friend. And as she'd learned over the past few months, tonight, just like every other night she attended a ball, she could use such a friend.

An hour and a half later, Isabelle was being spun around the dance floor in the arms of one of the most handsome gentlemen to grace a London ballroom. Not only was he handsome, young, and virile, but this particular duke was already married. How unfortunate she hadn't come into her fortune a few years earlier and perhaps the Duke of Gateway could have been hers. Oh well, surely there would be others. She just needed to look around a bit and she'd find the right one. She was sure of it.

The music ended, and simultaneously so did Isabelle's ability to feign enjoyment at being present at Lady Rutherford's ball.

Not fifteen feet away dressed entirely in black except for his perfectly pinned snow-white cravat stood the one person on the planet who had the ability to make her laugh, cry, feel loved and hated all at the same time.

***

Sebastian Gentry, Viscount Belgrave wished he were anywhere else at the moment. In the past five and a half years he'd been chased by an elephant in India, stranded in a battered boat during a storm in the Channel, and nearly impaled by a bull's horn as he was chased around a muddy ring in Spain. All three of those experiences seemed more pleasant than his current situation.

He glanced over to his friend Giles Goddard and was once again reminded of his many blessings. Giles was an odd sort who'd been dealt a difficult hand, to put it politely. Born to an elderly man who didn't wish to keep him around after it became apparent he wasn't destined to have the same sort of life as the others with his breeding, Giles was banished to Ireland and raised by nuns. If that wasn't bad enough, he was slow to speak and often considered by some to be low of intellect. To say that Giles had an easy time of it would be an outright lie. And other than Giles himself, nobody knew that better than Sebastian.

The two had met five years ago while boarding a steam packet bound for Ireland and had become fast friends during the journey. They'd spent the interim touring the continent, neither having a care in the world for when it would be the right time to return to London. But when Giles received some sort of summons to return to England in the early spring, Sebastian decided it was time for him to return, too. He'd been gone long enough. It was time. Time to face his past and whatever demons lurked there.

But that wasn't the reason he'd come to the ball, however. He'd come to the blasted ball because Giles had asked him to; and if there was one thing he'd learned from a chap as simple as Giles, you don't break your promises.

"Do you see her?" Sebastian asked, leaning over to his friend.

Giles shook his head slowly then gave a pointed look in the direction of a potted plant.

"Capital idea," Sebastian said. When they'd first met, Sebastian found Giles' quiet demeanor quite odd. But after five years of carrying the majority of the conversation, he didn't think it odd in the least.

Together the pair lumbered over to the spot by the potted plant Giles had indicated with his stare. Standing along the perimeter of the room would allow them the position to search the room for a woman named Lady Cosgrove.

Not that Sebastian had the slightest idea of what she looked like, of course. He'd better leave locating Lady Cosgrove to Giles. Instead, he'd stand and wait quietly until—

All of the muscles in his body tensed, then fell slack as every drop of his blood made one final thundering round through his veins then drained to his toes. There, standing not fifteen feet in front of him wearing the fullest, light blue gown he'd ever seen was Isabelle Gentry, Lady Belgrave: his wife.

Chapter Four

Though her mind commanded her mouth to speak, she couldn't. She opened her mouth once, then twice, as if to say something, but nothing came out. The only thing she could do was to open and close her mouth like a fish. And stare. Yes, she could certainly stare.

He was taller and leaner than she remembered him to be. Broader and more angled, too.

"Good evening, Belle," he said with a slight bow as he approached her.

Anger she knew she had, but didn't expect to have surface, surged inside of her at his informal, almost friendly greeting. She tore her eyes away, spun on her heel and retreated across the ballroom.

She was such a fool.

At least she felt like one and had no desire to allow him to think her one; or make her into a bigger one.

Instead, she wouldn't give him anything else to think of her.

Cutting him might be perceived by some—likely, himself included—a cowardly thing for her to do, she knew, but considering all the vile things that had befallen her during the year after their 'marriage', it was the best she could do. At least to her mind it was. Spurning him as he'd spurned her was fair, was it not?

On their way back from Scotland, they'd been involved in a terrible carriage accident. One that left the coach in shambles, the coachmen dead, and her unconscious.

She obviously didn't recall how long she was unconscious, but she'd been alone when she awoke some weeks later with intense pain in her back and both hips. Pain that was so sharp and crippling that something as simple as breathing made her cry, which only brought about more pain.

And through it all, Sebastian who'd been her friend far longer than her husband, was nowhere to be found.

True to his word as soon as they'd climbed back into the carriage outside the smithy's, he'd orchestrated their annulment and was gone. Never once did he call upon her or even ask how she was while she was recovering. Just gone.

Hurt and anger bubbled up inside of her. She hated him. Absolutely hated him. And his having the nerve to appear so devilishly handsome out of nowhere and speak to her as if nothing had happened between them was too much.

"Miss Knight."

Isabelle started and turned to see the soft green eyes of Simon Appleton, a quiet sort who defied the norms of most gentleman of his young age of twenty. Though he'd never sought Isabelle out outside of balls, routs, and musicales, it was clear he had some interest in her, or else he wouldn't always be the first to claim two of her dances for the evening and eager to suggest he take her to the refreshment room. She flashed him the best smile she could. "I was just looking for you—just in the wrong direction, apparently."

A broad grin took his lips. "Good. Then, I'd like to claim my dance now."

"Of course." Doing her best to control the slight tremor in her hands, she allowed him to lead her onto the floor. Following her injury, she didn't think she'd ever be able to dance again without pain, which wasn't a true concern of hers since she'd never really given dancing much thought as a young girl, given her position and all. But truth to tell, Mrs. Finch still loved to dance and often insisted Isabelle practice with her. Considering the break in her hips and how long it had taken her to walk again, Isabelle feared she'd let her companion down, but had actually found it very helpful with her walking and movement to spend so much time practicing dancing. It helped make her gait more even, too. So much so that it'd be hard for anyone to ever know how badly she'd been injured.

Her partner, Mr. Appleton, was a magnificent dancer even if she'd never seen him practice the skill with anyone other than her.

His green eyes sought to lock gazes with hers, and she struggled to keep her eyes on his, too apprehensive about the set of sharp brown eyes that she knew were watching her from the edge of the ballroom. She nearly laughed at her own foolish notion. *He* wasn't watching her. Sebastian's interest in her was very little. Very little? She almost snorted. Very little was too much. His interest in her was absolutely none.

So then why was he watching her?

To mock her, perhaps?

She shivered and a knot of raw emotion formed in her throat.

She surely hoped not. She'd suffered enough mocking at his hands these past years, and had no desire to have any more.

"Is everything all right?"

Mr. Appleton's question snapped Isabelle from her thoughts. "Of course."

He nodded as if he accepted her answer and flashed her a nervous smile. "As you may already know, Miss Knight, I attend these balls because I've now reached the age where I'm in search of a wife..."

Whatever it was he had to say after that was lost to Isabelle as a knot the size—and the approximate weight—of a cannonball lowered into her stomach. If she thought it difficult to breathe before with the emotion clogging her throat, it was nearly impossible now. "Mr. Appleton, please don't," she rushed, cutting off whatever words he'd practiced to say to her at that moment.

The way he blanched then turned red made her guilt grow.

"What I mean is..." *My desire to marry you rivals that of your desire to bed a sixty year-old scullery maid: none.* Were she younger and him someone else, she'd have said that very remark without concern to the consequences, but she couldn't. Her reputation couldn't survive such a scandalous statement. Whether she truly wished to find a husband or not, such remarks must stay quiet or she'd bring more rumors and scorn upon her head. "Mr. Appleton," she began again with a sigh. "I like you, I truly do, but I think we might be better suited as friends." Which was rather generous considering their acquaintance so far had been restricted to less than a dozen dances and a couple of trips to the refreshment room spread out over a handful of balls.

"I see," he said slowly, another nervous smile spreading across his lips. "I hadn't thought of you as a potential bride before."

Isabelle misstepped.

Mirth danced in Mr. Appleton's green eyes. "I, too, thought of us only as friends and was merely going to ask what you thought of Henrietta Hughes, but now that you've suggested..." He shrugged and flashed her a full grin that left her uncertain. Either he was lying to protect his pride or she'd been too distracted with the idea of marrying someone other than Edmund to see his attentions for what they were: just being friendly.

"Er...Henrietta seems nice enough, I suppose."

He quirked a dark brow. "You suppose?"

"Well, she is a bit...er...shy don't you think?"

"And what do you consider yourself?"

Isabelle almost misstepped again, and might have if not for Mr. Appleton's tightened grasp. "I'm not shy. I'm more...reserved." She forced herself to meet his eyes. She'd never been termed reserved a day in her life. Well, at least not until after the disaster that was her elopement... But Mr. Appleton didn't seem to know of that folly, nor the girl she'd been prior to said folly. Thank heavens.

"I'd say Henrietta is reserved, too," he remarked. "This is her what? Third season?"

Isabelle murmured something he'd take as agreement. Honestly, she had no idea how long Miss Henrietta Hughes had been on the Marriage Mart. She'd never met more than a fraction of the people who were here tonight and had only heard of a quarter. Well, *heard* might not be the correct word. More like she'd read about them. In scandal sheets, to be exact. And only then when Mrs. Finch instructed her to read such claptrap to her. As it was, Isabelle would happily never look at that section of the newspaper ever again.

Mr. Appleton chuckled and led her to the side of the room. Apparently the music had ended. She blushed and followed her escort's lead.

"You really are distracted tonight," he mused.

She bit her lip. Was it that obvious to him? It was quite

obvious to her since she kept getting lost in her own thoughts. Just like she was doing now, dash it all. She closed her eyes and took a deep breath. Then opened them again, refreshed. "What is it that you were saying about Miss Hughes?"

He shrugged again. "Nothing. Just that I find that perhaps she's reserved."

"I don't see why she'd have a reason to be, it's not as if she's haunted by a scandal," Isabelle said before she could think better of it, her eyes flaring wide.

Mr. Appleton eyed her curiously. "One wouldn't think that a little scandal in one's past would be enough to make a girl unmarriageable, would it?"

Isabelle stared at him, her eyes searching his face. What did he know? Was he still talking about Miss Hughes or was he now talking about her? She opened her mouth to say something, but immediately closed it with a sharp snap when a voice came from behind her, sending shivers down her spine.

"No, I shouldn't think so," came the soft, quiet voice of none other than Sebastian, Lord Belgrave, her no-good former husband.

***

Isabelle whirled around to face him, fire blazing in her green eyes.

Sebastian offered her his hand; the opening strains of a waltz just starting. "May I?"

She couldn't very well refuse and they both knew it. She swallowed in a way that made the center of her slender neck move and then took his hand.

He'd been watching her from across the room since she'd walked away from him without so much as a word of greeting. At first, he thought she might be as stunned to see him as he was to see her, but now that she'd had time to recover from her shock, he wanted to speak to her. She was his wife, after all, that made it his right to do so.

"How have you been?" he asked after he had her in his arms and began leading her about the floor.

Her fiery eyes scorched him. "Don't."

"Don't what?"

"Don't pretend as if we are friends when you know as well as I do that we are not."

"Hmm, and when did you become as stuffy as a matron with seventy-five years in her dish?"

Belle didn't answer, at least not with words. Her stiff body and piercing eyes said more than enough.

He pulled her closer, delighting in the way she seemed to resist, but still complied. "I do hope this isn't how you conducted yourself with your other dance partners or you'll never find a husband."

"No. It's only your arms I long to get out of. I melt to jelly in any other's embrace."

He almost chuckled at her words, and then actually did when her eyes grew large with what appeared to be horror that she'd actually spoken those words. "Do you no longer speak the first thing that comes into your mind, then?"

"I'm a lady now, Belgrave," she said in a tone he didn't recognize. "I temporarily forgot my manners when you provoked me, but I assure you, that I shall not again."

"Pity that." Why he said that, he didn't know. It was one of the things that irritated him most about her: her loose lips and stubborn streak.

"No pity. Ladies must remember to be mindful of their reputation."

"I see. And that requires them to mind what they say?"

"Exactly. What I just spoke was inappropriate and...and...I apologize."

He bit back a grin at the grimace on her face as she spoke those words. Belle had never been one ready to apologize. Ever. He cocked his head to the side. "Tell me, is your newfound desire to apologize for speaking your mind part of your pretending to be a lady?"

She glared at him, but simply said, "I am not pretending."

"No, I suppose you're not." He hoped she wouldn't challenge him on that for he'd hate to reveal so soon just how much of a lady she was. He sighed. But she wouldn't challenge him. He could see that quite plainly on her face. Her eyes said she wanted to demand he explain his cryptic statement, but only after she accused him of not being able to recognize a lady if there were a parade of one hundred of them led in front of his face. Her slightly downcast face, complete with closed lips and lowered eyelashes spoke volumes of her new position as a "lady". One who didn't issue challenges or demand answers.

A wave of an emotion he couldn't name—shame, embarrassment, anger, perhaps—washed over him. It was because of *him* that she'd become this stiff creature who felt being a lady meant she couldn't speak.

"Tell me, Belle, do you have an interest in the gentleman you were just dancing with?" he asked to change the subject and staunch his feelings.

"Mr. Appleton?" she asked with a slight hitch in her voice that he couldn't place. At his nod, she continued. "We're...uh...friends."

"I see." He twirled her around their spot on the floor. "And do you wish to become better friends with him?" He chuckled at her blush and pulled her even closer. "Is he the one you've set your cap on, Belle?"

"No." She tried to distance herself from him, but he wouldn't let her. "As I said, we're just friends."

"Are the two of you friends in the same way that the two of us are friends?" he asked before he could think better of it. But now that he'd asked, he wanted to know. He'd watched the two of them dance. Their exchanged smiles. Her missteps and his practiced hands holding her. There was certainly something there.

"If you mean to imply that I intend to trap him into a marriage he does not desire, the answer is no that I do not," she said abruptly, shocking him to the toes.

His shock so jolting and sudden, and her will so iron-strong, she managed to free herself from his hold with nothing more than a sidestep. And for the second time that night, she issued him a social insult that would undoubtedly make the scandal sheets tomorrow; meanwhile intriguing him all the more.

Chapter Five

It was nearly a week before Isabelle was 'at home' and accepting callers. The day after the ball at Lord and Lady Rutherford's house, her name had been bandied about in every gossip column in the country, and probably a few on the continent, too. Of course, she wasn't the only one mentioned, Sebastian's name was listed there, too. Just like five years ago when she'd first come to London. Also like five years ago, every feeble-minded author who thought to entertain the population with embarrassing stories and embellished anecdotes thought it prudent to mention *all* the known details of Isabelle and Sebastian's tumultuous relationship. Every single one of them.

"Would you like for me to have our engagement announced in the *Times?*" Edmund offered from where he sat on the blue settee that was nearby.

"Thank you, Edmund, that's very sweet, but no." She offered him a slim smile. "I don't want you to bear the shame of my actions."

"Actions you were provoked into performing," came a new voice entering the room, startling them both.

"Lord Belgrave," she said, wincing. Her voice sounded cold and waspish even to her own ears. Not that it mattered, it didn't.

"Belle," he greeted casually, bowing.

She forced herself to stand and make the proper introductions to her chaperone Mrs. Finch and to Edmund, but that was as far as her pride would allow for her pleasantries to go. As soon as Sebastian left today, she'd have to inform Clemmens, the butler, that Lord Belgrave was unwelcome here in the future. Had she thought he'd ever have the nerve to darken her door as it was, she'd have issued that command before now.

"Don't let my presence interrupt your conversation." Sebastian waved a hand between Isabelle and Edmund and took a seat.

31

Edmund cast her a questioning look and Isabelle shot daggers at Sebastian.

"I believe you two were talking about Belle's recent actions, presumably at a ball hosted by Lady Rutherford."

Isabelle would have liked nothing more than for Edmund to lay Sebastian out for his teasing tone and devilish grin. But Edmund wasn't that kind. His possessiveness of her was mild at best; he preferred to take the simple action—marrying her rather than to publicly defend her.

Unfortunately, marriage to a dead fish like Edmund was becoming less desirable by the day, if such a thing were possible, and though her matrimonial prospects were few, she'd rather keep looking or remain a spinster than to settle for an awkward marriage.

Mr. Appleton's—and even Edmund's—open disregard for her former scandal gave her hope that someone would come along who would accept her as she was. Love wasn't necessary, of course. She knew that would never happen, but high regard, or any genuine regard at all that didn't hedge on being overzealous, would be good enough.

"Hmm, silence," Sebastian said. "The mark of a conversation interrupted, I should think."

"Then perhaps you should take yourself elsewhere." Isabelle closed her mouth with an audible snap as her teeth hit together. Her face heated, then dissolved in flames when he chuckled.

"No. I do believe I like it here." He reached forward and poured himself a cup of tea like the uncivilized man he was, quirking a brow at her as he did so. "I've been away so long, it's always good to return home and chat with old friends—" he shifted his eyes over to Edmund— "and make new ones."

Isabelle bristled. "We are not old friends, Lord Belgrave, and you'd do well to remember that."

Sebastian turned his sharp eyes to her chaperone. "Mrs. Finch," he said loud enough for the nearly deaf woman to hear, "you grew up in the country, did you not?"

"Why, yes, I did," the greying woman said loudly, setting her teacup down on her saucer with a slight clink.

"And did you have any playmates?"

"Of course." A wistful smile came over her face, sealing Isabelle's doom.

"I see. And would you consider those playmates your friends?"

"The dearest I have," she said without hesitation.

"The dearest, you say." Sebastian lifted his eyebrow at Isabelle again. "Did you hear that, darling," he drawled. "We're not just old friends, but the *dearest*."

Isabelle scowled and turned her attention back to Edmund who returned her gaze. But neither could say anything with their annoying audience watching them with rapt attention.

Fortunately, they were all spared a certain death by suffocation due to lack of a sufficient amount of air when Clemmens opened the door and announced an impeccably dressed Mr. Simon Appleton.

Isabelle stood and graciously accepted the bouquet of hyacinths. She said a silent prayer that her shock at having him call upon her wasn't stamped on her face and made another uncomfortable introduction between Mr. Appleton and Sebastian. Mr. Appleton gave Sebastian nothing more than a cursory nod, then sat right next to Isabelle.

Isabelle's gaze shot to where his thigh was no more than half an inch from hers.

Were this any other day and her...er...former husband not have been in the room, she'd have tried to remain as impassive as possible and attempt to scoot away a few inches to allow them each room to breathe. But this wasn't just any normal day, and her former husband *was* here, staring at her, even. Besides, she suspected Simon knew of their connection—and how could he not for it was the recurring theme of all the gossip articles for the past week—and he was sitting there just to show his support. Not one to turn away from help, she met Sebastian's narrowed eyes and grinned like a five year old who'd just been let loose in a confectionary.

Sebastian lifted his brown eyes and cleared his throat, but didn't say anything.

"Isabelle, my dear, do you wish to make some sort of announcement?" Mrs. Finch asked with a pointed stare at Simon.

"No."

"Then I'd suggest you two separate."

Isabelle's face heated and she looked to Edmund to say something to help ease the tension from the room. He didn't.

"Of course, you're right, Mrs. Finch," Simon said with a swallow. "I nearly forgot myself—what with such a room full of prospective suitors and all. Speaking of which—" he turned back to face Isabelle and reached into his breast pocket— "I was wondering if you wouldn't mind looking over something for me?"

Ignoring Edmund's look of keen interest and Sebastian's arrogant stare, she took the folded vellum from Simon's fingers, barely catching his quick, inconspicuous wink.

She cleared her throat and took her time unfolding it.

"It's a...um—" Simon looked around the room, his cheeks coloring a bit, but his voice holding firm, confident— "I've been thinking to recite it to a certain someone at a certain event later in the week," he said as if to appease the interest in the room.

Isabelle could have kissed him for his diversion. Then granted him another kiss when she opened it up to find the writing on the paper he'd handed her was nothing more than a bill from his tailor.

Playing along, for no other reason than to follow the silly lead he'd created for them, she moved her lips and scanned the lines— heaving a sigh here and a smile there as she pretended to scan lines of beautiful poetry that didn't exist.

"It's quite lovely," she said at last, handing it back to him. "I think you'll have her eating out of your hand in no time."

Sebastian's snort drew her attention.

"Do you have something to say, Lord Belgrave?"

"Actually, yes." He grabbed a biscuit from the plate positioned on the table in front of him. "I was wondering if Mr. Appleton here would be kind enough to read aloud his poem or ode or whatever it is that he gave you so that I, too, might know what to say to make a lady swoon with delight."

Isabelle pursed her lips. She knew his words for what they were: a lighthearted jest, and had she not have once been married to him, nor one of those young ladies who were naturally attracted to him, she might have laughed. Instead, his comment stung. "I doubt there is anything you could say to a young lady to make her swoon with delight."

"Why Belle, I had no idea you thought I was so charming that all I have to do is be present to make a young lady swoon."

She lifted her chin a notch. "I do believe you lost all of that charm when you crossed the line from confident to arrogant."

"So you think I was once that charming," he parried with a cocksure grin.

Isabelle felt rather than saw all the eyes in the room focus on her. Lifting her chin a notch, she brought her hands to her chest and in a sing-song tone said, "Oh dear me, I never thought I'd see the day where the haughty Sebastian Gentry, Lord Belgrave, had to fish for compliments."

All eyes went to him and without missing a beat, he said, "Does that mean that you've spent your whole life thinking about me, then?"

"No."

"Are you sure?"

"Positive."

"Not even just a little."

"No. Not even just a little."

As if they were all thoroughly entranced by the exchange in the room, everyone else moved their attention to the other speaker with each exchange.

"It doesn't have to be for a positive reason that you thought of me, my dear. Just that you did," he said, grinning.

"And fill my mind with something more unsavory than what's found at the bottom of a privy? I should think not," she blurted before she could think better of it.

"Ah, then it was of fond thoughts, indeed," he concluded with a knowing grin.

She fisted her hands into her skirt. What was it about this infuriating man that made her forget herself and embarrass herself in front of others with her loose tongue? Not again, she vowed. She lifted her chin a notch. "Fond thoughts, indeed. Why, I must confess that only four months ago my carriage rolled past where a young lady had slipped on the ice on her front steps. A gentleman she seemed to know ignored her cries for help and walked right past her. It was that moment, I briefly gave into my girlish insensibilities and wondered whatever happened to you."

"Did you now?" A stoic look came over his face, transforming him to marble. "And how do you know that cad wasn't me?"

She looked down to examine her nails before meeting his eyes and giving a casual shrug. "Oh, wouldn't you know, he was far too handsome to have been you."

Chapter Six

Sebastian scrubbed his face with his hands, then spread his fingers and looked at the room around him through the gaps. When had his life come to this?

He'd accompanied Giles to that blasted ball with the sole purpose of helping his friend find Lady Cosgrove for whatever reason it was he was looking for her. If he'd known that Belle was to be there, he would have been more careful where he stood. In fact, he should have turned and fled as soon as he saw her. There had been time, she hadn't seen him until several moments later. But no, he hadn't. He knew she'd be there of course, in London that is, not necessarily at Lady Rutherfords's ball. That part was pure coincidence. But he knew she'd be in London having a Season. Both his father and hers had thought it necessary to inform him of the event.

He raked his hands through his hair. Both of their fathers were still adamant that he sign those papers and set her free. His father had never said it in as many words, but he was getting on in years, which meant that Sebastian would be the earl and in need of an heir—and a man cannot get a legitimate heir with a woman he was estranged from. Well, perhaps he *could* get an heir, but it'd be a cuckoo and Sebastian would look to the world a fool. So the need for a true annulment, followed by another marriage was necessary to carrying on his family line—in the family.

Thaddeus Knight, however, didn't give one fig about Sebastian's or his father's title, all he wanted was Belle's name cleared because, well, quite simply he was her father, and until everything was settled, he and the rest of the Knight family didn't dare associate with Belle.

He understood both reasons. He even understood their reasons for bestowing upon her a fortune in hopes of forcing him to return and set things to rights by finally granting her an annulment so she could remarry during the Season. He wondered, however, if they knew that by his returning and granting her the annulment they all sought that it would only bring scandal upon her head again? Or were they hoping that the sum they settled her with would be enough for a fortune hunter to turn a blind eye to her past and still wish to marry her?

A tightness formed in his chest. Lord Kenton, or "Edmund" as Belle so casually called him, seemed the sort to do such a thing. Why he'd be willing to, Sebastian didn't understand. The man had more money than most, a fact that could turn many young girls and their mama's blind about his age. But something just didn't seem to fit. His interest in Belle seemed mild, almost as if he was interested in her because he knew she was comfortable, familiar, a good friend.

A good friend? He nearly snorted. That's how she'd described Simon Appleton. Another peculiar man. His interest in Belle today seemed forced. Either he was pretending to like her or he genuinely does, but doesn't have an inkling of how to show it. Either way, he wasn't good enough for her. Where Lord Kenton was too old, Simon Appleton was too young. Where Lord Kenton was disinterested, Simon Appleton was too interested, almost to the point of an annoyance or insecurity.

Sebastian leaned back in his chair and dropped his hands to his sides. If she'd spent close to three months in London and her only prospects were these two, she was in a desperate need of help.

Or was she?

She'd been nothing but cold to him since he'd returned. Not that he could blame her entirely. He'd behaved like a selfish arse when he discovered her identity in Scotland, then hadn't been there when she needed a friend the most. Not for his lack of wanting to, mind you. He'd tried. Over and over he'd tried, but her father would have none of it, claiming the blame for Belle's situation was all Sebastian's doing. He was right of course. Belle might have healed faster and more peacefully if not for the horrible way he'd treated her before the accident. To her mind, she had nothing to come back to. Nothing but more pain and hatred. Bile surged up his throat and he took a deep, calming breath.

If nothing else, Sebastian owed Belle her own life back. That was the reason he'd returned to England, was it not? With her having a Season he would finally be afforded a chance to talk to her. Though he'd wanted more than anything to set things to right with her, she seemed unwilling to speak civilly to him. Perhaps, he should come at this from a different angle.

Perhaps the best way for him to make things right between them and restore their friendship was if he helped her find a match. Yes. That was exactly what he'd do. He'd help her secure a good match—not someone too old or too young. Nor someone as interesting as Hessians boot or more zealous than an eager pup. Someone young but mature, handsome but not vain; someone respectable but not a prig; intelligent but not demeaning. He might not have spent much time in London since his majority, but he was sure such a man existed and it would be his mission to find him. Then to make him fall in love with Belle. And why wouldn't he, she was... Well, Sebastian didn't exactly know what she was, nor did he wish to examine his thoughts of her too deeply. Instead, he needed to inform her of his plan.

***

"Is he the one, then?"

Isabelle jerked ramrod straight in the chair she'd been sitting in by the big open window in the library, leaning forward to do embroidery. Every muscle in her body clenched. "Lord Belgrave, what are you doing?" she asked of the arrogant beast who dared lean his head through the open window of Mrs. Finch's library.

He opened the window further and climbed inside. "I've returned to see you again."

"And you couldn't have done that by coming through the front door?"

He shook his head and flopped down on the dark green settee as if he hadn't a care in the world. Which likely, he didn't. "No. I couldn't come through the front door. Apparently, I've been banned entry through the front door." He shot her a triumphant look. "Now that I've answered your question. It's your turn to

39

answer mine."

"Who? Which one? What?" She asked in annoyance.

He shrugged and put his booted feet up on the squat oak table in front of him. "Mr. Appleton or Lord Kenton. Have you set your cap on either of them?"

She almost laughed at the absurdity, but the fact that he was alone with her in the library where they could be caught and her already tattered reputation further destroyed kept her laugh at bay.

He frowned. "Is there a reason you're refusing to answer?"

"Are you jealous?"

"No." He drew the word out just long enough to prick her pride.

"Well, then, you need not bother yourself to wait here any longer to hear my answer." She flicked her wrist in a shooing motion to indicate he could leave the same way he entered. The sooner the better.

"Ah, so they really are just friends as you'd claimed earlier."

Isabelle's chest constricted. Of course they were just friends. Gentlemen were always just her friends. Mr. Appleton. Lord Kenton. Him. All just friends. But the fact that all of them only wanted to be her friend in some awkward manner or another didn't bother her nearly as much as the fact that he was able to deduce that just by looking at her.

"It was your severe reluctance to answer that gave you away," he murmured.

She gave him a pointed look, one she hoped that he'd interpret that if he were sitting just *that* much closer to her, she'd prick him with the end of her embroidery needle. "Now that you know the state of my courtships, you may see yourself out."

"And miss spending some time with my dearest childhood friend? I think not."

"I hate to break your heart, my lord. But my sister does not live at this address."

That sobered the grin right off of his handsome face. He cleared his throat. "She... We... Er..." He speared his hand through his hair. "That's not what you think."

"So then you meant to come into my room that night and not hers?"

"Well, no." He frowned at her.

"Then it is what I think. The two of you had planned an assignation and I got in your way." She forced her best smile, even if it was wobbly. "As usual."

"The first part is correct," he said. "The second..." He shrugged. "She was always in the way, too."

"That doesn't make me feel better."

"It should."

"Well, it doesn't."

"If you must know, I only agreed to marry her because she begged me. Then half a second after I agreed, I wished that I hadn't. I went that night in hopes she'd change her mind."

"That explains your remarks about seeing up my nightrail," she commented.

He nodded. "I was hoping to upset her sensibilities and make her cry off. I knew that if I reneged she'd forever hate me and blame me for her having to marry Lord Yourke. But if she cried off, then it was on her."

"Such a gentleman."

He gave a lopsided shrug. "I try."

"As I remember it, you didn't seem so against the marriage after the vows were said and we were at the inn," she said tartly.

A wolfish smile split his face. "That's because by then primal urges were taking over."

"Ah, but they weren't too strong because as soon as you saw me your only urge was flee as soon as possible—even if you acted like a primate to do so."

His smile faded. "You have to understand. I was young and foolish. I didn't consider your feelings at the time, only mine. You rattled me, Belle. You have to know that."

"It's for the best," she said dismissively; not wanting to hear anymore. She knew he was a selfish cad. Now that he'd said it, she had no further wish to discuss this any longer, lest she reveal to him that the worst part was how he'd abandoned her when she needed his friendship the most. Not that it would have mattered too much, she supposed. Their friendship was probably only what she'd ever imagined it to be anyway. He'd told her almost every chance he found that he thought of her as an annoyance, while she'd regarded him with awe and fascination. Likely only because other than her sister, he was the only person close to her age who lived within walking distance.

"How about if I make it up to you?"

"That's not necessary."

"Yes, it is. Our friendship ended just after I behaved poorly, give me a chance to rise to the level of regard you used to hold me in."

That did it. His arrogance was just too much. *He* was too much. Everything was still just a game to him. She tossed her embroidery hoop to the side and stood to the full height her five-foot-two frame would allow then made for the door.

His arm snaked out and wrapped around her waist. "Not so fast."

She dropped her gaze to his offending fingers. "Release me, you cad."

"No." Without moving his hand from her person, he stood up and spun her around to face him, now with both of his hands on her sides, staying her. "You're here in search of a husband, are you not?"

She held his intense gaze, but didn't speak.

"Let me help you find one."

She laughed at his addled suggestion, then sobered. "You're serious."

"Yes, I am."

"No."

His lips thinned. "Why not?"

"Because you don't know anything about me."

"I know that you prefer purple to pink and violets to hyacinths. I know that you'd do anything to get out of eating any kind of pork. You have a fondness to dogs and hated Rachel's cat Felix."

"None of what you just listed is important to finding a husband."

He cocked his head to the side. "But you don't disagree that I was correct on those facts?"

"Perhaps."

"Whether you think they're important or not, you have to admit that I do know you. Now, let me help you find a husband."

"Why, so you can bandy it about that you rescued the girl who once trapped you into a marriage?" Try as she might, she couldn't disguise the sob that erupted in her throat at those filthy words.

"No," he said softly. "I subjected you to a life of scorn and I'd like to make it right. Please, allow me to do that."

"I don't think you can."

His smile returned. "You underestimate me, my dear. I'll be back tomorrow morning with a list of potential husbands."

Then, not allowing her a chance to argue, he released his hold on her and climbed out the same window he'd entered through.

Chapter Seven

Sebastian groaned. Thinking of potential husbands was tough work. Not to mention, he felt extremely foolish sitting by the fire and flipping through the latest copy of *Debretts* like some debutante preparing for her first Season. He scowled and not for the first time threw a glance over his shoulder to make sure he was still alone.

His tired eyes scanned the lines on the page and his scowl deepened. Were there no decent gentleman who were unmarried?

Apparently not.

Married. Gambler. Drunk. Drunk. Married. Addict. Womanizer. Drunk. Married. Gambler. Card cheat. Terribly dull. Too young. Married. Mad. Gambler. Impoverished.

He turned the page and sighed.

Drunk. Married. Devil of a temper. Decrepit. Married. Habitual skirt chaser...and married. On his Grand Tour. Compulsive liar. Sebastian blinked. Sir Wallace Benedict. There wasn't anything wrong with him, exactly. He was just...odd. Odd was acceptable. Compared to the other options, a little odd would be more than acceptable. He scratched Sir Wallace's name down and continued looking. One name wasn't enough.

Too young. Married. Married. In love with his hounds. Gambler. Obsessed with horse racing. Widower...with a brood. Married. Cad of the worst sort. Married. Betrothed.

He flipped the page.

Old. Drunk. Married. Married. Coward. Perfect. Sir Michael Smythe. He was young and loyal, he'd rightfully earned his title as a knight, and had a decent amount to his name so he wouldn't see marriage to Belle as merely a way to plump his coffers. Not to mention, he and Belle were already acquaintances. The report his man had sent Sebastian in Italy had indicated as much.

That gave him, or rather *her*, two choices. That would do,

wouldn't it?

No. Belle might not like these options. He needed as many as he could find.

Best to torture himself to find more now rather than have to repeat this torture another night.

He turned his eyes back to the page, but was saved from having to actually read it when he was interrupted by his friend.

"What brings you about?" Sebastian called to Giles by way of greeting.

Giles eased himself into a leather chair and slowly looked around the room, taking it all in. "You weren't there."

Sebastian sliced his hand through the air. "I had a more interesting engagement." That was true enough. He'd joined Giles at White's every afternoon since they'd come to London and to be frank, it was tedious. For a man who liked to travel and explore, sitting on one's hind quarters reading a newspaper or playing cards was only entertaining for so long. Every day for the past week he'd tried to gain entrance to Belle's and had been turned out. After he'd seen her there this morning, he didn't want to have her disappear before he could tell her his plan, so he'd skipped his club and returned to speak to her, which is when he'd found her in the library.

"Didn't miss anything," Giles said in his usual slow tone. "It was exactly the same as it was yesterday and the day before."

"And dare I suppose the day before that, too," Sebastian suggested.

Giles nodded with vigor then sighed in aggravation as he moved around to get more comfortable.

"Would you care to test out my new settee?" Sebastian offered.

Giles shook his head. "Settled." He dropped his inquisitive green eyes to where Sebastian still held open his copy of *Debretts*, prompting Sebastian to close it with a *snap*.

"Don't ask. You don't really wish to know."

Giles lifted a single brow.

Giles. A little slow in speech and action at times, but nothing was *wrong* with him. He just required a patient bride. Belle was patient. She would complement him in other ways, too. She could be the chatterer of the relationship, allowing Giles to stand silent like he preferred. Neither seemed too keen on London or Society.

Their only problem might be the difference in their sizes.

Giles was built like a tower at an unimaginable four inches past six feet. By far the tallest person that Sebastian had ever seen; a good eight to ten inches taller than most. Sebastian himself felt dwarfed standing next to him and he was taller than average, too, being an inch shy of six feet. Belle's five-foot-two inch body would look like a mere child in his presence as her nose would barely reach his sternum. He nearly snorted at the mental image.

"Ahhhh, a blinding grin!" Giles teased, holding his hands up in front of his eyes and acting wounded.

"Don't worry, you'll have a blinding smile of your own soon enough," Sebastian informed him.

Giles slowly dropped his hands, his brows knitting in confusion. "Why?"

"I think I've found you a bride."

"No," Giles clipped. His face lost all expression.

With the exception of when Giles asked him what a certain phrase meant that a prostitute was shouting out the window as they passed a brothel, they'd never spoken of women. Of course that probably had something to do with Sebastian not fully understanding the phrase, either. Giles, Sebastian assumed, had no interest in women because well, he just didn't. Likely he never felt he'd need any kind of knowledge because people of both sexes seemed disinterested in him in general.

Sebastian's disinterest in women wasn't as innocent, however. He was interested. Undeniably so. He'd lain awake many nights trying to make his throbbing erection vanish while ignoring the sounds of lovers through the walls. But, blast it all, he couldn't do a thing about it, he was still married!

She might not know they were still married, nor what he was doing and if he was in the arms of another, but he was married to her all the same and owed her that dignity even if he'd inadvertently stripped her of all others. He wouldn't be married to her much longer, though, he reminded himself. Soon, he'd find her a husband then he could sign the annulment papers free of guilt, then after that...

"Did you ever find the cousin you were looking for?" Sebastian asked to change their topic of conversation and the mindless drifting of his thoughts.

Giles shook his head, still penetrating Sebastian with his steady stare.

"Do we need to go out tonight to look for her again?"

"You won't be going anywhere," thundered the deep baritone voice of Thaddeus Knight.

Just as it did when he was a young boy running and playing with the man's daughters, Mr. Knight's voice made every hair on Sebastian's body stand on end. Reluctantly, he pushed to his feet. "How may I help you this fine evening, Mr. Knight?"

"Stay away from my daughter," his father-in-law blustered.

Sebastian let his eyes wander over the body of the man he'd been so fearful of as a boy. His ruddy cheeks and purple nose were still the same, if not a bit fattier. His hair had thinned and his grey eyes seemed colder than he'd remembered. Not that that was much. To Sebastian, Mr. Knight's eyes had always reminded him of a powerful, unyielding storm. One that Sebastian had thought to defy only once: refusing to annul his marriage to Belle. He'd heeded the command to get out of the man's home and never return, but he had stood his ground over where he put his signature. "Sorry, sir," Sebastian said as calmly as he could. "I can't stay away from her. She is my wife after all."

The older man let out a string of vile curses under breath. "Dissolve your marriage and find another."

"No."

Mr. Knight's breathing grew labored and raspy, his jaw set and his eyes narrowing to slits. *"Why not?"* he shouted.

If he were a boy, even one of nineteen still, Mr. Knight's tone and stance would have startled him and made him uneasy. Instead, he stood his ground. "I have no reason to discuss the state of my marriage with you, therefore, I won't. So if there is anything else I can do for you..."

"Give her the annulment, you blackguard," Mr. Knight demanded, crossing his arms.

Sebastian ignored his statement, sat down and opened *Debretts* as if he had a genuine interest in reading that claptrap again.

Not one to be ignored, Mr. Knight yanked the book from Sebastian's hands. "You listen to me, you filthy cad. You *will* annul your marriage and set my daughter free."

"And just why do you care?" Sebastian countered, not breaking eye contact with the older man.

"She's my daughter. I want what's best for her."

"As do I," Sebastian said softly.

"*You're* not what's best for her," her father raged with a sneer.

Sebastian shrugged. "I know."

Mr. Knight blinked at him, seemingly stupefied. "Then what are you doing?"

Without a word, Sebastian reached forward and plucked his copy of *Debretts* from Mr. Knight's loose grasp. "Finding her a new husband."

Chapter Eight

"No."

Sebastian looked at his father-in-law and shrugged. "I don't see why you have a problem with it."

"Because you think to just foist my daughter off on some bounder so you can be free of her."

"Isn't that what you just asked me to do? Sign the papers so she could be free of me?"

"Your insolence is intolerable," Mr. Knight snapped. "I just want you to free her, not pass her from one demon to another."

Sebastian grinned. He didn't realize he had such a reputation. Undeserved, of course, but he wouldn't argue. "I have no idea what I've done to deserve such high disrespect from you, nor do I care to know. However, what I do wonder is why you even care who she marries. Obviously you thought I wasn't good enough for her for some reason or another—not that I have wish to convince you otherwise. But, from what I recollect, you sent her off to live in the country as a companion—forgotten. It was only due to my mother's passing and her gaining a fortune that she is now in London and it's not even you who she is staying with. It seems to me that you've disowned her. So what does it matter who her husband is?"

"It is due to her impulsiveness that she married you. That I cannot change. Nor can I begin to repair the amount of damage that was caused to her reputation after that unfortunate event. But I can try my best to ensure she doesn't end up with another cold-hearted husband who doesn't want her."

Sebastian felt every one of those words like a blow to the jaw. It was no secret that he'd never been overly fond of Belle. She was an acceptable playmate, but he certainly didn't desire her like a wife. As he'd all but told her, he could have initiated intimacies with Rachel if he'd married her instead. But Belle? The feeling just wasn't there. Not that they were actually there with Rachel, but he surely would have had an easier time closing his eyes and pretending she was someone else. So docile and quiet, she likely wouldn't have noticed or cared since he'd rescued her from Lord Yourke.

"Mr. Knight, I won't argue with your ascertainment of my feelings for Belle. We are just friends. I will also agree that it was partially her impulsiveness that led to our marriage. However, I cannot in good conscience annul this marriage and throw her to the wolves again. I must first secure for her a good match."

"I don't give a damn about your conscience, Sebastian. Annul the damn marriage."

"I can't."

"Why? Are you afraid that Rachel won't wish to marry you when she realizes you've been married to her sister all of this time and you're hoping that if you secure Belle a good match that she'll be more inclined to rekindle the relationship?"

"She's already married," he said tightly. Not that he gave a hang one way or the other.

"And widowed."

Sebastian stared at the man.

"Don't think that I haven't learned that you were supposed to be stealing away with Rachel until Belle got in the way."

"Let me make this clear now so we don't have to have this discussion again, I have no interest in throwing Belle over to marry Rachel." *Nor did I truly wish to marry Rachel back then, either.* But there was no reason to say that. That would just be cruel.

"Then prove yourself. Annul your sham of a marriage and let Belle be free of you to marry who she pleases."

"Tell me, sir," Sebastian said, steepling his hands in front of his chin. "Why is it that she doesn't know that we're still married anyway? Were you hoping to keep her bounded off into the country where she could never learn the truth of it?"

"No," he snapped. "I wanted her to get married. And your father wants an heir. That's why we—" He broke off, but it didn't matter, he'd said enough to confirm all of Sebastian's suspicions.

"Do not worry yourself, Mr. Knight. Belle will make a good match this Season I guarantee it."

"What reason do you have to even care?"

Sebastian shrugged. "It's quite simple, really. We're friends. I was there when this scandal was created and I...er...wasn't there when she had to bear it. I'd like very much to be a friend to her now and help her make a good match."

"What qualifies you to know what a good match for my daughter is?"

"What qualifies you?" Sebastian challenged. "Belle was of an age where she could have come out before the whole Gretna Green incident, but she'd never mentioned to me that she was going to London. And believe me, I spent enough time in her company that if you'd planned to take her, she'd have said something."

Mr. Knight's nostrils flared. "There wasn't a reason to. Rachel was betrothed to my second cousin, Lord Yourke. Belle was too young...and spirited. She wouldn't have had a successful Season, I assure you."

"Well then, we are in perfect agreement, Mr. Knight. I shall make it my duty to see to it that Belle has a successful Season—"

"That is not your right," Mr. Knight shouted.

"I am her husband," Sebastian declared, jabbing a finger at his chest for emphasis. "My involvement in her affairs trumps yours and I assure you she will be happy with her match at the end of the Season." He stood and ushered a red-faced Mr. Knight to the door. "Now that we have that settled, if there isn't anything else I can do for you, I shall bid you farewell."

Mr. Knight looked at him as if he might like to rip Sebastian's head straight from his shoulders.

Sebastian kept his calm and offered the man a smile.

His father-in-law bristled, then marched out of the room.

Sighing with relief, Sebastian flopped down in his chair.

"I don't want her."

Sebastian snapped his eyes open. He'd quite forgotten that Giles was still in the room with him. Sebastian shifted and tried to act affronted, though he knew if he'd seen that display and knew he'd be doomed to a life with that ogre for a father-in-law, he wouldn't be too thrilled at the prospect of marriage, either. "Why not?" he asked with a forced smile.

Giles shook his head slowly. "She's yours."

***

The following morning, Sebastian shoved his list of three names into his breast pocket and started for the townhouse where Belle was staying only three blocks from him. The weather was warm, so he decided to walk.

Nearing the red brick front of the small townhouse Mrs. Finch was renting for their Season, he briefly considered using the window again, but thought to act civilized and try the door this time. If, however, she'd told her butler not to let him in, he *would* use the window. She could count on that.

"Good morning, my lord," Mrs. Finch, Belle's chaperone greeted him in loud tones after he was shown into the drawing room with no protest at all at the door.

"It's good to see you again, Mrs. Finch," he said loudly before taking a seat on the world's most uncomfortable settee on the opposite side of the room.

"Lovely weather, isn't it?"

To oblige her, Sebastian made a show of looking out the window then nodded. "Indeed."

It was hard to tell what Mrs. Finch thought of him. He was titled and reasonably wealthy, after all; but there was the minor issue of his past scandal involving Belle and the fact that Mrs. Finch had probably heard some very unfavorable things about him over the years with Belle as her companion.

He was spared from having to speculate further on the disconcerting topic when Belle practically floated into the room wearing a lavender morning gown with darker purple lace sewn around the cuffs of her sleeves. Her skirt was so voluptuous he'd have believed her if she said she'd stuffed a cloud under the fabric.

He immediately stood and greeted her, noticing how her smile didn't quite meet her eyes. She was still apprehensive around him, it would seem. Not that he could blame her entirely. He couldn't, but he'd have to ignore it.

He waited while she took her seat then resumed his.

"I've come up with a list of three names," he murmured without preamble just low enough to evade Mrs. Finch's hearing.

She lifted a single, dark eyebrow. "Possible names for your firstborn?"

"No. Potential husbands for you."

Her face went red and she cast a quick, not-so-discreet look to Mrs. Finch who seemed to just smile and nod. "Must we discuss this now?"

"Why not?"

Keeping her head tilted where Mrs. Finch couldn't see her expression, Belle cut her eyes toward her chaperone.

"She can't hear me clear over here."

"You don't know that."

He shrugged, then looked in Mrs. Finch's direction. Then, in his usual tone said, "Say, do you like to eat pickled pigs feet?"

Belle looked like she was trying to keep a straight face, and the left corner of her lips twitched slightly when Mrs. Finch nodded and said, "Of course, dear."

"All right," she said in a hushed whisper.

Sebastian straightened. "All right your choices are—"

"Pardon me a minute. My choices?" She crossed her arms. "I didn't realize it would be you and your infinite wisdom that would pick my husband."

"Of course it is." Sebastian shot her a grin, then seeing as how her lips were still pursed, he cleared his throat and said, "Belle, I looked through *Debretts* last night and of the dozens of names I found, only a handful were suitable. I think it's best we stick to one who is already suitable instead of you trying to reform one."

She quirked a brow. "Are you saying I couldn't?"

"Not at all. I just don't think one of the ones who need to reform would be worth your time."

Silence engulfed them.

Had he just complimented her? Moreover, had he meant it? He shook his head to clear the thought. Belle was his friend. He was supposed to think highly of her. There was nothing more to it than that.

"Anyway," he continued, "the three I think would suit you are: Sir Wallace Benedict, Sir Michael Smythe and Giles Goddard."

"No. No. And no."

"Why not?"

She looked at him as if he were the stupidest man in existence. "Sir Wallace Benedict has been jilted thrice and is rumored to still be madly in love with the first lady to do so, only agreeing to marry the other two because they'd each trapped him then abandoned him. My life is exciting enough already, I don't need that kind of excitement to add to it."

He lifted his eyebrows. "I had no idea your life was so exciting."

"I'd wager there's quite a lot of things about me you don't know," she returned.

"All right, so you're not so interested in a thrice-jilted baronet. What's wrong with Sir Michael Smythe? He was knighted just last year for his bravery."

Belle cocked her head to the side. "I do wonder how you'd know that, seeing as how you haven't even been in this country for at least five years."

He shrugged. "News does travel to the continent. It might be delayed, but it still reaches there." Especially when one has paid people to keep him apprised of what all was happening in England. He'd paid extra for any information available about Belle, but she didn't need to know that. "So what is it about him that disqualifies him from your list of potential husbands?"

A light patch of pink stained each of her cheeks. "He's...he's...he's..."

"Yes, he's a he," Sebastian agreed, making a rolling motion with his hand.

Her blush grew deeper. "Actually, *he* is not what *he* seems."

Sebastian made his eyes flare wide and turned his head to the side. "Is he really a she?"

She swatted at his arm. "No. Stop that."

"Then what's the problem? Everything I've ever heard about him has been very positive."

"Then you haven't heard everything," she said flatly.

He stared at her. "Does that mean you don't believe everything that you read?" *Especially the articles regarding yourself?*

"You of all people should know I don't read gossip articles," she said in a tone that would suggest she was trying to sound off-handed. Unfortunately for her, he'd spent too much time in her presence growing up that he heard the edge she tried to hide.

"So then are you telling me you've seen him do something...er...less-than-gentlemanly that would suggest he's not a good husband for you?"

She dropped her gaze to the floor. "Can we please just cross him off the list?"

A dull ache that Sebastian couldn't name formed in his chest. "Belle, did he do something to you?" The room began to spin around him as he waited for his answer. If Sir Michael Smythe did anything at all to her, Sebastian would destroy him. Then, himself. It was his responsibility to protect Belle. He was her husband still. That hadn't changed because he was commanded out of their house and blackmailed out of England. "Belle, tell me now, what did that man do that makes him an unsuitable husband?" He no longer cared if Mrs. Finch could hear their conversation. He needed to know.

Belle swallowed audibly and refused to meet his eye. "He and Rachel..."

"Are lovers," he finished for her.

She gave a simple shrug and looked down at her hands. "Apparently not everything made it to the continent."

He chuckled. "No. I guess not." He straightened. "How long?"

"Three months. But three months or three years or three encounters, it matters naught. I don't want to marry a gentleman who's carried on an affair with my sister."

"You married me, didn't you," he teased before he could think better of it.

Her eyes widened. "You and Rachel...did you two..."

"No."

She blushed and shook her head ruefully. "Not that it matters so much, I suppose. We didn't share intimacies, either."

Except kiss. It was on the tip of his tongue, but he thought better than to remind her of their blacksmith wedding ceremony. He ran his hand through his hair. "Belle, about my arrangement with Rachel—"

"I'm glad you agree Sir Michael's affair with my sister puts him firmly out for being my potential suitor."

He frowned. She clearly didn't want to hear what he had to say, and it was for the best. His attempt to soothe her pride would likely only make things worse between them. "Giles Goddard?"

"No."

"Why not?"

"I don't even know who that is."

Sebastian waved his hand through the air. "No need to worry on that score. I know every naughty deed he's ever committed—" he dropped his voice to a stage whisper— "believe me, the list is quite short." At her raised brow, he simply shrugged and added. "He's been a good friend of mine for a few years now."

"Well, then that is a definite no."

He twisted his lips in irritation. "Why?"

"Because he's a good friend of yours and any good friend of yours is certainly not a man I wish to be leg shackled to for the rest of my life."

Chapter Nine

Isabelle tried hard to hide her smile at the way Sebastian laughed loudly at her comment.

She didn't have to try any longer when she noticed that Edmund had entered the room and was standing by the door, his thin, grey eyebrows raised in question.

"Edmund," she chirped. She gestured to an unoccupied chair. "Do join us."

Mrs. Finch turned her head. "Oh, I didn't even see you come in. How have you been?"

"I've been well," he nearly shouted then took the seat Isabelle had pointed to. "And you Isabelle?" He slowly dragged his eyes to Sebastian, then back to hers. "Have you been well, too?"

She flushed. "Yes."

"I've been well, too," Sebastian offered, eliciting an inappropriate giggle from Isabelle and a sideways glance from Edmund.

"Indeed," Edmund murmured, a slight twitch to his lips.

"Yes, indeed," Sebastian echoed, grinning.

Once again, Isabelle released a little burble of uncontrollable laugher.

"And just what brings you by here...again?" Edmund asked.

Isabelle could have sworn Sebastian muttered something about someone's name—presumably his—being Belgrave, then raised his voice. "To see Belle."

Isabelle tried not to cringe at the use of his nickname for her: Belle. It wasn't really a name of endearment, he'd always grin and tell her he called her that because she was as loud and annoying as a bell. She stiffened. Then blinked. "Did I miss something?"

Edmund regarded her with a curious glance and she jerked her eyes away, embarrassed.

"Well, I'd best be on my way," Sebastian said with a smile and a sparkle in his brown eyes that spoke of all sorts of mischief.

Isabelle sat frozen as he stood and made his formal excuses to the room for the benefit of no one save Mrs. Finch.

"Is he the one, then?" Edmund asked without ceremony.

Isabelle started. "Who, what one?" Why did everyone keep asking her that?

Edmund waggled his eyebrows at her. "Lord Belgrave. Is he the one you're throwing me over for?" he teased.

"No," she said quickly, perhaps too quickly because Edmund began to chuckle. She frowned at him. He knew of everything that had happened between her and Sebastian. How could he sit there and even suggest such a thing? "We're just old friends, nothing more."

"Old friends," he repeated. "I see. So your friendship with him is the reason for the sharp banter yesterday and the coded messages today?"

She tucked a tendril of her red hair behind her ear. "I'd say that sounds correct."

Edmund shook his head. "If I didn't know better, I'd think there was still something there between the two of you."

"But you do know better," she said, scowling. There had never been anything between them at all except a form of friendship when they were younger, and that only came in the form of him tolerating her as best he could just so he'd have a playmate. For her part, she'd done the best she could making sure not to annoy him more than was necessary and not allowing herself dream up any sort of misguided notions that he might one day fall in love with her and become her husband. He was a lord and she was common, not to mention poor. It wasn't done.

Truly, she'd done her best to accomplish both tasks—though not always as well as he, or she, might have liked. Though she annoyed him, he always helped her out of any scrape she got into. Just like now. Although, she must admit, him helping her snag a husband was significantly less endearing than when he'd helped her climb down from a tree he'd told her was too high for her to climb.

"Indeed." His word drew her from her trance and he picked off a small string from his buckskin trousers and let it flutter to the floor. "And what of Mr. Appleton. Is he just a friend, too?"

She released a breath and fidgeted with the lace that circled her sleeve. All friends. Only friends. "Yes, Edmund, Mr. Appleton is just a friend, too."

"Now, *that* I believe."

She jerked her gaze to his. "What is that to mean?"

He waved her off. "Every fool can see that you and Mr. Appleton are just friends—even if he does pretend to write you poetry meant for another lady."

She blushed. "He was just trying to save me from Sebastian."

"Sebastian," Edmund murmured, reminding Isabelle of a parrot. "I see that the two of you are still on very informal terms. You call him by his first name and he calls you Belle."

"Only when he's irritated with me."

"I disagree. I don't think he was irritated with you today. Or yesterday."

She dismissed his statement with a quick shrug. "It must just be a habit he hasn't broken."

"Perhaps, but have you ever wondered if he spells it Belle, like the last part of your name or Bel, like the first part of his title?"

Isabelle narrowed her eyes at him. What had gotten into the man? Was he cracked? Who thought about such things? Edmund, that's who. She shook her head. Sebastian only ever spoke to her, one didn't think of how something was spelled while they were speaking. At least she didn't. Edmund might be different, but she was fairly certain if he did that, he was truly a rarity. She couldn't tell him that though.

"I'm not sure which spelling he'd use if he were to write it—" probably 'B-e-l-l' if she had to guess— "but I'm curious as to why you'd care."

"I'm just trying to educate myself on my competition."

Isabelle laughed. "Sebastian isn't your competition."

Edmund lifted a brow. "Then who is?"

If she had a genuine marital interest in Edmund, she'd

consider playfully teasing him by listing off the three names Sebastian had suggested, but since she saw him as only a friend and had no need to flirt with him, she just told the truth. "There isn't any."

His face softened. "Isabelle, I told you that—"

"I know," she said a little sharper than she'd meant. She gave him her best smile despite the tears that were now welling in her eyes. "I know. There just isn't anyone."

"You still have plenty of time, Isabelle. It's barely been three months, and you haven't met every eligible gentleman yet."

"I know." She remembered the three unsuitable choices that Sebastian had listed off, and blinked back the tears. She didn't know if those were truly the only genuine options or if those were the only ones he thought would take her.

"Then if you know, why are you so upset?"

Despite herself, she grinned. "I don't know." And that was the truth. She had no idea why she suddenly felt so sad and alone. She'd spent her entire girlhood following Sebastian around. Not necessarily dreaming of marriage to him out of any great love, but they'd been friends. Friendship, she'd learned from seeing her own parents get along, and his arguing constantly, offered a great basis for a marriage. But now, she knew friendship was all she'd ever had, but for a reason she couldn't name, she wasn't ready yet to settle for it.

"Is it Belgrave?"

She groaned. "No. I don't wish to marry him."

"I wasn't asking that. But since you brought it up..."

She pursed her lips.

"All right, I'll take that as a no." Edmund shifted and crossed his arms. "What I meant to ask is if he upset you?"

"No. Not intentionally."

"So then he did," Edmund surmised.

Isabelle sighed. "He's offered to help me find a husband and his prospects are...well, they're not very promising."

"Who are they?"

"Sir Wallace Benedict, Sir Michael Smythe and Giles

Goddard."

"Belgrave has been away too long. Sir Wallace and Sir Michael aren't right for you and I don't happen to know who Giles Goddard is, but his name alone does not recommend him."

"He's a friend of Sebastian's," she murmured forcing a slim smile.

"A friend, you say."

She nodded. What was he trying to imply?

"And have you met this friend?"

Isabelle turned her head to the side and frowned. "Actually no, I haven't."

"Then how do you know he exists?"

"Why wouldn't he?"

"Perhaps Belgrave was giving you two impossible choices so you'd choose the third one."

"Why would he do that?"

"It's simple—"

Not to her it wasn't. The workings of Edmund's mind were oftentimes—like now—very tiring.

"—Giles Goddard doesn't really exist. Belgrave is using his name as a front and he plans to be the one you fall in love with."

Isabelle stared at him, flabbergasted. "And why would he want me to fall in love with himself? Last we spoke, that was the absolute last thing he wanted to have happen."

"Perhaps he's changed his mind," Edmund countered with a shrug.

"Uh huh. Besides the part where I don't believe that's his real intent, I'm also supposed to believe he invented a man to accomplish this...this...scheme?"

"Absolutely." He gave her a serious look. "As you said you've never met him."

"No, I haven't," she said carefully. "But I read his name in one of the articles about the Rutherford ball last week. You can't expect me to believe the author invented him and Sebastian latched onto the name."

"I didn't say that."

"Oh, are you saying the author was referring to Sebastian's imaginary friend as Giles Goddard, then?"

"You never know." Edmund forced his shoulders up, twisted his lips into an overdone frown and made his eyebrows shoot toward his hairline. "Authors are some strange folks, Isabelle."

Chapter Ten

Three days later

Isabelle stared at the unread invitation on the silver salver. She'd received many invitations since coming to London, but she had an idea this invitation wasn't as ordinary as the rest. If she had to guess, she'd say that it was issued at the request of Sebastian.

Of course it *could* be another ordinary invitation. It looked just like the rest on the outside, which is all she could see...

But it had arrived later than all of the others.

She snatched the invitation up and broke the seal.

...join us for a dinner party...eight pm...419 King...

She read over it again, but didn't recognize the name of the hostess: Lady Norcourt. Perhaps she's fictitious, she thought with a giggle.

Oh wait, no, she wasn't imaginary. Lady Norcourt was Mr. Appleton's mother. Of course Isabelle didn't know all of the details, only the ones she'd gleaned from reading the gossip sheets to Mrs. Finch and having her fill the gaps, but Simon Appleton's mother, had married the octogenarian baron Lord Norcourt when she was fifteen. Isabelle didn't know if there was a child borne of the union or not. Since she'd never heard of a Lord Norcourt she assumed probably not.

The dowager Lady Norcourt shocked the *ton* and fell from grace when she remarried a man named Walter Appleton who was rumored to be her lover within a month of the late baron's death. Then she shocked the *ton* again when less than seven months later Simon was born. Mrs. Finch speculated—as did a number of people Isabelle would assume—that Simon was the late baron's son and had she not married Mr. Appleton, he'd have inherited the barony. But her own selfishness had taken away her son's birthright.

One would never know that such a heavy sin hung between them all, however. Some of the rumors must have been true for the most part because Mr. and Mrs. Appleton seemed genuinely happy together. So happy that Mrs. Appleton hadn't kept her title of Lady Norcourt though it was acceptable for her to do so and Simon had never seemed bitter about not inheriting his due. Perhaps he knew the truth of the situation, and his parents truly were having an illicit affair. She'd never know and doubted anyone else would, either.

Isabelle sighed and set the invitation down. Well, at least if she attended Mr. Appleton would be there, too.

And so might Henrietta Hughes, she thought with a smile. Not that the hobby of matchmaking had ever excited her before, but for some reason she'd like to see Simon Appleton happy. Mr. Appleton deserved—

She frowned. How did Sebastian know Lady Norcourt or Katherine Appleton? Even more curious, were they even the same person or had there been a male issue somewhere that the title had passed to and there was a new Lady Norcourt? Hmm, now she *had* to go!

***

Sebastian thought he might suffocate and it had *nothing* to do with how tightly he'd tied his cravat. It was the atmosphere in the room. Even more unsettling, Isabelle hadn't even arrived yet.

In front of him stood two grown, or somewhat grown, gentlemen, one of which was acting like a petulant child.

Of course, had Sebastian been Mr. Appleton he might have been a little upset, too.

"Since when have you decided to play the role of Lady Norcourt?" Mr. Appleton asked of his mother.

Katherine Appleton, alias Lady Norcourt, who unbeknownst to Sebastian was the dowager baroness Giles had claimed a relation to when Sebastian had sought his help in finding a titled lady to host a dinner to invite Isabelle to, clasped her hands in front of her. "Giles has asked that I play hostess at his dinner party, Simon. I

64

don't suppose that one night of being Lady Norcourt will harm anything."

Simon Appleton folded his arms across his chest and cast a sharp look at his mother and Giles, who apparently was his half-brother or a similar relation. "Perhaps not for either of you."

"Simon," his father, Mr. Appleton warned, placing his hand on Simon's shoulder.

Simon shrugged him off. "Thank you for the invitation, Lady Norcourt," he said to his mother with a sneer. "However, I just remembered that I have another engagement I am expected to be at tonight."

Sebastian doubted that, but had no plans to question the man, and apparently neither did anyone else as he strolled from the room.

Mrs. Appleton, or Lady Norcourt, as she was apparently referring to herself for the evening stood, wringing her hands. She cast a hesitant glance to Giles, then to her husband. Her eyes were wide and full of hesitation or hurt or concern or unease. Something. Blast it all, Sebastian was a man, he didn't know what emotion the woman was feeling, but whatever it was it had made her look like she was about to swoon.

Her husband walked up to her and murmured something in her ear before whisking her from the room.

"I didn't know you had a brother," Sebastian said without ceremony as soon as the Appletons were out of the room.

"He didn't, either."

Sebastian grinned at his friend's remark. "No, it would seem that he didn't." He idly scratched his temple and studied his friend. Giles often wore the same expression. Unless he was completely befuddled or upset, then it just went blank. "Did you know?"

"A while," he admitted quietly. "Never met though."

Sebastian nodded. That was obvious. "How long have you known?"

"Twenty years."

Sebastian's jaw would have dropped in shock if he weren't so shocked that he couldn't move. They'd been inseparable for the past five years. Why in the devil had he never heard of this? Not that he should be too surprised. He hadn't even known that Giles was a lord, either. Not that it mattered one way or the other to Sebastian what rank his friend held. He was more surprised Giles had hid it so well. "I see," he said slowly. "Is Simon twenty?"

"Yes."

"And his mother is your mother?"

"Yes."

"And his father?"

Giles shrugged.

"Do the two of you share only the same mother?" Sebastian guessed, though to be honest with the brutality of a wild bull, Simon and Giles shared several traits with Mr. Appleton. All three men had dark brown hair and emerald eyes. All three were of a similar height. Sebastian hadn't made note of the similarities before, but now it seemed all he could think of.

Giles shrugged again.

Though it really wasn't any of his concern, Sebastian would have to remember to ask for a tour of the townhouse at some point and see if there was a portrait of the old baron. Not that that meant too much. He'd glimpsed many portraits that didn't resemble the subject other than the lady was wearing a dress and the man was painted wearing breeches.

"Thank you for hosting," Sebastian said to change the subject.

Giles nodded, but didn't say anything. He didn't have to. Sebastian had spent enough time in his company to take note of his stiffened spine, clenched fists and narrowed eyes that had no object in sight except the open air in front of him. This could only mean one thing: Giles was upset. Just as much or perhaps more so than Simon Appleton had been.

Sebastian doubted, however, that the reason was the same.

Simon had seemed upset about meeting his brother, and perhaps the fact he had one and had lived his entire life not knowing about it. The lies and betrayal must have hurt. Giles, on the other hand, was more likely upset by the cold dismissal he'd received. It wasn't anything new, mind you. Many people

SECRETS OF A VISCOUNT

dismissed Giles out of hand and the man never even seemed to mind. But this was different. Simon Appleton was different. He wasn't some random fool Giles had encountered, but his own brother.

"Giles, would you rather if we had the butler send everyone away or I acted as host?"

Neither of those options would be well received, but the man did not look in a position to receive guests.

Giles shook his head. "I'll be host."

"Very well." What Sebastian—and likely everyone else who'd ever encountered him—wouldn't give to know the thoughts in Giles' head.

"She's here," Giles said abruptly.

Sebastian twisted around to see out of the window as Belle's carriage pulled up. Rooted to the floor, he stood frozen as she descended the carriage wearing a red satin gown with a billowing skirt and a low swoop neckline that offered him and everyone around a generous view of her breasts. Something in him tightened, irritation at her dressing thus, he'd wager since he'd never desire *her*. He swore under his breath and stalked from the room behind Giles. As soon as he had a moment alone with his wife, he'd have to inform her that her goal was to dress in a way that would snare her a husband, not get her ravished and left with a bastard in her belly.

Chapter Eleven

Sebastian was less than hospitable.

But then, why should Isabelle be surprised. He'd never been very good at minding his manners and his sneering and growling only proved it.

"We need to talk," Sebastian said with a grunt after she'd finally been properly introduced to his friend Giles Goddard—which, by the way, she was convinced she'd made the right decision in marking him off her list. It wasn't that he was completely undesirable. In fact, he was quite handsome on the whole. Tall with brown hair and a chiseled face that matched his barrel chest perfectly. He wore white breeches, a yellow waistcoat, a pale blue coat and had an emerald pin the same color as his eyes in the middle of his flawlessly tied cravat. He was quite striking. But he was also quite...brooding wasn't the right word, though he did appear to be doing that, he was more...tense. His posture reminded her of a fire poker: stiff and unyielding. Perhaps he was nervous?

Sebastian's squeeze of her arm just above her elbow brought her to present. Right. He wanted to talk.

"Very well, my lord, what shall we talk about?"

He pursed his lips. "Giles, we'll go make use of the chess table for a spell, if you don't mind."

Isabelle allowed Sebastian to lead her into a large drawing room that had two card tables and one chess table set up for play. "I didn't realize this would be such a large party," she murmured.

Sebastian pulled a chair out for her. "It won't be." He grimaced and lowered himself into the chair opposite her. "As it is, Sir Wallace's engagement was announced in the paper earlier this week. Apparently, he attended a house party hosted by Lord and Lady Watson last month and the festivities have ended with the announcement that he and Lord Watson's sister are betrothed." He shook his head. "Not that it matters too much, you'd already said you're not interested in him."

"No, I wasn't." She gestured to the board. "Are we to play or discuss the social calendar of Sir Wallace?"

"You have the white pieces," he reminded her.

She bit her lip. She'd always hated chess and now she knew why: she couldn't remember all the rules. Especially the most basic one of who went first. "Right." She moved one of the men in the front row forward a space.

Sebastian mirrored her move and waited for Isabelle to pick up her piece. "I don't like your gown."

"Excuse me?" she demanded, setting the ivory pawn down with more force than necessary.

"It doesn't fit you."

Isabelle glanced down at her gown. Even though she wore no less than three yards of petticoats underneath her skirt touched the floor just enough to nearly trip her every time she took a step. Her sleeves were capped, a perfectly acceptable fashion to wear at a dinner party. "I beg your pardon, but in no way does my dress not fit right. The modiste sewed it to my exact measurements."

"Yes, that's obvious," he said, leveling his eyes on her chest.

She dropped her gaze to where his was on her chest and flushed. Her neckline was low enough to allow half of her bare bosom to be glimpsed by anyone who looked her way. "I don't know why you should care, you have no need to be looking."

"Perhaps not, but when you put so much on display, it's all anyone can notice."

Isabelle's flush deepened and she readjusted her shawl to cover her breasts better. "There. Now, you shouldn't be too distracted to take your turn."

He scowled at her. "I never said I was too distracted by them. I was merely commenting that there is a thin line between class and crass. You're walking it."

She moved her piece and shrugged in a way that made her newly positioned shawl fall. "I daresay, you'd be the one to know since you crossed it ages ago."

69

"Fix your shawl," he ground out, moving a chess piece. "You don't want a potential suitor to think you've loose morals."

Isabelle laughed. "Loose morals? I'm hardly showing anything."

"It's too much."

She narrowed her eyes on him. They might be alone and he her friend and former husband (what a strange combination *that* was), but there were topics even they shouldn't discuss. She expected that he knew that as well as she did, but he always did like to push her over the edge into the pool of impropriety. She licked her lips. "I'd imagine you've shown far more of yourself to those of my sex than I've shown to those of yours."

"You think so, do you," he drawled. He crossed his arms and lowered his lashes, but was still looking at her. "If I remember correctly, there isn't much more space between where the edge of your bodice is and where your nip—"

"Don't you say it," she hissed. Mortification overtook her and she abruptly stood from her chair. Six years ago on that better-forgotten morning when he'd glimpsed her naked, she did have small breasts and he'd have been absolutely correct. The fact that he remembered such, however, unsettled her in ways she couldn't possibly name. "I don't know why you'd care to dredge up memories of my naked body, but if reminding me of my shame and flinging the past in my face was your intention in striking up a friendship with me, I am better off with no friends than a snake like you."

***

Sebastian sat stock-still as Belle swept the room. She deserved this moment, he granted. He'd been an arse. He deserved her wrath and much more. He should have never gone so far as to make mention of how he remembered her breasts to look, but damn if seeing her in that dress tonight didn't bring back memories of the day she'd stood before him wearing nothing but the drops of water that were running down her naked body.

At the time he couldn't have possibly cared less at seeing her naked. She'd held no appeal to him that way. Now... Now he was stuck sitting in his friend's drawing room with a large erection he didn't want to explain the origin of straining against the front of his trousers. "Devil her," he muttered in irritation.

Footsteps coming down the hall pushed him into action. He rose and adjusted his coat to conceal the unwelcome visitor below his waist, then walked as gracefully as he could to the hall to join the others.

Belle was on the arm of a gentleman Sebastian didn't recognize. Served him right, he supposed. Had he been a bit more diplomatic in explaining about her dress, he'd get to sit by her tonight at dinner. He started. Why the devil did he care if he sat by her or not? He shouldn't. He'd arranged this torturous dinner party to help her meet a young gentleman who'd suit her. He'd expected that to be Giles, but clearly Giles wasn't in the most charming of moods.

Sebastian took a step back and waited until two ladies came down the hall together. Because Simon Appleton had excused himself early, there was to be one extra lady tonight. Wordlessly, Sebastian came up behind them, then cleared his throat and offered them each an arm.

It was an awkward exchange, to be sure, but the easiest way to manage it.

In the dining room, he was seated between the honorable Miss Louisa Hunt, daughter of Viscount Grindle and Lady Mary Craven the eldest daughter of the Duke of Craven.

"What lovely cheekbones you have," Lady Mary complimented after he adjusted the napkin in his lap.

"Pardon me?"

"Your cheekbones, my lord. They are quite lovely. Very high and rigid. Sharp."

Sebastian fought the urge to touch his cheek and block her view of his face before she said anything more asinine, but reached for his empty glass instead. He frowned. The footman had better get over here to fill his glass soon. He'd never been one to indulge in the spirits while taking meals but tonight he might begin.

He was ready to stab himself with his own knife just to put an end to the tedium before the second course was served and he still didn't have anything good to drink. The footman had given them all some fruity punch. He scowled at the offending glass.

"Does lace make you itch when you dance with a young lady, my lord?" Lady Mary asked, her eyes wide and intent.

He didn't even want to know why she wanted to know such a ridiculous thing. "No," he said slowly.

Her lips formed the biggest frown he'd ever born witness to. "Pooh."

"You want the lace of your gown to make your dance partner itch?" he asked for no other reason than to see her talk again so her awful frown would disappear.

She shook her head sadly in a way that made her golden curls sway. "I was hoping that's why the gentleman don't like to dance with me."

Sebastian stared at her. "That's possible," he allowed, though he doubted it. It probably had more to do with her inane chatter and awkward compliments.

"Perhaps I should wear less lace on my gowns and wear them more like Miss Knight," she murmured.

Sebastian's eyes shot to Belle.

"Do you like her dress, my lord?"

Sebastian jerked his gaze back to Lady Mary. "It's very...er...eye catching. So puffy and all."

She giggled. "I do believe that is the first time I've ever heard a gentleman use the word puffy."

Sebastian made his eyes flare wide, though he hadn't meant what he'd said as a compliment and was rather surprised she took it as one. "Please be mindful of my reputation as a libertine and exercise the greatest caution of who you divulge that particular secret to."

Lady Mary giggled again like he knew she would. Except this time, it was louder and suddenly her pale face went bright red. Then she snorted. Loudly. Not once, not twice, but over and over. *Snort, snort, snort, giggle, giggle, giggle, snort, snort, snort...*

Sebastian sat frozen in terror. He'd expected her to giggle a little at his jest, but not turn into a madwoman. *This* was likely the reason men didn't wish to dance with her.

Suddenly she rapped him across the knuckles with her fan. "Lord Belgrave," she giggled. "You—" *giggle*— "are—" Whatever she thought him to be was lost in another round of ferocious giggles and snorts.

Not wanting to seem too rude, but wishing for a distraction now that the entire table was staring at him and Lady Mary, he turned his attention to Miss Hunt. "Is she always like this?" he whispered.

"Yes," she whispered back, her lips twitching in amusement. "She's just nervous."

"She's likely to sever her own tongue if she keeps carrying on," Sebastian remarked.

Miss Hunt grinned at him. Then she did it, she dissolved into a fit of giggles to rival her friend's!

Sebastian lifted his eyebrow at the host. "Giles, did your men taint the punch?"

"No." He frowned and blinked at Sebastian. "Was he supposed to?"

And at that, peals of laughter from half the room filled the air.

Chapter Twelve

Isabelle wasn't jealous precisely of the way the two ladies on either side of Sebastian cooed and fawned over him. Nor was she jealous of the attention he showered on them. However, if her dinner companion could be even a tenth as interesting as Sebastian seemed to be to those ladies, she'd jump onto the table and begin singing. She nearly snorted, that alone would be more entertaining than the conversation she was engaged in.

"The duck is splendid, no?" Mr. Frisk said from beside her.

"Quite." She cast a sideways glance down toward the end of the table where Sebastian sat chatting with those two featherbrains. She twisted her lips. The one on his left was showing far more of her fleshy bosom than Isabelle.

"So tender and succulent, no?"

Isabelle whipped around to turn her attention back to Mr. Frisk then realized he was talking about the duck! "Yes. Quite."

"Tell me—" he speared another piece of meat and lifted it to his lips— "have you ever tasted anything so divine?" He closed his eyes and chewed so slowly Isabelle thought she might fall asleep before he finished.

"No, I don't think I have." She shook her head and said a silent prayer that the meal would pass quickly.

It did. Pass, that is. But not 'quickly' at all, unfortunately.

However, by the time the meal was done, the torture had only just begun.

"Shall we play charades or cards?" Mrs. Appleton, who was also apparently Lady Norcourt this evening, asked.

Cards was the consensus with a vote from everyone except the two simpletons seated beside Sebastian.

Once in the drawing room, partners were announced.

"Lady Mary, why don't you partner Lord Belgrave," Mrs.

Appleton announced. "And Miss Knight, why don't you partner Lord Norcourt."

Not sure whether to be relieved that she wouldn't have to sit across from Sebastian and be forced to look into his chocolate eyes for the next hour or annoyed at the obvious attempt at matchmaking that Isabelle had little doubt Sebastian was behind, she walked next to Giles and allowed him to help her into a chair. She'd never played a card game of any type before and desperately prayed that Giles, Lord Norcourt didn't mind if they lost.

Giles pulled a deck of cards from the drawer in the underside of the table and tossed it on the table in Sebastian's direction.

Sebastian unbound the cards and shuffled.

From the corner of her eye, Isabelle watched Lady Mary as she stared at Sebastian's hands while he shuffled the cards.

"I think that's enough," Sebastian said, handing the deck back to his friend.

Giles shook his head. "You."

The two men locked eyes for a moment as an unspoken message passed between them, and then Sebastian picked up the deck of cards and began passing them out to everyone.

Isabelle picked up her hand of cards and looked at them, not sure what on earth she was looking at. Unsure what she was supposed to do, she moved this card here and that card there until the thirteen cards she held were lined up in numerical order: three, four, four, five, seven, nine, nine, nine, Jack, Jack, King, King, Ace. Biting her lip, she locked eyes with Giles and mouthed. "What do I do?"

He knit his brows in confusion, his face otherwise blank.

She wanted to groan. She pointed to her cards, then gave a quick shrug.

"I don't know," he said tonelessly, but not at all trying to quiet his answer.

Were he anyone else, she'd might have questioned if his answer was genuine, but something about the look on his face hid nothing: he didn't know how to play the game any better than she did. She pressed her lips together so not to embarrass him with the little giggle in her that begged to be released. What a pair these two were.

She cleared her throat and racked her brain for the words to ask Sebastian to inform her (and his friend) of the rules without drawing too much attention to her lack of knowledge. Fortunately, she was saved when Lady Mary fluttered her eyelashes at Sebastian and said, "I hope you're a good player, my lord. I have a terrible time with this game. Mama always says I need a strong partner—which I have no doubt you are."

Isabelle stared at the girl and her shameless attempt at flirting while Sebastian appeared to be choking. The only one who didn't seem to care was Giles. "What are the rules?"

Sebastian cleared his throat. Twice. "You have to get a trick."

"Like a magic trick?" Lady Mary asked with an obnoxious giggle.

Giles winced at the shrillness of her reaction and Sebastian twisted his lips and if she wasn't certain she could have sworn he muttered something under his breath about the best magic trick he knew would involve her disappearing.

Isabelle grinned at him and he flushed, then shrugged. He'd never been one to speak so bluntly. At least she had never heard him make a comment like that. Perhaps his years of travels had changed him.

"No, a trick is having the trump—"

"Like Gabriel?" Lady Mary asked.

The entire table went quiet. Was Lady Mary completely addled or did she think acting like a simpleton was a good way to get a gentleman's attention? The stone-hard look on Sebastian's face should be enough to tell her it wasn't working. "Gabriel?" he asked in a tone that held a slightly annoyed edge.

Lady Mary nodded her head. "You know, the archangel Gabriel from the Bible. He blew his trump."

Sebastian's lips thinned and Isabelle had to duck her head to hide her grin and squeeze her empty hand into a fist to keep from laughing, her entire body shaking uncontrollably with mirth. Squeezing her eyes closed to clear her mind and regain her composure, her body began to move less as the giggles left, only to be provoked again when someone—likely Lady Mary—made a loud "*doot-de-doo*" trumpet noise and Isabelle lost it completely.

***

Sebastian stared stupefied at the tableau in front of him.

Giles' face was an odd mix of shock and humor—almost as if he couldn't quite make sense of why this well-bred woman was acting like she belonged in an asylum.

Lady Mary grinned in between bursts of annoying cackles and snorts.

As for Belle...

Genuine giggles were pouring out of her mouth, filling the room with a sound sweeter than anything he'd ever heard. While that drew his attention, it was her body's reaction, however, that kept it. Shaking almost violently with mirth, her shawl had fallen from its former position and he was almost certain her breasts were about to pop right out of the top of her gown.

Without thinking, he reached for her arm, catching her just above the elbow. It didn't stop her shaking as she tried to wiggle free.

"Let's go," he barked, giving her arm a slight squeeze to let her know what he meant.

Avoiding the curious glances of everyone in the room he gained his feet and helped her to hers, then led her across the room.

"Stop giggling like a madwoman," he hissed when they were almost to the door. "You're a lady, act it."

That sobered her instantly and she moved to pull away from his hold. He had no intentions of letting her go and tightened his grip a fraction, keeping her at his side. He needed to remind her, a bit more gently this time, that her dress was vastly inappropriate, especially when she carried on that way.

They crossed the threshold of the drawing room and entered the hall and immediately Belle jerked her arm from him and started down the hall. He closed his empty hand into a fist. He should have known she'd do that. Scowling at her back, he walked after her. "Belle, stop."

77

She kept walking.

"Belle, I said to stop."

She walked on.

He wrapped his arm around her waist, picked her up, and then carried her into the library and straight to a settee where he put her down with less grace than she might have preferred.

Just as he suspected, that didn't deter her and she immediately began pushing to her feet. "How dare you!"

"How dare I?" he repeated in the same tone she'd used, jabbing a finger toward his chest. "You're the one making a public display of yourself."

"By finding something humorous? I think not." She twisted her lips. "Now, you're dragging me from the card room like some highhanded husband who'd just found his wife having an affair will make me a mockery for certain."

He crossed his arms. "I wasn't acting as a highhanded husband —"

"No, because you willingly gave that role away without a second thought many years ago."

Her words stole the wind right from his lungs. "I was trying to protect you."

"Protect me? From what?"

He gestured toward her low-cut bodice. "Yourself."

She stared at him a moment, then he'd swear she pushed her chest out further as she stepped toward him and let her shawl fall to the floor. "While I cannot begin to comprehend why *you* have such an interest in my body—" she reached for the long end of the gold chorded bow on the front of her bodice and began to slowly pull the string— "I should like to remind you that as neither my father, nor my husband, you have no say over who I might share my body with." She gave the chord one final tug and the knot slipped loose, allowing the center of her bodice to fall open about an inch.

Sebastian's mouth ran dry.

"I believe you might recall having seen me without my clothes once, but perhaps you've neglected to notice that my body isn't the same as it was back then..."

No, he hadn't neglected to notice. He was noticing right now and it was making him break out in a cold sweat as his blood raced through his veins. But nothing short of a miracle could make him take his eyes away from where she'd pulled her bodice open just a fraction more, offering him only a slight, almost teasing, glance at the valley between the rounded globes of her breasts.

"As the only one who has control of my body—" she continued, reaching for his hand— "I can share with whoever I want." She brought his hand to her warm skin and like a seductress he'd have never thought her to be, she slowly moved his hand in a way that dragged his fingertips across the plane of her chest, with each sweep she made, moving them just that much closer to her breasts.

"You're playing a very dangerous game," he practically growled at her; his fingers itched to take advantage, but he couldn't. Not yet. Her game was too intriguing for him to stop playing it.

"Am I?"

"Yes." This time he did move to take advantage of what she was offering him and pressed the pads of his fingers into the softness of the side of her breast where she'd last stopped his hand. His erection nearly doubled in size where it was pressed against the softness of her stomach.

Something flickered in her eyes, but before he could name it, it was gone. Then suddenly, so was his hand from her body as she squeezed his wrist and thrust his hand away. "You are the biggest hypocrite. You're not interested in protecting me from the unwanted attentions of men who might see me. You're only interested in protecting yourself. How tragic it would be that the lofty Lord Belgrave desired the young lady whom he'd once spurned and condemned to a life of shame? I do hope you enjoyed this because it is the last time you'll ever be afforded such liberties from me."

"And why did you afford them to me at all?" he asked around the blood thundering through his ears.

"To see that my theory was correct," she spat as she retied her bodice. "And it was."

He scoffed and reached forward to turn her chin up so she'd have to see his eyes. "You don't know anything about what you think you do."

"No?" Challenge flashed in her eyes. "I know plenty. The very idea that someone else might be allowed to enjoy my body rankles you. I didn't know why before—" she shot a triumphant glance down below his waist where only a moment ago a large erection had tented his trousers— "but now I do."

"Any man would react that way," he said with a snarl.

"Not one who didn't hold any interest," she retorted. She cocked her head to the side. "What I wonder, is why you have any interest at all when we both know you shouldn't."

No, he shouldn't. Shame washed over him. "You're right. I should not have reacted that way. I beg your forgiveness."

She sliced a hand through the air. "I don't want your apologies. I want you to admit the truth."

"Which is?"

"That your interest in me is beyond that of a friend."

He pressed his lips together. "No."

"Why not?"

"Because it's not true. I only care for you as a friend."

She arched her brow at him.

"As I told you before, any gentleman would have responded that way." He forced a shrug. "Breasts are breasts, Belle. Any man presented with a pair and given the freedom to touch them would do so. It doesn't matter whose they are."

"Liar."

Sebastian bristled. "Not at all. Go play that trick on any of the gentleman here tonight, they'd all have the same reaction. Even Giles."

Her face turned scarlet. "You haven't changed a bit."

"Were you hoping I had?" he teased, giving himself pause. Did she have an interest in him? He dismissed the idea immediately. There wasn't a single reason for her to like him and she'd made sure he was well aware of that.

"Yes, I had," she said, inclining her chin. "I'd hoped we'd be friends. But instead all you've done is given me a shabby list of potential husbands and acted like the highhanded lord you are. If not desire, then I am at a loss for your reasons for being so highhanded with me. Nonetheless, I shan't abide you or your pompous attitude a day longer." Then, without another word, or bothering to pick up her shawl, she spun and walked from the room.

Sebastian should go after her. He knew that, but for some reason he couldn't as part of her words kept tumbling over and over in his mind: why was he being so protective of her? In all fairness to Belle, Lady Mary's bodice was even lower than hers had been and he hadn't once been distracted by what she'd revealed. He fell into a nearby chair and covered his face with his hands. Breasts weren't just breasts. Every set did not hold as much appeal as any other. At least not for him. He groaned. He *did* desire her.

No. He forced himself to sit up straight and hit the arms of the chair with his open palms. He would not allow his desire for her to get in the way of helping her. She deserved to have a husband and be happy. He owed that to her.

He sighed and took to his feet. At least now he knew why he'd been so protective of her: lust. He shook his head, leaning down to pick up her shawl. Lust wasn't such a powerful thing. He could deny himself. He'd done so for years. What were a few more months?

He ran his fingers over Belle's black velvet shawl and nearly groaned. It had better only be a few more months. Likely after what had happened tonight she'd refuse to receive him again for a while, postponing his torment.

Scowling, he slipped out of Giles' townhouse through the window with the simple intent of going home to end the current torment he currently had at the memory of his hand skimming the top of his own wife's breast.

What a positively infuriating existence he was currently living.

Chapter Thirteen

Isabelle had once heard Edmund use the term swallow hole to describe a giant hole in the ground that had magically formed on his estate, causing a few bushes and a poor helpless cow to fall into the deep hole with no warning. If it were possible to pray these things into existence, Isabelle would get on her knees this second and begin pleading with God for such a phenomenon to occur this very minute. Instead, she ran down the side of the street, swiping at the tears that were spilling from her eyes.

How in the world could she have acted so boldly, giving Sebastian just one more thing to hold against her?

And what about everyone at the dinner party? Would it be remarked upon that she had not returned to the room after Sebastian had removed her in such a way? Of course it would, she thought as she yanked open the servant's door of Mrs. Finch's town home and raced up to her room.

Closing the door behind her, she shut her eyes, leaned against the door and sank to the floor in a boneless heap.

From across the room she could hear the faint ticking of the clock that rested on the top of a little bookcase she had. The ticking so soothing and comforting, it was just what she needed.

The footfalls in the hall, however, were not what she needed.

Whether it was her maid or Mrs. Finch or heaven forbid Edmund, she was not in the mood to see anyone just now and prayed they'd keep walking past.

A soft knocking on the door dashed her hopes.

"Isabelle?" Mrs. Finch said through the door. "Isabelle, are you in there?"

Was it possible that if she didn't answer that Mrs. Finch would leave? Probably not. "I'm getting ready for bed."

"Would you like to talk?"

Isabelle cringed. It wasn't that she didn't like talking to Mrs.

Finch. She did. Mrs. Finch had always been a good listener and for the most part trustworthy with a secret. But frankly, there just wasn't anything to say. "No, Mrs. Finch. I'm tired and would like to go to sleep."

"All right, dear. We'll talk tomorrow."

Isabelle sighed in relief then forced herself to stand and do her best to undress without knotting any of her tapes or crushing her gown beyond repair.

Fortunately, getting out of her gown was easy enough.

Her corset, however, was not so easy.

She reached around her back and stretched her fingers as far as they'd reach, trying to grab the end of one of the ties. She almost had it; she just knew it. She gritted her teeth and arched her back, reaching. Taking a deep breath and holding it while squeezing her stomach even tighter (if such a thing were even possible while wearing a corset) she strained her arm to reach. She felt the end of one of the ties, but just couldn't get a grip on it.

She dropped her arm to her side, needing a break.

Catching her breath, she tried another tactic: reaching overhead. She reached her left arm over her head and behind her back, using her right hand to help push her arm as far as her shoulder would allow.

It was no use, but that didn't stop her. She was determined to get that tie. There was no way she'd survive the night if made to sleep in a corset.

With a grunt, she tried to reach again.

She clenched her teeth together and strained.

Tears welled in her eyes. Blast it all, she was so close, yet just couldn't reach.

Letting out a cry more appropriate for a battlefield, she gave it one more try.

"What a fetching view this makes," came a man's voice, stilling Isabelle.

Her eyes flew to the window where Sebastian's head was coming through the curtains.

"I'd say I'm surprised to see you at this late hour, but when I remember your love for entering into rooms I'm inhabiting through the window I have to admit that I should not be." She suddenly felt naked and vulnerable and crossed her arms in front of her chest.

He flashed her a look of confusion then let himself into her room. "Perhaps you ought to keep the windows closed if my presence offends you so."

"I did once, but varmint that you are, you still found your way in."

"Ah," Sebastian said, closing her window. "I remember it being closed, but not locked." He set the lock on her window as if to prove a point and a shiver ran over her. What was he doing here anyway?

Inclining her chin, she said, "If you're looking to have a dalliance, you've entered into the wrong bedchamber. Mrs. Finch is two windows to the left."

Sebastian nearly choked at her statement and it was all Isabelle could do not to grin. "Gads, Belle, is that all you think about?"

Her humor fled as suddenly she was transported back in time to the day they were married and in a similar situation, with him being just as condescending. Painful discomfort came over her. "Out!" she demanded, pointing toward the window.

Sebastian ignored her and walked over to her. "Turn."

She stood frozen. "No. I said to get out."

He acted as if he didn't hear her and walked behind her.

She spun around to face him and swatted at his hands. *"Get out!"*

Sebastian's eyes grew hard. "Do you intend to sleep in your corset tonight?"

"If I must."

His eyes left hers and made a slow path down her barely covered body. "I can only imagine the marks and bruises you'll have when you awake."

"Well, imagine them all you'd like, just do it elsewhere," she snapped.

"All right," he said, nodding. He took a step back, then

another, then wordlessly strolled over to her bed and made himself comfortable. "I'm elsewhere."

Were she half the docile creature he'd wanted her to be, she'd have gasped and become flustered by his boldness. Isabelle was not. "You intend to spend the night in my bed?"

A grin that could only be described as wolfish spread his lips. "I hadn't intended to when I first entered, but how could I refuse your sweetly worded request?"

Willing herself to stay calm she nodded once, then with all of the dignity of a queen wearing nothing but her corset in the company of her former husband, Isabelle walked to her bureau and removed that scrap of fabric made of silk and gauze she'd found in the top drawer the night she'd first arrived. It was black gauze with red lace—clearly something from someone's *trousseau*. "Be sure to make yourself comfortable," she murmured to Sebastian. "But you might wish to put this on." She tossed the scandalous nightrail at him.

He picked up the nightrail with his tanned hands and held it up to let it unfold. He arched a brow at her. "Why would I be the one wearing this?"

Isabelle shrugged. "Because it's Edmund's favorite and he'll expect to see it tonight when he comes for his regular visit."

***

A rush of emotions overcame Sebastian: anger, rage and jealousy, among the most prominent, but none of which he had any right to feel. He balled up the nightrail and tossed it to the floor. "You won't be needing that tonight."

"No, I won't," she agreed. "You can wear it."

He pursed his lips. "The devil you say. I'll not be wearing that —" he glanced at the offending garment— "and neither will you." *Unless I'm your sole audience.* His body stilled and his blood turned to ice. Where had that come from? He didn't want to see her in that. From the corner of his eye he glimpsed her standing with her arms crossed under her full breasts. Full breasts? He took a deep breath to calm himself and clear his thoughts. But it didn't work. Yes, she had full breasts. He'd know. His mind still remembered the way her breasts had felt under his hold.

With a curse he stood and crossed his arms, willing his eyes to look anywhere but at his half-naked and highly delectable wife. "Have you shared intimacies with Lord Kenton?" he asked for no good reason other than the jealousy of wanting her to confirm that she'd cuckolded him.

"I'm sure I haven't done anything you haven't," she said with a shrug.

His gut tightened as if someone as big as her father had just punched him in the gut. He couldn't determine if his reaction was because she'd cuckolded him—and with someone she had no real interest in no less—or that she spoke of it as if it were an inconsequential matter. Blast it! Why did it even matter? He didn't plan to stay married to her. Pride, perhaps. Once he found her a proper husband, they'd have to annul their marriage and it was likely the truth would be exposed.

"I don't know why you'd care," she continued in a tone that held a waver.

"Because you—" he broke off. Wait. She didn't know that they were still married. The realization made him feel a little better about her transgression, but not much. Pride, what a damnable thing. He cleared his throat. "Young ladies should be virgins on their wedding night," he said by way of explanation. "He should have waited."

"I see," she said slowly, cocking her head to the side. "Dare I ask if you plan to be a virgin on your wedding night?"

"I don't see how that's any of your concern."

"Nor do I see how the state of my virginity is any of yours. Everyone knows you and I married in Gretna Green, surely no man actually expects that I'll come to his bed as a virgin."

She had a point. Even couples who had their Gretna Green marriage annulled—usually at the urging of their parents—faced a scandal and questions. Mostly the young lady. Gentlemen always had a way of escaping such scrutiny; ladies did not. No matter how many details were or weren't revealed about their elopement, one thing was always assumed: the young lady was no longer chaste.

Of course nobody, not even a chit as outspoken as Belle could ever contradict this or offer an explanation, even if it were the truth.

He closed his eyes for an extended blink. So caught up in his own jealousy and irritation at his sudden, but not-so-slight attraction to her, he'd forgotten to really think about how everything had affected her. "I'm sorry."

"It's of no consequence now."

He pushed down the little niggle of guilt at hearing the slight unevenness of her voice. It was of consequence, but brave girl she'd always been, she wanted to pretend it didn't matter. Another wave of remorse for all his actions concerning her washed over him. "Might I still be allowed to help you find a husband?"

She snorted. "I didn't realize your help was ever truly a request."

Sebastian frowned. "It is." He raked a hand through his hair. "I just want to right my wrongs, Belle. Please, let me do that."

Belle dropped her eyes to where she was drawing lazy figure eights on the floor with her pink-tipped toes. "Will you help me find an honorable husband this time?"

"Giles is honorable," he retorted, flabbergasted. The man might be a little awkward at times, but he was honorable.

She met his gaze. "Perhaps honorable was the wrong word. I mean...suitable."

He bit back a smile. "All right. I take it you're not interested in Giles. What of his brother?" He froze. What was he saying? There wasn't anything wrong with Simon Appleton, so to speak, but the man was...well...he was too young and a bit stuffy by Sebastian's estimation.

"His brother?"

"Mr. Appleton," he said through clenched teeth, cursing himself for even bringing that man into this.

She nodded slowly as if suddenly everything made sense to her regarding the dinner hosts. "He'd be a fine catch for a lady in my condition, I suppose," Belle said slowly, stealing Sebastian's breath away.

He dropped his eyes to her abdomen. "Are you..." He trailed

off, hoping she'd take his meaning.

She stared at him blankly, then dropped her gaze to see what he was looking at. She gasped, and then jerked her head back up, her eyes wide with what he assumed was horror. "That is none of your concern!"

"I'm just trying to help you, Belle. If you're pregnant that changes things. Finding a husband who is willing to marry an unchaste bride is one thing. Finding one who is willing to take on another man's bastard is something else."

"And we all know how you'd react at the prospect of entering a marriage with an increasing bride." The condemnation on her face only compounded the sting in her words.

"That's not a fair statement, Belle," he said defensively. "If I loved her and the circumstances surrounding her impending—" he waved a hand through the air— "grand event were something she had little control over, I wouldn't hesitate to marry her. But to marry a woman who is increasing because she has given herself to a man by choice—whether out of some disillusion of love or for gain—isn't a marriage most gentlemen would be delighted at the prospect of entering into."

"And yet, ladies are expected to pretend their husbands haven't visited the bed of every lightskirt in the country and don't have any by-blows."

"Well, if she wants to marry the gentleman, then yes."

Belle threw a pillow at him.

He ducked. "Nobody says you have to marry a scoundrel." He paused. "If chastity is such an important quality for you when pursuing a husband, then Giles is the right gentleman for you." He offered her a smile. "I can say without question that he'd be faithful to you, too."

"Something I'm sure you'd struggle with," she mumbled under her breath.

He clenched his hands into fists, though he didn't dare tell her the truth. "You might be surprised. You might not intend to keep your vows, but if I make a promise, I'll keep it."

Her throaty laugher filled the room. "And what of our

marriage? You couldn't get back and break that promise fast enough."

Was it just him or was there a trace of hurt in her tone? He shook off the thought. "I didn't make that promise in good faith," he admitted with a sigh. "As you well know, I thought I was marrying—"

"Rachel," she finished for him. "Yes, I know." She took a deep breath and shook her head. "Regardless, you did make vows and weren't very concerned about keeping them."

"I don't believe I truly made those vows. I thought I was vowing to marry Rachel, not you."

She winced at his words. Not a lot, mind you. In fact, it was so minute that he wouldn't have noticed it himself if he hadn't been staring at her so closely. "Yes, I know. There is no reason to ever speak of this again." She let out a sigh. "If I agree to allow you to help me find another husband, will you please leave?"

"That will help, yes, but there is one other thing you need to agree to before I'll leave."

"And what is that?"

"Let me help you remove your corset."

***

Isabelle's breath hitched. "Wh-what?"

"Your corset," he said, gesturing toward her. "It cannot be comfortable to sleep in such a contraption, I wouldn't think."

"N-no."

"Then allow me to help you remove it."

She cleared her throat, praying her voice would come out even, but not truly convinced. "Remove it?"

Sebastian stared at her as if she'd just said the silliest thing ever spoken. Then, without a word of warning, he began walking toward her.

Isabelle stood frozen, her feet rooted to the floor, unable to carry her away from him.

He came to stand behind her, his tall, broad body so close she could feel the heat radiating off of him. Her skin tingled and she fought to keep the feeling at bay as he reached up and systematically undid the ties on the back of her corset. Though his skin never once touched hers, hers heated up as if he had.

"Done," he practically barked, taking a step back.

Isabelle flushed then reached behind her for the ties. He'd only loosened them. Not a lot, just enough to allow her to remove her corset without further assistance. She flushed again. Of course he'd been careful to only untie the ties, and not actually press her to do anything further was because he didn't want her. He'd said earlier that one set of breasts was just like any other. He probably felt the same about the female body in general. Only her body wasn't good enough for him at all. She held no appeal to him and though it shouldn't and was preposterous to think otherwise, the knowledge of disinterest cut to the bone.

"I'll come by to call upon you tomorrow."

The words, "Please don't", were on the tip of her tongue to speak, but not trusting her voice, she just nodded.

Chapter Fourteen

Isabelle pulled the pillow over her face tighter.

Unfortunately, though she couldn't see Tilde, it did not mean she or her announcement actually went away.

She tossed the pillow off. "Can you please tell everyone that I'm unwell and in need of some time to recuperate?"

The young housemaid that Mrs. Finch had ordered to come up and inform Isabelle that a gentleman caller was here to see her shook her head wildly, her eyes wide. "I cannot lie," she whispered in a strong French accent. "It is not allowed."

Isabelle wanted to groan. Why did Mrs. Finch have to hire a maid who had been raised in a convent? Sighing, she pushed her feet into her slippers and stood. "All right. Tell them I'll be there in just a few moments, please."

Tilde's eyes narrowed on Isabelle and she bit her lip.

"Yes?"

"I won't be lying, will I?"

"No. I'll come."

Looking relieved, the maid bobbed a curtsey and left the room.

Isabelle shook her head. Tilde was a good sort, if not a bit religious at times. At first it irritated Isabelle because she felt like she was constantly under scrutiny with Tilde because of her past, but she'd since learned that Tilde was too steadfast in her beliefs to even read a scandal sheet, let alone stay in a room long enough to hear gossip.

Sighing with resignation, Isabelle stood and straightened her skirts. Tilde had come by a few hours ago to help her dress for the day. Since then, she'd spent the day sitting on a chaise, staring out the window in hopes the world would just fade away.

It didn't.

It was custom for a gentleman to have to wait for a young lady to enter the room, would it be so horrible to make him wait so long he left? She admonished herself for her thoughts. She might not wish to speak to Sebastian, but it didn't mean she needed to be completely rude in her attempt to go about it.

When at last she could walk no slower, she screwed up her bravery and entered the drawing room.

"Mr. Appleton?" she gasped when she saw him sitting across the room with his hands on knees, staring at the floor.

Simon rose, his cheeks turning slightly red. "Excuse me, I was woolgathering."

"I'm sorry." She offered him a small smile. "I didn't realize it was you or I wouldn't have taken so long."

He grinned. "I shall take that as the highest compliment."

"As you should." She took a seat. What had brought him by today? He'd left the dinner party early last night. Had he come for information? Unease swirled in her stomach.

"Isabelle," he said a moment later, startling her. "I wanted to explain to you about last night—"

"There's nothing to explain."

He looked at her askance. "Yes, I think there is."

Isabelle sucked in a sharp breath. She really didn't think he needed to explain anything, but his tone and the rigid expression on his face kept her words firmly in her mouth. "All right."

Simon let out a deep exhale and rubbed his hands together. "Giles Goddard and I are...related." The way he choked his last word, made Isabelle's heart melt like a pastry that had just come out of the oven. "We have—" he took another deep breath— "a common relation. My mother."

"I take it you didn't know of this until last night?" Isabelle ventured.

He nodded. "I know it sounds petulant—" he shrugged— "but I can't help it."

Isabelle lowered her lashes. As odd as it might seem, she could understand his hurt. It rivaled that of the hurt she felt at being abandoned and betrayed by everyone she'd ever thought loved her to be packed off to the country. She started. Those two were not the same thing at all. Besides, she didn't have anyone to blame for her being sent away except herself. She was the one who'd brought scandal to her father's house.

"Had it been my father," he continued, "it would be easier to accept. But my mother?" He shook his head and sighed, pain and confusion stamped all over his face.

Instinctively, Isabelle reached her hand toward his forearm to comfort him.

Swallowing, he covered her hand with his and gave her a gentle squeeze. "I wanted to tell you this because I have something to ask you and I don't want to be dishonest or you to get hurt if this scandal ever breaks."

Isabelle went numb. What could he possibly ask her? Never mind. She had an idea of what it could be and though she knew she'd never have a love match, only a marriage of friendship and mutual respect, for reasons she couldn't name exactly, she wasn't sure she'd find either of those things with Simon Appleton. The brutal truth was, she didn't hardly know the man. Dances hadn't really allowed them any time to talk and this was only the second time he'd come to see her. "Simon, please don't."

"Isabelle, I think you already know that I care a great deal for you—"

Stop! Stop! Stop! She wanted to scream it as loud as her throat would allow, but couldn't embarrass him that way. Neither could she allow him to continue to embarrass himself this way. She opened her mouth to stop him, when suddenly she was struck dumb. "Wh-what did you just say?"

He offered her a half-smile. "I said that I have no ulterior motives. I don't need your money and I genuinely don't care about your previous scandal and neither will my family. "

She'd known all along that fortune hunters of the worst sort would surround her this Season. She also knew that money made people ignore scandals if they wanted the funds enough. This wasn't anything new, but for some strange reason, hearing it from someone else made everything seem so real. So definite. So cold and ugly. "But what about Miss Hughes?" she heard herself ask.

He pursed his lips. "I never had a true interest in her, you had to have known that." The color heightened in his cheeks. "I was embarrassed that you were about to deny me publicly and I just selected the first debutante I could see." A self-deprecating smile played over his lips. "Isn't it obvious how much I adore you?"

Yes, it was. She cleared her throat. "It's hard to know what's genuine."

Heedless to their quiet, nearly deaf chaperone in the room, Simon reached for her hand. "I am. I adore you. I genuinely want to marry you—even without your fortune."

"Why?" The word was out before she even realized she wanted to ask the question.

"Because I think we'd be a good match."

Was it a declaration of love young girls dreamed of? No. Was his proposal even in any way romantic? No. But it *was* truthful. And genuine. She wrung her hands and bit her lip. Hard. He was right. So very right. Everyone would look the other way for her money, but what would her life be like after she married? Would her husband grow to resent her? Would he scorn her once the money had run out?

She shook her head to rid herself of the confusing thoughts. Did any of this matter? Edmund had already offered her the same thing and though he wasn't anywhere within a quarter century of her age, she was friends—of sorts—with him and already knew they could live an amiable existence if necessary.

"Simon, I—I—I—" She what? She hadn't accepted Edmund's offer, and he was the only one under some false illusion who assumed she would if the Season didn't turn out well. She licked her lower lip where she'd just crushed it with her teeth. "I promised Edmund that I'd entertain his suit if I didn't find a suitable husband this Season." It was all she could do not to choke on her own tongue as she said those words, but it seemed the only thing he might be willing to accept.

"And you've found a suitable husband. Me."

A smile pulled at the corner of her mouth. "I know you're offering, but not for the right reasons."

"The right reasons?"

She nodded. "I think you're embarrassed about—" she waved her hand through the air in a circular motion, hoping he wouldn't make her put voice to his mother's indiscretion— "and because of that you're making a decision because you're upset."

"No, I've wanted to ask you for a while," he pointed out. "Just as recently as the Rutherford's ball. I just wanted to tell you the trouble surrounding my family so you wouldn't feel trapped in another scandal you were unprepared for if the story ever breaks."

She nodded slowly.

"Is there something about me you find disagreeable?" he asked abruptly.

"No." That was true enough. She didn't know him well enough to know if he was agreeable or disagreeable, if one were honest. "But I've told Edmund—"

"That you'd agree to marry him if you don't find another match," he finished for her. He flashed her a rueful smile. "I'm not asking you to give me an answer today, but at least think about letting me court you in earnest."

She swallowed. "I—I suppose I can agree to that."

His grin grew so wide she thought he might strain the muscles in his face. "The thinking or the courting?"

She laughed. "You can court me." She raised a finger. "But, you may not propose marriage to me again unless you are certain you cannot live through another day without me and I have made it clear I feel that way about you."

"I can do that." He grinned and suddenly pushed to his feet. "I need to be off. I have a courtship to plan."

Oh dear what had she agreed to?

***

Less than three and a half hours later Isabelle's mind raced and her fingers trembled as she reread the lines of the invitation she'd received only a few minutes prior. A house party? Surely not.

"Won't it be splendid?" Mrs. Finch asked in a sing-song voice.

Yes, splendid. That was exactly what it wouldn't be. She sighed. Sebastian was behind this. He had to be. For who else would want her to attend a house party? Even as an heiress, she wasn't the kind of young lady most wanted their daughters to associate with. The only people interested in her were gentlemen— and even that wasn't as successful as she'd once hoped it might be.

She folded the invitation and placed it back on the silver salver before taking a seat on the green settee and picking up her dreaded embroidery. She hated embroidery. Almost as much as she hated Sebastian at present, she thought when she nearly pricked herself. Or had she nearly pricked herself because she was thinking of him? No. Absolutely not. That was not at all what had happened. He was just annoying and tedious, just like embroidery. That's why she was thinking of him. It had nothing to do with the way he'd set her blood to racing with a single glance or burned her skin with his touch. Nor how he'd cut her to the core with his implication last night.

She groaned. She must put him out of her mind before she left bloodstains all over the fabric. Simon. She'd think of Simon and his promise to court her in earnest and not ask her to marry him again until the time was appropriate. Could he be behind the invitation? Before she'd even finished the thought, she knew that wasn't possible. He was merely a gentleman. It didn't matter what his mother's position was, she rarely ever associated with those of rank unless they were her friends, most of whom were lesser gentry, not a marchioness like Lady Cosgrove.

"Is something wrong, dear?" Mrs. Finch asked; her face contorted in confusion that made her usually slight wrinkles deepen.

"No, Mrs. Finch. I'm just having a difficult time."

"Gentleman can often create such difficulties, I'm afraid," came Sebastian's deep voice from the door. "Particularly when I'm the one they're thinking of." He winked at her and she was tempted to throw a pillow at the insufferable man.

"Oh, do come in," Mrs. Finch encouraged with a hesitant smile.

Sebastian was in the room before she could finish, then, as if he were a welcome guest and the dearest friend to Mrs. Finch, he unceremoniously took a seat on the settee next to Isabelle and stretched his long legs out in front of him, grinning.

She willed herself to remember her manners and not poke him with her needle. "What has brought you to calling at such an early hour?"

He frowned. "It's not so early, is it?"

"Not for most of us, but for those who lose large quantities of sleep each night to build up their pride, it might be considered early yet."

Sebastian arched a brow at her. "And how would you know about my sleeping patterns?"

She flushed and chided herself. She'd played right into that snare. Clearing her throat, she glanced toward Mrs. Finch. "Have you come to discuss the potential of the house party?"

He blinked. "House party?"

"Yes. The one Lady Cosgrove is hosting."

"Lady Cosgrove?" He furrowed his brow and narrowed his eyes as if he were truly confused. "Giles' cousin?"

Well, now that made sense. "Yes."

"I didn't know she was hosting a party. May I see the invitation?"

Isabelle retrieved the vellum and handed it to him. His light red lips moved as he read the lines, the crease between his brows growing deeper with each line. When he lowered the invitation from his face, Isabelle pressed her lips together to keep from giggling at the look of bewilderment on his face.

"Do you know Lady Cosgrove?" he asked.

"No." Nor did she really find it so exciting to be invited to a house party where she'd have to spend an entire ten days in the company of some of the highest ranked people in the country, but for now, it was rather amusing that she'd been invited without him even knowing about it. "But I do look forward to going," she lied with a dazzling smile.

"And am I right to assume that Lord Kenton will be there, too?"

Isabelle fought to keep her smile firmly in place, but couldn't help but wonder if it was just her imagination or if his words had come out with a slight dose of bitterness. Was he jealous? Her skin prickled at the thought. No, it couldn't be, she reminded herself. She was the last person he wanted. He'd even told her that he'd have stayed married to her sister. Her mouth suddenly became as dry as cotton. "I'm sure he will," she said as best she could, considering it felt like her tongue had become paralyzed in the last three seconds.

He pursed his lips and nodded. "I see."

She doubted he did, but didn't wish to discuss this any further —for her lack of ability to speak more than anything else. Perhaps now would be a good time to tell him of the events of this morning and how she no longer needed his help to seek a husband. Truly, Simon wasn't the kind most unattached ladies would fawn over by any means with his young age, but with his kind and genuine demeanor, he'd ultimately be a good match to her. She just needed a chance to grow accustomed to his eagerness, hence her agreeing to a courtship.

"Can I take you for a walk in the park?" Sebastian asked suddenly; his voice just loud enough for Mrs. Finch to hear.

"Oh, I believe that is a wonderful idea," the older woman said with a clap of her hand. "The weather is just perfect for a stroll in the park." She paused for a moment, then added. "Be sure to take Beatrice with you."

Isabelle wanted to groan. Beatrice had at least seventy years in her dish. Ancient by anyone's standards. Though propriety in all things was her biggest concern in life, the poor woman could hardly see any longer and frequently had to stop and sit to rest. Unfortunately, she took her duty as a servant of doing her best to be unseen and unheard so strongly she didn't like to inform those she was with that she needed one of these little rests and would just sit down. In short, she was a dear woman but a terrible chaperone.

Chapter Fifteen

Under the watchful, cataract-covered eye of Belle's chaperone Beatrice, Sebastian handed Belle her bonnet with his left hand and gripped her parasol with the right. He doubted she needed both, but she seemed bent on having them so who was he to argue? They'd done enough of that in their lifetime and they were about to have another bout, of that he was certain.

"I don't think you should go to this house party," he said without preamble as soon as they were off the steps of Mrs. Finch's townhouse.

"Oh, you don't, do you?"

"No. I think house parties create...opportunities."

"Such as those that lead to marriage?"

"Sometimes, but not without scandal." He stepped behind her so they could walk through a narrow walkway. "You don't need any more scandals, Belle."

"No, I don't," she agreed in an arch tone. "But I do need a husband. I see no reason why I shouldn't go."

Sebastian reached for her wrist to stay her, then moved to stand in front of her. No matter that there were other people wanting to keep passing. "I don't think you should go."

"I don't care what you think. I'm going."

"I understand that you don't care what I think, but you're not going."

Something flashed in her eyes. "What makes you think you have any right to tell me where I can and cannot go?"

Because I'm your husband! The words were on the tip of his tongue, but he couldn't say them. They quarreled enough as it was, if he mentioned that, she just might kill him. "I'm helping you find a husband, am I not?" He didn't pause long enough to allow for her to respond. "If I'm to do that then you need to listen to me. I don't —"

"Need to bother with my finding a husband any longer," she cut in smoothly. "Simon Appleton came to see me this morning and has offered his suit."

Every muscle in Sebastian's body went rigid. Simon Appleton? The man wasn't good enough for her by half. "No. I forbid it."

She sputtered with laughter. "You forbid it?"

"Yes." He ground his teeth. "That boy is...is...well, he's just that, he's a boy."

"He's twenty."

Sebastian frowned. "That does not raise him any in my opinion. He's still a boy."

"Are you saying he's too young to make such a commitment to a young lady?"

"Yes, he is," he burst out. "He's too young to be able to make any kind of promise regarding providing for her and offering her fidelity."

"I see." She drew her words out in a way that made his skin crawl with uneasy anticipation. "I suppose that's why you're still not married, then."

He crossed his arms and narrowed his eyes on her. "This isn't about me."

"No? You were only a year younger than him when you were prepared to marry Rachel."

Gritting his teeth, he said, "You already know I didn't wish to marry her that night."

"Ah, yes, you've mentioned that, but you still arrived and even went through the ceremony."

"I made her a promise and felt I needed to keep it. No matter how much I didn't wish to," he said around the unease nearly choking the life right out of him.

The tip of her pink tongue poked out and moistened her lips. "Are you saying that had you married her, that you'd have been a doting and faithful husband?"

"Yes," he bit out, praying she wouldn't press him any further on the matter. Though she was still his wife, he'd only held up one of her two criteria for a husband. Not that he hadn't at least tried to be doting. He'd come to see her—only to be turned out and later blackmailed to never return.

Belle heaved an exaggerated sigh, pulling him from his drifting thoughts. "I do thank you for mentioning this, I'll be sure to ask Mr. Appleton how true his intentions are regarding a wife and his ability to keep his breeches fastened." She shrugged as if she hadn't a care in the world and said, "Perhaps he'll be at the house party and I can ask him then."

"The devil you will," he practically growled. "You won't be going to that confounded house party."

"Yes, I will." Challenge danced in her eyes. "And if you don't like it then you can stop calling upon me."

"Belle, I don't—"

"No." She lifted her hand to halt his words. "I'm not going to argue with you about this anymore, and on the street no less."

He reached for her wrist and she pulled away. "Belle, let me —"

"Let you what?" she snapped. "Let you explain to me why your way is always superior to mine? Let you get involved where you are not needed?" She shook her head. "No. No more. Nothing has changed about you. You're upset with everything I do. The only difference now is that I don't care what your opinion of me is. I'm going to that house party and I'm going to let Simon court me whether you want him to or not. Now, if you'll excuse me, I must get back to pack." Just as she finished those words, she spun on her heel and walked to where her chaperone was sitting on a bench. Belle said something to her and the older woman stood, then together they made for the direction of their townhouse.

Sebastian knew Isabelle wouldn't like it, but he didn't care and followed her to her home anyway. When she immediately— and firmly—slammed the door in his face, he set out to go do another thing Belle wasn't going to like: secure himself an invitation to that blasted house party.

***

Giles lived a good two miles from where Belle was staying,

but Sebastian didn't mind the walk. It gave him time to sort things out and get some fresh air.

Actually, it didn't.

By the time he arrived at his friend's bachelor lodgings, he was no closer to understanding his dislike for Belle agreeing to entertain Simon Appleton's suit nor had he yet shaken the suffocating sensation that had taken hold of him since receiving that news. Furthermore, he had no wish to discover the connection between the two.

The one thing he didn't like, but could actually do something about was Belle's invitation to the house party. He'd never actually attended one, but he'd heard enough rumors about them and had read of at least one unexpected engagement that had been announced at the end of almost every single one. That was the last thing Belle needed. And with her penchant to find herself in the middle of a scandal, he could almost be certain it would be her engagement announced at the end of the party.

His gut tightened in time with his fingers gripping the brass knocker of Giles' door.

Two swift bangs and then he let himself in. Certainly not the most proper or acceptable thing among those of his class, but he and Giles had been friends long enough that pleasantries and formalities were wasted on either of them.

"Sebastian," Giles clipped by way of greeting when he glimpsed Sebastian coming down the hall. He opened the closest door. "Come."

Sebastian followed Giles inside the room he'd indicated and took a seat in one of his black leather chairs. He looked around the room, noting the open windows, uncovered wooden floor, the clear desk, and precise location of the furniture. Either the room was never used or Giles' had too many servants with not enough to do.

"I didn't like it," Giles said, lowering himself into the chair behind the desk. He swiped his hand across the clear top of his desk. "It was cluttered and dark in here before."

"It certainly isn't now." Sebastian ran his hands over the soft arms of the chair. "I need another favor."

Giles' expression stayed the same. "The house party?"

Sebastian nodded, then frowned. Giles had never been overly perceptive. How did he already know what Sebastian wanted? "I take it you've been invited?"

"Yes." He pursed his lips. "It's the reason I have been searching for the blasted woman. She wants to introduce me to Society there."

"Introduce you to Society?" Sebastian repeated, perplexed. "Isn't that for debutantes?"

Giles shrugged. "She thinks it's time I respect my title."

"I see." And he did. Until just a few days ago he didn't even know that Giles *had* a title. It wasn't his place to say anything, but as a baron, he did have a responsibility to his title and those he represented to take his place and mind his affairs. "Is that why you wanted to come to London to find her?"

"Yes. She needs to know that I have everything well-in-hand."

"Do you?"

"Yes." He crossed his arms defensively. "It's what I pay an overseer for."

"Indeed," Sebastian murmured. "But there are other responsibilities owed to your title."

Giles blinked.

Sebastian scowled. How could he word this without this leading into an extremely uncomfortable conversation for them both? "All right, you're keeping a man of affairs to keep things straight with your estate manager and anyone from the barony that might require your attention." At Giles' nod, Sebastian swallowed his nerves and went further. "I don't think Lady Cosgrove is concerned so much about that, but about your securing the family line."

Giles' face didn't change and Sebastian thought he might have to further explain himself when suddenly Giles spoke. "I know. That's the point of the house party," he said as if Sebastian was the one confused in all of this.

"You plan to attend, then?"

"No. I tried to tell her not to host one and now I cannot find her to tell her to call it off." He shrugged. "You're welcome to use my invitation. I won't need it."

Sebastian almost smiled. "I don't think that will work."

"I don't think she'll turn you out once you get all the way there." He turned his attention down to his fingernails. "Since I've never met Lady Cosgrove, I doubt she'd know the difference anyway."

"You've never met her?"

Giles shook his head. "The night we met was the first time I remember being in England. I'd always stayed in Ireland until then."

Hundreds of questions swirled through Sebastian's mind. Questions he knew would never be answered for him. Something was certainly amiss as far as Giles' parentage and family connections were concerned. There was no other reason for so many things to not add up. But it wasn't his place to ask. "If you've never met her, then why is she so adamant to see you reclaim the responsibilities that go with your title?"

"Connections?" he said with a shrug.

He was right though. Giles might merely be a baron and Lady Cosgrove a countess, but it always helped one's social standings to be able to tout connections to other peers, even if they were of a lower rank. "You despise your title, don't you?"

Giles lowered his lashes and continued to study the grain of wood on the flat of his desk. "Don't you?"

"That's a fair question," Sebastian allowed. "I wasn't running to the continent because of my title. I—my father is still living. My title is just honorary. My responsibility to it isn't the same as yours."

Giles scoffed. "You still need an heir."

"Indeed." That was the only responsibility he had to his title as of yet. The only one his father would allow him to fulfill. Allow? No. *Urged* him to fulfill. He had a suspicion the reason Father had been so adamant about not expressing interest in Sebastian learning the other responsibilities that would one day come when his father died and left him the earldom was because of the tension his presence would create. Father might have been an earl, but with Rachel married to Lord Yourke who, though only a baron, was a second cousin to some old duke, there could be tension. Not to mention the blackmail that Mr. Knight had threatened Sebastian with if he ever appeared on the Knights' doorstep again without the annulment papers signed. Had Mr. Knight truly informed the authorities of Sebastian's assumed activities, it wouldn't just be a scandal that would once again befall them, but legal entanglements, too. He shook off the thought. "My father is still young enough that he could remarry if he wanted to secure another possible heir badly enough."

"My cousin can inherit," Giles said easily enough. He leaned back in his chair and ran the pad of his thumb along the edge of his desk, appearing not to have a worry or care one way or the other. He snorted. "Simon could inherit for all I care."

Sebastian bristled at the mere mention of the man's name. "I don't think you'd really want that."

Giles' left shoulder tipped up. "It might make him more amiable toward me."

"I don't think so."

Nodding, Giles pursed his lips. "Don't need him anyway."

"No," Sebastian allowed. "But I don't think he hates you as much as you think. I think he was merely shocked."

Giles' impassive expression didn't change, making Sebastian wonder why he'd even bothered to defend the man. "I'll go to Telford tomorrow to see my cousin about the invitation."

Sebastian nodded. It was all he could ask for.

Chapter Sixteen

In the week that passed leading up to the house party, Isabelle could hardly sit still. Not for her own titter and excitement, mind you. It was Mrs. Finch who was all aflutter making plans and running errands in preparation for Lady Cosgrove's house party.

If anyone, whether ladies or gentlemen, had come by to call upon them they truly had not been at home.

Finally, they were on their way to Telford and Isabelle could breathe.

The only thing that would make it slightly better was if it was fresh air she was inhaling, but the air of the stuffy carriage would have to do. It was far better than being turned into a pincushion for the modiste.

"I think you'll find your husband this week," Mrs. Finch said.

Isabelle offered the older woman her best attempt at a smile. Because of the tardiness of the invitation, she hadn't had a chance to speak to Simon Appleton again before leaving this morning, but if he were there as she expected, then yes, Mrs. Finch was right. She turned her attention out the window at the passing trees and fields. Was the prospect of marriage to Simon so bad? With his light brown hair and sparkling green eyes, he was undeniably handsome, if not a bit taller than most. If he aged like his father had, he'd still be devilishly handsome even when they were half a century old.

But what of his personality? He was nice enough. All right, perhaps a bit *too* nice. Not that that was a bad thing necessarily. It was just odd. Yes. Odd. He was odd. Almost like Giles Goddard, Lord Norcourt. She almost choked on a giggle. Now *that* man was odd. But once again, not in a bad way. Just in a way that made her feel uncertain. There was no denying their family connection.

The carriage jerked, jarring Isabelle from her thoughts. When she'd regained her composure, she stared across the carriage at

Mrs. Finch and a small wave of sadness came over her. They'd kept each other company for five years now. If she married, Mrs. Finch wouldn't have anyone. Her heart clenched and instinctively she reached across the carriage for Mrs. Finch's wrinkled hand. "Would you like me to read to you?"

Mrs. Finch put her free hand over top of Isabelle's, a twinkle in her eyes. "Depends on the author."

Isabelle bit the inside of her mouth to keep from smiling. In recent years there was a particular author who'd become all the rage. All the rage to everyone except Mrs. Finch who'd once claimed novels written from the pen of (name withheld due to threat of being murdered by an old woman yielding a cane) were the most droll claptrap ever scribbled. "How about *Where Art My Love* by Michael Foxtrot?"

Mrs. Finch nodded her approval. "That's acceptable." She narrowed her eyes. "But if you try to sneak in a passage by that Dreadfully Droll Busybody, I'll take it from your pay."

"Ah, but I am an heiress now," Isabelle teased.

"Then I shall allow you to only go on walks with the oldest gentlemen in attendance at this party."

Isabelle grinned. She'd never been able to have such lighthearted exchange with anyone. A bubble of emotion suddenly formed in her throat. "Mrs. Finch, just because I have a fortune doesn't mean I have to marry."

"Yes, you do," Mrs. Finch said matter-of-factly. Her tone and face softened. "I won't live much longer and from what I hear it's not considered polite by the *ton's* standards for a young girl to be a companion to a gravesite."

Despite herself, Isabelle smiled. "I know. But it just all seems so...sudden and definite. You offered me a post when I had nowhere else to go and I feel as if I'm abandoning you."

"Abandon me, dear," Mrs. Finch said with a wide smile. "While I enjoy your company well enough, I believe you'll enjoy the company of a husband more than that of an old prune of a woman."

Isabelle tried not to giggle. "But, how do I know which one is the right one to choose?"

"That, I cannot tell you, but you'll know."

Isabelle wasn't so certain. The two who'd shown any interest in her beyond her money were not quite right. Edmund was old and his interest was friendly at best. Simon was just the opposite. Very enthusiastic about his interest. She exhaled and reclined against the squabs. Was that such a bad thing? It was certainly better than the cool interest of Edmund or the utter disinterest from Sebastian. She scowled. Why had he even entered her thoughts? Their last disagreement had firmly put an end to any sort of relationship, friendship or otherwise, they might have ever had. Which was absolutely for the best. A cynical tyrant like him was the last person she wanted to be around while looking for a husband.

"He's the one," Mrs. Finch said, ripping Isabelle from her thoughts.

"No, he's not," Isabelle said quickly. "Wait. H-how did you know who I was thinking about?"

"Well, I don't know specifically," Mrs. Finch allowed. "But whoever it is who can put that sparkle in your eyes—even as defiant as it might be—is the right one."

"No, he's not," Isabelle said flatly. "He just—" she gripped her hands into two tight fists and gritted her teeth, searching for the right words— "Sebastian, he just—"

"Brings out your passion?" Mrs. Finch suggested at the same time that Isabelle said, "Infuriates me."

Isabelle frowned. "If he strikes any passion, it's not the good kind."

Mrs. Finch harrumphed. "Passion is passion, my dear. It's all in what you do with it."

"I see. I suppose then you'd like for me to read—" Isabelle shuffled through her reticule for a novel by the author who shall remain nameless and flashed the cover in Mrs. Finch's direction then shrugged. "It does illicit a certain passion in you."

"Passion that makes me want to rip someone apart," Mrs. Finch retorted.

"Ah, and my passion for Sebastian is about the same."

"No, my passion makes me want to rip the author apart, your passion makes you want to rip his clothes off. There's a difference, dear."

Isabelle's jaw dropped.

"Now, are you going to read to me or do you need to be further scandalized into submission?" Mrs. Finch asked with a wink, looking rather pleased with herself.

"I suppose you and Mr. Finch were a love match," Isabelle mumbled as she numbly thumbed through the book to find where she'd left off yesterday.

"Actually, no, but I had more than enough lovers in my time —"

"'*Sophie crept down the stairs...*'" Isabelle read almost loud enough to drown out Mrs. Finch's half-chuckle, half-cackle.

Isabelle read that blasted book until the sun was so low that she couldn't decipher the words on the page. Not even bothering to stop when the coachmen stopped to change horses.

"Either your feelings are stronger for him than you wish to admit or your sensibilities are overly sensitive," Mrs. Finch said with a yawn. "Not to worry. Once you marry that strapping lad, you'll enjoy such scandalous remarks—especially when they're quickly followed up by putting words into actions."

Isabelle doubted that. Moreover, she doubted she'd ever see him again after their parting words. Which was just fine with her.

***

Sebastian stared at the blazing fire that filled the hearth in his study. A week had passed since Giles had left for Telford and no invitation had arrived. He closed his eyes. Perhaps it was better this way. No, no it wasn't. He surged to his feet. House parties were not good places for scandal-prone young ladies such as Belle. He scrubbed his hands over his face. She was only involved in a scandal when he was present. The thought shook him to the core. It was true. The only time her name had ever appeared in the scandal sheets was when he'd provoked her or had in some other way been involved.

He flopped back into the chair he'd recently vacated and steepled his hands in front of his lips. A million thoughts raced through his mind—most of which supported his earlier revelation: *he* was Belle's biggest provoker.

Perhaps she was right and she'd be better off without him there...

Chapter Seventeen

Isabelle stretched her lips into the biggest smile she could muster and walked into the breakfast room. She needed to make an honest effort with Simon—starting with breakfast.

"Good to see you this morning, Isabelle," Simon said with a low bow and a wink, presumably because of his display of regard for her.

"It's good to see you this morning, too." She allowed him to lead her to the sideboard. Mrs. Finch's coach had arrived in Telford just after dinner yesterday evening and she hadn't a chance yet to greet any of the guests. They'd have been there earlier had it not been for a sudden lightning storm that had forced them to seek shelter at a nearby inn. No matter. She'd allow Simon to take her around to make the acquaintance of all the guests today.

"Grapes?"

Isabelle started. "Oh, of course." She held her plate still while Simon put a small cluster of green grapes in the center for her. When he was done, she allowed him to give her a serving of coddled eggs and kippers.

"Where shall we sit?"

Isabelle scanned the table. It was long enough to seat no less than forty guests. And yet, she noticed that there were only two other people in the entire room with them? "I—I don't want to disturb Mr. Mason as he reads so—"

"We'd best sit alone, then," Simon finished for her, winking.

Isabelle forced a smile at his logical jest. He was right though. Not only would they disturb Mr. Mason if they sat next to him and chatted, but they'd disturb him if they sat at the other end of the table and had to yell for Lord Wycoff to hear them.

Simon led her to the middle of the table. "How is this?"

"Most excellent." She allowed him to pull her chair out, then sat and let him push her up to the table.

Wordlessly, he took a seat next to her. "I heard about your unfortunate delay." He shifted in his seat. "I hope you don't mind that I asked Ophelia if we could make use of her stables for a picnic today."

Isabelle raised her eyebrows. "Ophelia?"

"Lady Cosgrove sounds too impersonal for my mother's dearest friend and I detest using the word 'Auntie'," Simon said with a grimace.

A genuine smile curved Isabelle's lips. "I see, and do you call her Ophelia to her face?"

He flushed. "No. She'd order me a birching."

Isabelle would have laughed if not for the sudden change in Simon's posture. She followed his gaze to where Giles Goddard had just entered the room. "We can leave if you'd like," she whispered.

He shook his head and swallowed. "No. You finish."

A hush fell over the room as Isabelle started eating her breakfast a little faster than was polite and Simon watched his half-brother fill his plate.

Isabelle sucked in a breath of anticipation. Where would Giles sit? Would he be so bold as to sit with them? Or would he be made to sit alone? A small weight lowered itself into her stomach. Following her accident, she'd been left alone so much she couldn't stop the pang of sympathy she felt for Giles at being made to eat alone and before she could stop herself, blurted, "If you'd like to join us, that spot is free."

Giles' eyes widened and Simon bristled. Isabelle cast him an apologetic look. "I couldn't *not* invite him," she whispered.

Simon nodded tersely; his jaw clamped so tightly a muscle in his cheek ticked.

"Miss Knight, Mr. Appleton," Giles greeted, taking the vacant seat directly across from Isabelle. He avoided eye contact with either of them and went about placing his napkin in his lap and setting his silver to rights.

"What are your plans for the day?" Isabelle asked in hopes of dissolving the thick tension that had engulfed them.

Giles' head snapped up. "Mine?" he asked, pointing his index finger into the center of his chest. At her nod, he said, "Avoid Lady Cosgrove at all costs."

Isabelle wanted to giggle, but the serious expression on his face told her he wasn't trying to be humorous. "Isn't she the hostess?"

Giles took a bite of his coddled eggs. "She thinks I need a wife."

It was odd really, but just then Isabelle felt some sort of kinship to him. Lady Cosgrove thought he needed a wife and everyone in Society thought she needed a husband. She could certainly understand his frustrations with the woman and desire to avoid her matchmaking schemes.

"Well, you're not going to find one here," Simon said unapologetically, giving a pointed look at Isabelle.

Giles shrugged. "She's already taken."

"Yes, she is," Simon agreed. He drummed his fingers on the table, likely to remind himself not to reach for her possessively.

Which was a good thing because just then if he'd tried to publicly claim her as his future wife, Isabelle just might snap. She took a deep breath. She needed to stay calm. She was allowing him to court her with the possibility of marriage, wasn't she? Isabelle dabbed her mouth with her napkin and studied her plate as they continued their meal in an uncomfortable silence broken a few minutes later by another unwanted distraction: Edmund with an older lady she wasn't familiar with on his left arm.

With an air of confidence she'd never seen before, he swaggered, yes, *swaggered*, into the room and led his companion to the sideboard.

Isabelle had rarely felt jealous of anyone, and she certainly didn't have any jealousy right now, it was more curiosity. What was it about the greying woman wearing the crimson gown that made him become so...so...excited?

From the corner of her eye, she watched the two as they chatted then went to the sideboard to fill their plates.

They turned from the food and Edmund froze, his eyes

growing as big as Mrs. Finch's tea saucers. "Isabelle," he said with a wide smile. He carefully put his plate on the table and straightened his coat. "I'd like you to meet Lady Vessey. Lady Vessey, this is my friend, Miss Isabelle Knight."

Lady Vessey lifted her brows and murmured a greeting that dripped with sickening sugar, then turned her curious brown eyes toward Edmund, a silent message passing between them.

"Shall we join you?" Edmund asked.

"Actually we were about to go outside to play a round of pall mall," Simon announced.

Unfortunately for Simon, and Isabelle if she were to be honest, Simon's words were punctuated with a heavy rumble of thunder that all but shook the house.

"Perhaps this afternoon," Edmund said, grinning. He took a seat on the other side of Isabelle and Lady Vessey took the place opposite of him to the left of Giles. The only way this arrangement could get any less comfortable would be if Sebastian walked in and planted himself in the chair on the other side of Giles.

Blessedly that did not happen.

Instead, Isabelle had to pick at her food under the watchful gazes of Edmund, Simon and Lady Vessey while Giles seemed completely unaffected by the awkwardness of the situation and made a comment every now and then about how runny the coddled eggs were or something about the hardness of the kippers.

A grander breakfast she couldn't have possibly imagined.

An hour later Isabelle was still sitting in her quiet torment when Mrs. Finch breezed into the room. "There you are!" she said, beaming in Isabelle's direction.

"Good morning, Mrs. Finch."

"Good morning to you, too." She looked at the crowd gathered around Isabelle and pursed her lips. "I see you have already met Lady Vessey."

"Of course we've met and we're on our way to becoming the dearest of friends," Lady Vessey declared, smiling up at Mrs. Finch.

Mrs. Finch didn't look moved. "Edmund dear, would you be a

sweetheart and escort me to the sideboard?"

Edmund was off his seat in less than a second and helping his aunt.

"Are you ready to go?" Simon whispered.

Actually, she was. And from the looks of it, Giles was, too. She knew Simon wouldn't like it, but she extended him the invitation to join them in the drawing room where game tables had been set up. After a brief moment of confusion, complete with a blank stare and an extended blink, Giles accepted.

"I'd suggest we play a game, but I don't know any that can be played with three."

"I won't play," Giles said. He pulled a slim book and a pencil from the breast pocket of his bottle green coat and made his way to a chaise near the big window.

Simon shrugged and pulled a chair out for Isabelle. "Chess or draughts?"

"Draughts."

Simon took his seat and pulled out the drawer in the side of the table. "Here you are." He pushed the ivory draughts over to her side of the table then started setting out his.

She took her time to line them up in a perfect order. With the storm raging outside there was no reason to hurry. "Shall I go first?"

"Of course."

She slid her first draught forward.

"Hmm," Simon said as if he'd just been given a vexing mathematical equation and told to solve it. A moment later, he slid his piece forward.

Without nearly as much thought, she moved another of hers and waited for him to move one of his.

"Are you enjoying the party thus far?" he asked, pushing one of his draughts to an empty square.

"Oh, yes, the hour and fifteen minutes I've been out of my room have been heavenly."

Simon choked on his laughter, blushing. "I suppose it is a little early to be asking that, isn't it?"

"Just a little." She moved her piece, not really sure if it was her turn or not.

He didn't contradict her and jumped one of her pieces. He smiled at her, his eyes fixed just beyond her left shoulder.

"Aha," she said, jumping not one but two of his men.

"How the—" He snapped his fingers. "I see what you did there. I'll have to watch you more carefully now."

"That might be wise," *and not just for this game.* Though she was able to keep the last part of her comment contained, it didn't make it any less true. His not-so-discreet glances over her shoulder to where Giles appeared to be drawing was most bizarre.

"Your turn," Simon said with an amused smile playing on his lips.

Isabelle took her turn and watched his tense face from below her lashes. Something about Giles really upset him. "I've moved," she said a moment later.

He started. "Indeed." He lowered his fingers to the board and moved another of his draughts with decidedly less interest than before.

"Perhaps we should go to the blue salon and see if Lady Cosgrove is organizing any games?"

"Brilliant idea, Isabelle." Grinning, Simon abruptly stood and helped Isabelle to her feet. "Sorry we couldn't finish our game," he said when they were outside of the card room.

"It's all right."

He lowered his voice to such a low whisper she thought she might strain herself to hear it. "I just don't know what to make of him."

She gave his arm a gentle squeeze that seemed to surprise him. Ignoring the look of shock on his face, she said, "Then perhaps you should talk to him."

Simon swallowed audibly. "I don't think so. We have nothing to say to one another."

"I think you might." Perhaps once they spoke, Simon would be a little less distracted. As it was, she wasn't sure which was worse: his being overly eager to court her or his distracted demeanor. Neither endeared her to him the way it should.

Chapter Eighteen

Isabelle eyed the tray of discarded biscuits that sat beside the cold pot of tea on the sideboard. It would seem the maid had forgotten to collect the tea service after the afternoon tea. She licked her lips and wondered just how hard those biscuits would be. Just a little hard would still be edible, but it wouldn't do for her to break one of her teeth just to escape dinner—no matter how tempting it was to do just that.

The remainder of the day had not gone any better than the morning. Simon wasn't completely unbearable, at least not on purpose, but he'd been so distracted it was hard to talk to him. While it was true that most marriages of the *ton* were cold or arranged between two people who could barely tolerate each other, neither she nor Simon were truly of Society. Sure, she was now an heiress and his father was a wealthy enough cit that his deep coffers afforded them some invitations by some of the lower gentry, but once they married that wouldn't matter any longer. She paused. Well, there was his mother's connection to Lady Cosgrove, a countess, by way of her first marriage, which is likely how Simon was invited to attend this house party. But again, once they married, they'd both be regarded as common cits again and would have to spend more time in each other's company than those of rank. She needed to know she could grow to care for him even just a little. It wouldn't be fair to either of them, especially him, if she could only ever see him through a veil of reserved tolerance.

Unfortunately, if she had to sit next to him for dinner tonight, she just might call the whole thing off—which would be just as much to her disadvantage as his.

In the corner of the room, she spotted a stoic Giles with Lady Cosgrove on his arm. Lady Cosgrove said something to a young lady who tittered and rapped Giles with the end of her fan. Giles winced. Isabelle bit her lip. She should do something. The poor man wasn't used to the way young ladies flirted.

Murmuring something she hoped passed as an apology to Edmund, Mrs. Finch and Lady Vessey, she walked toward Lady Cosgrove. Simon's gaze bore into her from across the room with each step she took, but she couldn't stop. As odd as he might be, Giles needed a friend. Not that they were what most would consider to be bosom friends. She nearly snorted. They were the furthest thing from it, but from what she could gather, a friend, no matter how little they knew each other, would be appreciated.

By the time she reached Giles and Lady Cosgrove, it was quite clear that Lady Cosgrove was vexed at Giles' reaction to Lady Mary's forward flirtations.

"Miss Knight," Giles greeted with a nod in her direction before she'd even come to a stop.

"Lord Norcourt, Lady Cosgrove, Lady Mary." Isabelle flashed them all her best smile.

Lady Cosgrove's lips spread into a coy smile. "Miss Knight, it is so wonderful to see you made it for dinner tonight. I trust you had a good day in my nephew's company."

"I did. He was the perfect gentleman." *Could she tell Isabelle was lying?* She forced a wider smile. "Although, I must confess a secret." She heaved an exaggerated sigh.

Lady Cosgrove arched a brow. "Oh?"

"He is quite impressed with you. I daresay, you are his favorite lady in attendance."

Lady Cosgrove's smile grew if such a thing were possible. "If you'll excuse me, I think I shall go see what my dear boy is about. You wouldn't mind escorting Miss Knight to dinner would you, Lord Norcourt?"

"Not at all." Giles offered Isabelle his arm as Lady Cosgrove sauntered off to go find Simon. "Thank you," he whispered.

"You're welcome," she returned. "Just remember that if I ever need to be saved, I'm charging you with the responsibility to do it."

"I can't save you," he said a moment later. "That's someone

else's job."

She eyed him askance and before she could ask him to elaborate, Clarke, the balding, rotund butler announced dinner.

If the seating arrangements at breakfast had been uncomfortable, dinner was what most would term unbearable and those stale biscuits seemed like a better alternative by the minute. To her left sat Giles, to her right was Edmund and across from her was none other than Simon with his hurt and slightly shuttered eyes.

Though Giles had been her escort, it wasn't proper for her to ignore the others, and yet, she just couldn't decide which would be easier to carry a conversation with.

Her father had once told her that her indecision would lead to her own destruction one day, and dash it if he wasn't right. He'd also scolded her for her impulsiveness. And her stubbornness. Or whatever attitude she seemed to be displaying at that very moment. It wasn't any great secret that her father didn't think very highly of her.

"I do hope the weather is more agreeable tomorrow, don't you, Miss Knight," Simon said, breaking into her thoughts.

Perhaps equating her indecision in this matter with leading to her own destruction might be too harsh of a word, but the way her stomach tensed at the implied meaning in Simon's tone and sharp eyes, made her feel as if she was on the path to destruction.

"Of course. It'll be nice to get outside in the fresh air," chirped Lady Vessey from the other side of Edmund.

Simon leaned back to allow a servant to fill his wine glass, his eyes never leaving Isabelle's. "I should think a round of pall mall would be in order if the weather is to be so nice."

"Of course," Isabelle agreed, feeling a bit of sympathy for both Simon, who was clearly trying to stake his claim, and Giles who was undoubtedly just trying to survive the week the same as she was.

Charades followed dinner. Usually it was her least favorite game; but tonight she adored it for the only talking was in the form of guessing what was being acted out. No idle chitchat to be made.

The only false pretense to be upheld was a smile that Isabelle had a strong suspicion rivaled a grimace.

When charades were done, so was Isabelle. Thankful for the reprieve and praying that tomorrow tensions would fade away with today's storm, she and Mrs. Finch made a hasty exit.

"Thank you for leaving with me."

"Oh, I only left so we could have time for you to give me all the details of your day with Mr. Appleton."

Isabelle sighed and sank down onto the feather mattress. "I don't know what to say. He's so... He's just..." She opened and closed her fists. "I don't know how to describe it."

"He doesn't evoke your passion," Mrs. Finch said, sitting beside her. Her warm brown eyes were full of compassion.

"Well, no, but I don't need that. I just need him to—" She shrugged. "I don't know how to describe it." And that was the truth. She didn't need any sort of great declaration of love from him. She only wanted him to be his real self. Neither tripping over himself trying to please her, nor so distant and distracted that he acted like she wasn't there. There *had* to be a middle ground somewhere. She blew out a deep breath. "Perhaps I should just take Edmund up on his offer."

"You don't sound very excited about that."

Isabelle started. Licking her lips, she reached for Mrs. Finch's hands. "I'm so sorry, I didn't mean to insult your—"

"Nonsense. I wouldn't wish to marry him if I were your age, either."

"So you won't be angry if I don't accept his suit?"

"Angry?" Mrs. Finch shook her head vigorously. "Heavens no, I'd be more angry if you did."

"But he's your nephew," Isabelle pointed out.

"And he's still old enough to be your grandfather." Her lips formed a tight line. "Besides, I don't think he's worthy."

Isabelle half-scoffed, half-choked on a giggle. "Not worthy? I think if anyone isn't worthy it'd be me. He's titled after all and I come with more scandals attached to my name than there are dukes in England."

"Even so, he's not worthy."

Isabelle wondered what she'd meant, but didn't think it was her place to ask Mrs. Finch to reveal something about her nephew that she'd rather not. "Do you think Simon is?"

Mrs. Finch patted her hand, then stood. "That's for you to decide."

Chapter Nineteen

Isabelle wanted to leave for London tonight. Never in her life had she ever believed she'd have such a thought, but as she shed her dressing robe and sat in her nightrail on the edge of her bed, she had to admit that it was true.

Between Simon's terse actions and Edmund's keen gaze, she was going mad. Today hadn't been a single bit better than the day before. In fact, it had been worse. Everywhere she and Simon went he was constantly looking over his shoulder. He wasn't too obvious, mind you, but she'd noticed. He was likely looking for Giles, but who Isabelle had seen every time she'd chanced a glance was Edmund.

She'd wondered what he was about, but decided she probably didn't want to know. If she had to guess he was just trying to see if there was any real possibility that Isabelle would want to pursue a relationship with Simon as opposed to accepting his offer.

Which, despite her earlier talk with Mrs. Finch, she still wasn't sure who the better choice was after all.

Isabelle exhaled in frustration and fell backward across the counterpane.

"Is it so taxing to decide which suitor to encourage?"

Isabelle shot up as straight as an arrow and crossed her arms over her chest to shield herself as best she could. Sebastian stood just outside her open window, grinning at her. "What are you doing here? And why do you always come visit me through the window?"

Sebastian climbed inside her room and made himself comfortable sitting on the windowsill with his back pressed against the frame. "I didn't think you'd let me in if I were to just knock— and if you did, I'd hate for someone to see us and be forced to marry. Again."

"Yes, that would be tragic," Isabelle agreed. She'd reached for a pillow and held it over her front. "You never answered my question. Why are you here?"

"I wanted to talk to you."

"And that couldn't have waited for tomorrow?"

Sebastian crossed his ankles and knocked the sides of his boots together. "Since I'm not an invited guest, I don't think that would be wise."

Isabelle didn't know whether to laugh at the addled man for being such a coxcomb that he'd resorted to coming to a house party where he wasn't invited and sneak around to avoid being seen or feel pity for him that he had nothing better to do with his time than to come spy on her. "Now that you've seen me and know that I'm neither betrothed nor courting an eminent scandal you may go home."

"Belle?"

Isabelle started at the softness in his tone as he said her name. "Yes?"

"Is anyone courting you?"

She fought to keep the scowl off her face. "Yes. Simon Appleton. We're...er..." She sighed. How did she explain this? "We have an understanding."

"An understanding?"

"We're courting with the idea that we'll become betrothed." Hadn't she already explained this to him in London? So much was said that day, she honestly couldn't remember.

Sebastian let out a soft chuckle. "Isn't that the goal of all courtships?"

Isabelle would throw that blue pillow at his head if she didn't need it to keep herself covered. "You know what I mean."

"I suppose." He uncrossed his ankles and brought his right foot to the floor. "Are you happy with the idea?"

"Of marrying Simon?"

He nodded.

"I suppose so. There aren't many other options."

"No, there isn't," he agreed slowly. "You could always wait a year? Your fortune didn't come with any demands of how soon you had to marry, did it?"

"No." She idly ran her fingers over the gold fringe that edged the pillow. "But I don't see the point in waiting. I don't think there will be very many more gentleman wishing to get married next year."

"Likely not. But neither do you need to rush."

She almost laughed. Almost. "You do realize that I'm two-and-twenty and I have one of the worst sorts of scandals attached to my name? I might be fortunate enough to make it through this Season on the favor that my newfound fortune has granted me, but I doubt I'll get another such reprieve."

"And of all the gentlemen you met in London, Simon Appleton was the best?"

"Yes."

"And you're not just the slightest bit more excited that he's taken such an active interest in you?"

Isabelle sighed. "I don't know. At first, his interest was annoying and now..." She shrugged.

"Now?"

"Now, it's almost like his interest in me is feigned. No, not feigned. I think he's still genuine. He's just...distracted."

"Distracted with other young ladies?"

Was it just her or had his voice just held a slight edge. Isabelle shook off the thought. "Actually, no."

"No?" Sebastian choked.

"No," Isabelle confirmed. "He's been preoccupied with your friend Lord Norcourt."

"Ah." Sebastian crossed his arms. "I should have guessed that would be the problem."

"And just what *did* you guess was the problem."

He waved her off. "Never mind that. What we need is a plan."

"A plan?"

Sebastian's answer was to tap his foot and drum his fingers on his jaw.

A sense of dread built inside Isabelle. This couldn't be good. "I don't need any help. I'm sure once we all go back to London he'll be as attentive as he was before."

"I think what you need to do is make sure he knows you exist," Sebastian announced as if he hadn't heard her protests.

"I believe he's well aware of my existence already. He's just not as attentive as he once was." She twirled the gold fringe some more. "That could be my own doing. I told him not to ask me to marry him again until he had absolutely no doubt I'd say yes."

"Perhaps then he's changed his tack and is just trying to be elusive in hopes of attracting you more."

"That would be a preferable method, but I don't think that's his goal. He's constantly staring at Giles or looking over his shoulder for him."

"Have you asked him why he's so interested in Giles' activities?"

"No, but I suggested they should talk."

Sebastian groaned. "Men do not 'talk', Belle."

"Well, these two need to. Simon is either jealous or confused at Giles' sudden appearance and it's coming in the way of our courtship."

"A bit of both, I think," Sebastian said. "Giles mentioned to me that while he's known all along that Simon existed. It would seem that Simon didn't know." Frowning, he continued. "I'm not sure exactly how that would work. You'd have thought at some moment over the past twenty years Lord Norcourt would have been mentioned, so perhaps he'd heard of him, but it wasn't real until the other night. I don't know nor do I wish to ask either of them about it. That's not my concern. You are."

A chill ran up Isabelle's spine at the way he'd said those last two words. "I know you mean well, Sebastian, but no, I'm not your concern any longer."

He twisted his lips into a partial smile. "Regardless of what you might think, I still have an obligation to you."

Another chill ran up her spine. One far less appealing than the last. *An obligation?* Just who did he think he was? Moreover, just who did he think she was? "There is no such thing. You aren't obligated to do anything for me any more than I am obligated to scrub the floor of this room before I leave for home."

"You know what I meant. I agreed to help you find a husband
—"

"I've already told you, I don't need your help any longer."

"Oh, so it doesn't bother you that your only suitor is distracted by another man?"

"Get out," she snapped.

"Not until you let me give you some advice."

"I don't need your advice. It's time for you to leave."

"Make me."

Isabelle got off the bed and walked over to him. "So help me, Sebastian, I'd push you out this window if I didn't think hitting your head on the floor of the balcony would kill what few cells you still possess in that brain box of yours."

He grinned at her. "Try it. My head is thick enough to protect me. Should you actually make me fall, that is."

She ground her teeth, desperately tempted to take him up on his challenge.

"Come on, Belle," he goaded.

Gripping her pillow in front of her, she debated her options. If she were to earnestly give him her best shove, she'd have to drop the pillow. Was that his goal? Surely not. He'd seen her in far less than a thin nightrail and had openly told her his response would have been the same no matter who it was showing herself to him that way. He didn't wish to see her that way again. He was just trying to provoke her, and it was working. "Remind me to lock the window of every room I stay in, in the future," she murmured, taking a step back.

"But then I couldn't give you any more advice. You think about it tomorrow while you're being ignored." He flashed her a smile and easily swung his body out of her window and onto the balcony, leaving her both relieved and unsettled at the same time.

Chapter Twenty

Sebastian said a brief prayer of thanksgiving as he jumped from the balcony of Isabelle's room. Had she been any higher than the second floor, he'd have had to find a different way into her room. A second floor room was easy enough, especially since she had a balcony. Now he just had to walk to the front of the estate and count the number of windows to find which room belonged to Giles.

Rounding the front of the three-story, brown brick, E-shaped estate, Sebastian stopped. Philip, the footman he'd bribed earlier, said Giles was staying in the room connected to the third balcony from the northwest corner of the house. Sebastian counted the balconies and made his way to the room with the wide open curtains. That should have given Giles away without Sebastian having to pay a coin. Unlike most who liked their bedchamber nice and dark at night, Giles preferred to keep his curtains open as wide as they'd go to allow moonlight to flood the room.

Sebastian spotted a brick about three feet from the ground that poked out of the wall a little further than the rest. He put his booted foot on it and gripped another brick above his head with his left hand to stabilize himself enough to reach the bottom lip of the balcony with his right hand. Latching on, he pulled himself up and with a maneuver he'd rather never give the details of where he learned it, he swung himself up onto the balcony, his back slamming the wooden planks with a hard *thwack*.

"Impressive," Giles greeted.

"Thanks," Sebastian panted. He took another two breaths then stood. "I need to talk to you."

"It must be urgent."

"No."

Giles lifted his eyebrows then turned to open the door that led to his room.

Sebastian followed him inside, feeling suddenly like a fool. "I hope you don't mind I came by. I needed to talk to you."

Giles flopped down on a chair, leaving Sebastian the choice to either stand or sit on Giles' bed. Sebastian stood.

"Are you aware of what's going on at this party?"

Giles blinked. "I think so."

"Lady Cosgrove is trying to find you a wife." Sebastian almost groaned. Of course she was. That's what every lady, no matter what her age or rank, took it upon themselves to do for any unattached man of their acquaintance. "What I mean is that I think she's gravely serious in her pursuit for you to get married." There, that was a tactful way to say it without saying too much.

"I know."

"Do you want to marry?" Sebastian had always just assumed that Giles' lack of interest in ladies in general was just part of who he was: not interested. Perhaps Sebastian had been wrong. That, or Lady Cosgrove had said something to Giles when he'd come to Telford to seek Sebastian an invitation that made Giles suddenly decide he wanted to get married.

"Never thought about it before."

"All right," Sebastian said slowly, trying to make sense of everything. "So you're thinking about it now. At this party?"

"Yes."

"And?"

"And?"

"Have you found a lady who strikes your fancy?"

"She's taken."

Sebastian bit back a grin. Perhaps Lady Cosgrove was onto something by hosting this party for Giles after all. "All right, so you have a lady in mind. Can I ask who she is?"

Giles started. "No."

Sebastian held his hands up in front of himself. "All right, all right, keep your secrets." He crossed his arms. "Would you like some advice?"

"No."

"You said she's taken. Is she the only one you have an interest in?" He had a hard time believing any of the ladies who'd come to this party were otherwise taken with any of the unsuitable pack of gentlemen who'd been invited so she must have a suitor waiting for her in London.

"It's not really an interest. She's just the only one I'd consider."

"I see and does she know this?"

"No."

"Perhaps if she did—"

"No!"

Sebastian stilled at the sharpness in Giles' voice. He'd never heard the man use such a tone before. Ever. "So what of the others? Do you plan to get to know them or wait until you get back to London?"

Giles shrugged. "Don't have a choice."

"What do you mean you don't have a choice?"

"I must marry."

"Must?" Sebastian scoffed. "Nobody *must* marry."

"I must. Lord Cosgrove has demanded it."

"Lord Cosgrove?"

Giles tapped his fingertips together. "He was one of my father's closest friends and has control of my money. He says I won't get any more unless I marry."

"He controls your money?"

Giles nodded. "My father thought." Giles swallowed. "He thought I wouldn't be capable of running the barony so he set everything into a trust that Lord Cosgrove controls."

That certainly explained why Giles had grown up in Ireland and had no real interest in coming to London until very recently. "If your father didn't think you were capable, then why is Lord Cosgrove so adamant that you marry."

"An heir."

Sebastian pondered how to ask what might be better left unspoken: if Giles wasn't good enough for the old baron to raise as his son and not capable to run the barony then why did his male issue matter?

As if reading his mind, Giles said, "The delivering physician said my condition wouldn't pass down to my children."

"Did he say what makes him so certain of that?"

"I don't know."

"Are there any conditions surrounding the wife you choose or just that you pick one?"

Giles' blank expression was his only response, sparking a glimmer of hope in Sebastian. Perhaps his earlier suggestion wouldn't be met with as much opposition this time.

"What of Belle?"

"Belle?"

"Isabelle Knight," Sebastian clarified.

Giles shook his head. "No, she's taken."

Ah, so that's who Giles had been speaking of earlier when he'd mentioned a female he'd been interested in but couldn't pursue. "It might not be the easiest task you embark on, but if she's willing to entertain Simon's suit, then I don't see why she couldn't be persuaded to entertain your suit."

"No."

"No? Why the devil not? Do you think she's really that taken with Simon?"

"No."

"All right, then you can just woo her a little—I'll even help you."

Giles blinked. "Why?"

"Why what? Why help you or why her?"

"Both."

"You're both my friends and I think you'd be a good match for each other."

"No."

Sebastian refused to give into the temptation to groan. "Why not?"

"She's taken."

This time, Sebastian did groan. "No, she's not. She's only allowing Simon to pay her court because—"

"Not him."

131

"Then who? Lord Kenton?" he said with a snort of disbelief.
"No. You."

***

Sebastian couldn't shake the uneasy feeling that had settled over him the second Giles had made his final statement the night before. Belle was not his. They might be married, but she wasn't *his*. Sighing, he rolled out of the bed he'd occupied in the gamekeeper's cottage and scrubbed his fingers over his face. With any luck he'd be able to spot Belle and Simon playing lawn games or some such nonsense and get a better idea of what was going on between them. Giles might have some misguided notion that Belle belonged to Sebastian, but it was quite clear he was the only one who felt that way, and if Belle wanted to pursue a courtship with and possibly a marriage to Simon, he'd do what he could to help her succeed.

Luck might not have been in his favor when it came to receiving an official invitation to the party, but he'd been quite fortunate when he'd happened upon Belle and Simon selecting mallets for pall mall.

"I think I'd like the red one this time," Belle said.

Sebastian pressed up against the side of the shed and craned his neck so he could hear better.

"Here you are," Simon said. "I shall take the blue. No, the green." Wood tapped together, presumably from Simon putting the blue one back on the rack and taking the green.

"Thank you," Belle murmured.

From the corner of his eye, Sebastian could see the firm line of her lips. Was she upset already? Why?

"We'll play bowls later," Simon said, a hint of apology in his tone.

"It's all right. I understand."

Simon drummed his fingers against the wood of either the handle of his pall mall mallet or the wooden rack. Sebastian didn't know which and it wasn't important enough for him to chance being seen to peek.

"This was a bad idea," Simon said at last with a sigh. "I should

132

have known better and just stayed in London to court you there."
He sighed again. "I just thought—"

Sebastian desperately wished he could see the expressions on their faces.

"It's all right," Belle repeated. "Are you ready to play?"

Sebastian's heart constricted. She was really trying. It was her oaf of a suitor who wasn't worthy. Sebastian started and thrust the thought away immediately. It wasn't his place to decide who was worthy of her—even if he felt Simon wasn't. It was her decision and her choice could have been far worse, to be sure. Simon wasn't a bad sort from what he'd heard of the man. He was just distracted. With the right action Belle could steal his attention. Then, they all could move forward with their lives. Yes, all she needed was some advice and now that he knew exactly what was going on between them—which really wasn't so bad, Simon was just preoccupied with wanting to avoid Giles—Sebastian could give her advice to hold his attention no matter who was around.

Pleased with his new strategy of how to help her, Sebastian slinked away to wait for darkness when he could go see Belle again.

Chapter Twenty-One

Isabelle seriously considered begging Mrs. Finch to take her back to London. If she had to play one more game of pall mall, that's exactly what she'd do. Three days. Yes, three days straight they'd had to play that blasted game. Once was all right, twice was tedious, thrice was exhausting and if it came to a fourth time, she just might do herself in!

"Did you win?"

Every muscle in Isabelle's body clenched. She should have locked her window! Slowly, she turned to face her handsome intruder. "Actually, I did."

"I'd offer you my felicitations—" Sebastian let himself in and closed the window with a *snap*— "but I don't think you really won. I think Giles' did and he wasn't even there."

Isabelle scowled. "How do you even know?"

"I saw you two."

"I see. So you no longer just climb into my room, you've taken to spying on me in the daytime, too?"

"For good reason." Sebastian sagged against the wall and swept her with his gaze.

She suddenly felt naked, keenly aware that she was wearing only her wrapper. She crossed her arms over her chest. Though why she bothered, she didn't know. It would seem that Sebastian was making a habit of seeing her in scandalous states of undress. "What do you want?"

"To help you." He cleared his throat. "I think he's sincere with his motives, Belle. He's just distracted."

She frowned at him. "I told you that before." But evidently he hadn't believed her.

"You just need to be more attractive than the distraction."

"Why thank you, Sebastian. I'm so glad you told me that," she said sarcastically. "If only I'd known..."

"Ah, that's the Belle I know!" He pushed off from where he was leaning against the wall and made his way to her bed. "Come join me."

"I think not."

He shrugged and took a seat on the edge. "Soft."

"You're not staying. You can go back to whatever hole you crawled out of."

Chuckling, he said, "I think you just need to flirt with the man."

"I've tried."

"Tried? You can't *try* to flirt. You either do it or you don't."

"I do."

"Come show me."

"Absolutely not!"

"Belle, I just asked you to show me how you flirt, I didn't demand you share your bed with me—though in a literal sense, I would be ever thankful."

"That won't be happening." She narrowed her eyes on him and his giant grin. "Either request."

"All right. If you won't show me how you've been flirting. I'll show you how you should be flirting."

Isabelle half-groaned, half-giggled—quite an odd combination, to be sure. "And how do you know how a woman should flirt?"

He gave her a queer look. "I am a man."

She blushed. Well, yes he was a man, but that didn't mean he was an expert when it came to the attraction between the two sexes, did it? "That might be how you like to be flirted with, Simon might prefer differently," she pointed out.

He continued to stare at her as if she were cracked. "This will work—no matter who the chap is."

Even you? She started. Why had she thought *that*?

"The first thing you need to do is smile more."

"I do. I smile quite a lot, actually."

"Not that I've seen," he said with a dubious look. "When I saw you today, your lips were pressed together into a line straighter than one of your father's arrows. Now, tomorrow you can't do that. You need to smile."

"All right. I'll smile more," she mumbled.

"Try it."

"Pardon me?"

"I said, try it. I think you need to practice so I can help you."

"Help me smile?" she said in disbelief. "Do you intend to come hold my lips in proper position, then?"

"If I must. Now, smile."

"If I do, will you leave?"

"No, not until I'm satisfied. Now, give it a try."

Feeling every bit the fool, Isabelle stretched her lips into the widest, fullest smile she could.

"Excellent grimace, now, let's try a smile this time."

Isabelle relaxed her face and let out a shaky laugh. "I cannot smile if there's no reason to."

"Then you're going to have a very difficult time obtaining your Mr. Appleton's attention." He stood and walked over to her.

"What are you doing?"

A slow, wolfish grin split his face. "I know how to get you to smile."

Isabelle took a step back and tightened her hold on herself. There was a gleam in his eyes she almost didn't recognize. "What are you doing?"

"If I recall correctly—" he took another step toward her— "you're very ticklish."

"Don't you dare!"

"Then smile," he murmured, taking another step toward her.

Isabelle took a step backward and collided with the wall. *Drat!* She extended her right hand toward him to keep at a distance. "All right, all right, I'll smile." She forced another smile.

"That's not good enough." He reached for her hand, taking another step toward her, bringing their bodies mere inches apart.

Her breath caught and her stilted smile vanished. "Take a step back, please."

He didn't budge.

136

She swallowed. "Sebastian, please."

Something passed over his face. Something quick and heated. Something she didn't recognize. "All right, try again," he said raggedly, taking a half-step back.

She tried again, but it was useless. Her lips had suddenly turned to stone for her cheeks couldn't pull them apart. "You're making me nervous."

He released her hand and took another step back, leaving her further distracted by his sudden absence.

She blinked off the thought and tried again to smile.

"Better, but a little less—" he stretched his lips into something similar to a snarl— "and a little more this—" He relaxed his facial muscles just enough to allow his lips to fall into a nice frame around his white teeth without showing so much of his gums. "See the difference?"

She nodded. Many things might have changed about Sebastian since they were children, but his wide, boyish smile hadn't. "I'll try again." She tried again.

"Almost," he murmured, bringing his hands up to cup her face. "Just a little more."

Isabelle stood frozen as his gentle thumbs moved her lips a little wider into what he'd consider a perfect smile. She was an idiot. A complete idiot. What was she doing?

"Just like that."

"All right." She batted at his wrists until he removed his hands. "I think I have it now. You may go."

"Belle?"

Isabelle swallowed and crossed her arms. "I think I have it," she repeated, stretching her lips into the same position he'd just had them.

"Indeed you do, now for the next step."

"The next step? What is this a performance?"

"Of sorts, yes. You have a very beautiful smile, Belle, but that alone won't win his attention. You need to also—"

"Flirt," she cut in, flushing. "Yes, I remember that part. I'll be sure to rap him on the knuckles with my fan at dinner and bat my lashes at him enough that we can all be sure there's no bug taking up residence under my eyelids."

"And giggle," he added with a wink.

"That won't be happening."

"Why not?"

"Forced giggling is absolutely the worst form of flirtation."

"Then you'd better find Simon to be talented of the comic arts because gentlemen enjoy that sort of thing."

Isabelle grinned. "Oh, so then you did enjoy sitting next to Lady Mary at Lady Norcourt's dinner."

"No. But that smile right there, that's the one that will steal his heart."

Chapter Twenty-Two

As much as Isabelle hated to ever admit such a thing, Sebastian was right. The only real option open to her right now was to attract Simon with her female wiles enough to distract him from his dislike for Giles.

How absurd!

Even a week ago had someone told her she'd be the one falling all over herself to capture Simon's attention and not the reverse, she'd have laughed. Now, she wasn't laughing. No, she was sporting what she hoped would be her best grin.

She'd stayed up half the night looking at her reflection in the mirror and practicing her smile and batting her lashes. She was truly going mad. There was no other way to describe this idiocy.

"Good morning, Mr. Appleton," she greeted, coming into the breakfast room.

Simon's head snapped up. "Isabelle," he breathed. He swallowed convulsively just as she'd hoped he would upon seeing her in her red brocade dress and sophisticated upsweep. He rushed to the sideboard and helped her fill her plate. "You look quite lovely this morning."

"Thank you, but I'm sure you say that to all the young ladies." Was that considered a flirtatious statement or asking for trouble? She really wasn't sure.

"I might say it, but I only mean it when I say it to you. You are undoubtedly the most beautiful creature here."

"Oh, you don't have to flatter me," she cooed, batting her lashes up at him.

"Of course I do. I owe it to you."

"Owe?"

He nodded slowly. "I've been dreadfully inattentive to you and your needs these past few days and if we're to marry, I need to make a better impression, wouldn't you say?"

She offered him her best attempt at a sweet smile. It was all she could do.

"Let's sit at the far end."

Isabelle followed him down to the end of the table and took the seat he'd indicated.

Breakfast was tolerable. As promised, Simon had been far more attentive to her than he had been over the past few days. Then again, Giles was nowhere to be found.

"Shall we play bowls?"

"I'd love to," Isabelle said, silently adding, *but only if we get to play the whole game this time.* She bit the inside of her mouth. She needed to be more understanding. Truly, how would she feel if she were in his position?

"Would you like me to show you how?"

"Oh, that's all right, I know how to play." She took the bowl from him and walked up to the little strip of wood that designated where the bowler stood and rolled her bowl down toward the waiting white ball known as the jack.

"Very good," Simon commented, coming to stand next to her and watch her bowl roll straight for the jack.

Her bowl veered slightly to the left and rolled right past the jack. "Oh drat!" she said with a snap of her fingers.

Chuckling, Simon picked up his bowl and rolled it toward the jack.

It stopped within inches of his target.

"Would you like to know my trick?"

Isabelle opened her mouth to refuse. There weren't any tricks to bowls, but right before she could refuse, she caught a glimpse of Sebastian hiding on the other side of a large shrub; he was nodding his head wildly.

She turned to face Simon and batted her eyelashes at him. "Yes, I'd love to know all of your tricks, sir," she purred sweetly, smiling.

He grinned, but not in a way that would suggest he was flattered. If she didn't know any better, she'd think he was laughing at her!

"Let me retrieve our bowls," he murmured. A moment later he came back with one large bowl balanced in each hand. He flashed her a smile, then his attention caught on something beyond her left shoulder.

Tension coiled inside Isabelle. Had he just seen Sebastian? Slowly, she cast a glance in the direction Simon had just been looking and saw Edmund leaning against a tree smoking a cheroot.

A dull ache built in her chest. She needed to talk to him. Even if Mrs. Finch didn't think he was a worthy match for her, she needed to explain her situation with Simon to him. He'd been so kind to her over the years, it was the least he deserved. He removed his cheroot from his mouth and gave her a slight nod, then walked off.

"I should probably go talk to him," Isabelle said quietly.

Simon twisted his lips. "I'm fairly certain he's not too concerned."

"Oh?"

He put one of the bowls down. "I think he already knows, Isabelle. He's been watching us all week."

"He has?"

Simon nodded, a smile playing on his lips. "Yes. He was a little less obvious about it earlier in the week, but now—" He shrugged.

"I probably should talk to him about—" she swallowed— "us."

A wide smile spread across Simon's face. "Does that mean—"

"I'm still considering it," she said carefully before he could embarrass himself or make her embarrass him.

"That's all I ask." He ran his hand over the top of the bowl. "All right, let me show you that trick."

"Right." She bit her lip. She'd have to make time to talk to Edmund tonight. He'd always been adamant that he wouldn't force her to accept his suit and that if she found another that he wouldn't interfere. But she still needed to talk to him. It wasn't fair that she wasn't honest with him about her courtship with Simon, as strained as it might be.

"Here, you use this bowl," Simon said suddenly, extending the bowl in her direction.

Isabelle took the bowl from him, catching a quick glimpse of where Sebastian was peeking his head out from around the hedge again, frowning. She knit her brows. What did he have to be unhappy about?

"Grip the bowl like this," Simon said. He gripped the bowl in a way that didn't look any different than how she'd done, so she mirrored the action. "Good. Now..."

Behind Simon a good twenty feet, Sebastian emerged from between the two hedges and cupped his hands as if he were holding a bowl, then moved his arm back, lowered his hand and pretended to bowl.

"All right, try it," Simon said, breaking into her thoughts.

Isabelle licked her lips. She hadn't heard a single word he'd said other than how to grip the bowl. "Can you show me again?"

In the background, Sebastian came closer to them, shaking his head without ceasing and making the same bowling motion.

Without thinking, Isabelle sent her bowl rolling forward in a direction completely opposite of where the jack was.

Simon was speechless.

Sebastian gave her a nod of approval from where he stood not ten feet away.

Simon handed her his bowl and said something about going to get the other bowl.

Sebastian's eyes went wide and he shook his head.

Instinctively, Isabelle reached her free hand out to stay Simon, shocking them both.

Sebastian looked relieved. He gave her another nod and made a slow retreat back to the safety of his hedge.

"Why don't we just use this one?" Isabelle suggested around the giant bubble that had just formed in her throat. Share the bowl? She willed herself not to shudder at the thought of him touching her. It wasn't that she found him disagreeable exactly, but she still wasn't sure she wanted to marry him and if someone suspected his helping her was inappropriate they'd be announced within a trice.

"No, it'll be easier if we each have our own," Simon said, pulling himself away from her hold.

Sebastian lifted his eyes heavenward and threw his hands into the air, then disappeared behind the hedge.

"Have you seen Sebastian?"

Isabelle almost jumped out of her skin, if such a thing were possible. She wasn't sure if she was more surprised that Giles knew his friend was here or that he'd crept up on her that way. She turned to face him and nearly laughed. He looked all out of sorts. "Are you all right?"

Giles nodded slowly. "Yes."

"A-all right." She felt Simon come up behind her, bringing a sense of discomfort over her. "Just a minute ago," she said in answer to his original question, then she pointed toward the hedge.

Giles nodded his understanding. "Simon," he greeted, bobbing his head in the man's direction before walking toward the hedge.

"What the devil is he doing?" Simon muttered, staring at his brother's retreating form.

In spite of the oddness of the entire situation, a bubble of laughter built up in Isabelle's chest. "We should probably go back inside."

Simon gave her a grateful look. "Indeed. Perhaps we can find someone who'd like to play cards."

***

Isabelle wasn't sure if it was to her good fortune or fate trying to torture her that the only people interested in playing cards were Edmund and Lady Vessey.

"Have a seat by me, dear," Lady Vessey said.

Isabelle and Edmund exchanged looks. Clearly neither of them knew who she was referring to as 'dear'.

"Why don't you sit by Lady Vessey," Edmund said, the tips of his ears pink.

Isabelle lowered herself into the chair next to Lady Vessey and smoothed her skirts while Edmund and Simon took their prospective seats across from them.

"Whist?" Edmund said, shuffling the cards.

"Ooooh, you know I adore Whist," Lady Vessey said with a clap of her hands.

Edmund coughed and Simon grinned.

Edmund shuffled to his satisfaction then dealt the cards. Isabelle picked hers up and stared at them. She didn't know the rules and hoped someone would be kind enough to explain them.

"Oh, can I go first, Edmund?" Lady Vessey asked, a smile curving her lips.

Edmund's eyes widened, then narrowed and darkened. Then he swallowed.

Isabelle stared at the pair. The game, or at least the rules, didn't appear to be very important any longer. It was without question that Lady Vessey was flirting with Edmund, and if the way Lady Vessey's full skirt was moving was any indication, the flirtations weren't just above the table!

"I think that'd be permissible," Edmund practically barked.

Lady Vessey made a little sound of satisfaction and picked up a card from the facedown pile, then took one of her others and put it on the table. Edmund wordlessly made a similar action, his eyes fastened on the cards in his hands and his jaw tight. Simon was next. He also selected a card from the down-faced pile and immediately put it back on the table.

Isabelle bit her lip and did the same thing she'd seen the others do, not paying attention to what she'd picked up or put down.

All four took another turn.

Then another.

Nobody said anything, but looks were enough. Lady Vessey kept peeking over at Edmund under lowered lashes; Edmund kept his eyes fixed on his cards even when it wasn't his turn, but the fire burning in his eyes was still visible; Simon's expression was the most difficult to interpret. At one moment it looked like he was about to boil over with nervous discomfort, then a second later, he almost looked sympathetic for some reason.

Isabelle shook off the thought and reached forward to retrieve her next card when suddenly something large and warm that felt decidedly like a stocking-covered foot landed right on top of her slipper. Blushing, she licked her suddenly dry lips and plucked up her card. She put the one she'd just picked up in line with the others in her hand and held them in front of her like a fan. She looked over the top of her cards at Simon. She narrowed her eyes on him. She'd assumed that their companions were touching feet under the table, but it didn't mean that she and Simon needed to do it, too.

In fact, while it would seem that Lady Vessey seemed to like the exchange, Isabelle didn't. His foot was heavy and it might just be her perception, but it almost felt moist. She clenched every muscle in her body to keep from shuddering, then wiggled her toes and tried to pull her foot back. It didn't budge.

"You need to play a card, dear," Lady Vessey reminded her.

Isabelle grabbed the one on the end and tossed it on the table without a second thought, then narrowed her eyes on Simon and began wiggling her toes, making sure to really push up with her big toe so he could feel it in his arch and release his heavy hold.

No such luck.

She pressed her lips together. Truly, having his foot on top of hers was most unsettling. It was mildly uncomfortable a moment ago, but now it was really bothering her. She clenched her jaw and lifted her eyebrows, suppressing the urge to make an unladylike noise though she was very much so tempted.

Simon's eyebrows shot to his hairline and he shouted something, but his foot stayed firmly in place.

"Well, show us your cards!" Lady Vessey, said throwing hers down on the table.

"My cards?" Isabelle laid them out for everyone to see: a three, a jack, a six, and a king.

"That's not a trick!" Lady Vessey exclaimed.

"A trick?"

"I thought you had a trick and were trying to give me the signal," Simon said with a shrug.

She had no idea what he was talking about and handed her cards back to Edmund, noting the unusual look in his eye.

Edmund handed the cards to Simon. "Care to shuffle,

Appleton?"

Simon took the cards and scooted his chair back from the table a few inches. Odd the foot stayed firmly in place.

Isabelle was certain her eyes had nearly just bulged, and Edmund's slight grin confirmed they had indeed. His lowered lashes confirmed Isabelle's other suspicion: it was *his* foot! Why the devil was his foot on top of hers when Lady Vessey was so openly flirting with him? Surely he didn't think to try to reassure Isabelle that he still planned to keep his earlier promise by...by...such an indecent gesture!

She caught his gaze and gave her head a slight shake, not enough to draw anyone's attention, but enough to tell him she wanted him to stop this nonsense. He didn't. In fact, he was the one now moving his toes. She could feel them rubbing her ankle. It took every ounce of control she possessed over her body not to cast up her accounts or run screaming from the room. There was one thing that was indisputable: she was going to have to ring for a bath tonight.

Simon finished shuffling the cards and began dealing.

"Perhaps before we begin, the two of you should work out a better signal," Lady Vessey suggested.

"I'm sure they'll be fine, my lady," Edmund said, killing any hope that Isabelle was about to get a reprieve from his daring foot. As if to make sure of it, Edmund quickly drew a card to start.

Simon shrugged and waited to take his turn.

"Say, you don't mind if we join you, do you?" Giles asked from the door. Without waiting for an answer, he walked in and took a seat in one of two vacant chairs by the window.

Behind him, Sebastian sauntered in, creating a wave of unease completely unrelated to the sweaty, unwanted foot on top of hers. What was he doing here? She had to bite her tongue to keep from asking that very question as he made his way to the chair next to Giles.

"We'll play the winner," Sebastian said.

"That should be amusing," Lady Vessey said, licking her lips.

Everyone took their turn and it was time for Isabelle to go. She picked up the top card and quickly dropped it on the table without even bothering to look at the cards in her hand.

"Dropped like a lady who knows what she wants," Sebastian commented.

Isabelle stiffened. Was he mocking her? Surely it hadn't escaped his notice just whose foot it was on top of hers under the table. Her skirts were full, but from where he sat, he had an unobstructed profile view of where everyone's feet were positioned under the table. Did he think it was amusing that both Simon and Edmund were showing her affections, of a different variety of course? "If I know it's not the one I'm looking for, there's no reason to hold onto it." A smile pulled on her lips. "You might recognize that tactic, I did learn it from you after all."

Silence encompassed the room as the impact of the words she'd just spoken rocked Isabelle to the core.

Lady Vessey seemed to be the only one who didn't seem to understand her meaning other than perhaps a superficial game tactic and she took her turn.

Edmund sat still a moment longer as a shadow passed over his eyes. He reached forward to grab his card, simultaneously removing his foot from Isabelle's.

Isabelle would have sighed with relief, if not for the inner tension that had recently gripped her and held her captive. If Sebastian dared to come to her room tonight she was going to brain that man and she'd use the Bible if she must to do it.

Chapter Twenty-Three

It was everything Sebastian could do to keep an impassive face as he watched the players at the card table—particularly Belle. She was rather fetching when she was unsettled. He closed his eyes. He wasn't here to think of how fetching Belle was to him. He'd agreed to help her find a suitable husband and that's what he needed to be concerned with. Not what she did to him.

Beside him, Giles let out a deep exhale and leaned his head back, staring up at the ceiling as he was often wont to do when there was nothing else in the room that interested him.

Sebastian would have to send the man an entire barrel of whisky after this party to show his appreciation for Giles allowing him to join without permission from Lady Cosgrove. Come to think of it, that was probably enough of a token of appreciation in itself since Giles was no longer expected to sit in the drawing room with a gaggle of debutantes. Or his mother. Apparently that was another caveat of this party, Giles' mother, though not a very prominent and engaged guest, had taken to coercing Giles to spend time with her whenever she could manage it.

At the card table, the game continued. Cards, that is, not the game that had previously been being played under the table. Odd. When had Lord Kenton retracted his foot? No matter. Hopefully it was enough of a hint for Belle to become daring enough to try the same tactic with Simon.

Or not.

She stared at her cards in a way that might suggest they held the answer to some secret riddle. Her feet both firmly planted on the floor in front of her. What he wouldn't give to understand the workings of her mind. Did she not understand now was a prime opportunity to capture Simon with her wiles?

His gaze shifted to Simon. If it were possible, he looked even more unsettled than Belle. What the devil— *Giles.* Blast it all, he hadn't thought of that. Actually, this was probably the best time for Belle to distract the man and capture his attention.

Sebastian cleared his throat.

Belle ignored him and took her turn.

He cleared it again. Louder this time.

She cast him a scowl over her shoulder, then turned her attention back to the game.

Not so easily put off, Sebastian put his fist to his mouth and prepared his body for the internal abuse it was about to take at the account of Belle's stubbornness and his will to capture her attention. *Cough, cough, cough. Hack! Hack! Hack!* With his free hand he started banging his open palm against his chest. *Cough, cough! Hack, hack!*

"Choking on a biscuit over there, Belgrave?" Lord Kenton asked.

Sebastian shook his head. *Cough, cough.* Blast it all, now his coughs were genuine!

A firm hand smacked him on the back, startling him to silence.

"You're welcome," Giles muttered.

Sebastian looked over to Belle. She was staring right at him, scowling. Good. Not the scowl, of course, she needed to get rid of that post haste. He cocked his head to the side and shot an overdone smile at her.

She pursed her lips.

He lifted his eyebrows and stretched his smile wider.

Her nostrils flared and it was all he could not to laugh.

He sent a pointed look to Simon, still smiling like a simpleton.

The corners of her lips pulled apart in a smile that rivaled a grimace, but now wasn't the time to point that out. He nodded his approval, then crossed his ankles and tapped the sides of his boots together.

Her smile vanished and she gave him a quick shake of her head as if to say, *"Absolutely not!"*

He nodded slowly and looked back over at Simon.

Scowling at him once more, she turned her eyes away from

him to pay attention to the game.

Sebastian knocked his boots together again.

Belle seemed not to notice.

Sebastian hated to be an annoyance, but he wasn't above it. He lifted his fist back up to his lips and cleared his throat, a warning.

Belle swallowed visibly and slid her slippered foot closer to her suitor's, stopping merely an inch away.

A little further. But she didn't move it further, prompting Sebastian to clear his throat once more.

"Perhaps you should pour yourself a drink," Lady Vessey suggested.

"Indeed," Belle agreed, a genuine smile turning her lips.

Sebastian knocked his boots together—his last warning.

Belle licked her lips and reached for her card, simultaneously lifting her foot and bringing it down on top of Simon's.

The young buck's entire body jerked and eyes lit up as if he were truly startled. He cleared his throat. "Excuse me," he murmured. Then as if he'd just solved a complex equation, said, "Trick!"

***

Isabelle didn't know who she wanted to brain more: Simon or Sebastian. She didn't have the trick, whatever that was.

"I don't think she has the trick, old chap," Sebastian said easily, pulling a chair up to the table. He took a seat. "Would anyone object if I help Miss Knight?" When nobody spoke within a half-second after the words were out of his mouth, he tossed her cards toward Simon, saying, "Why don't we start this hand over."

Twisting his lips, Simon collected everyone's cards and shuffled.

Meanwhile, the insufferable man Isabelle had once foolishly been excited to be eloping to Gretna Green with moved his chair even closer to her.

"Must you sit so close?" she all but hissed.

"If I'm to help you, I must," he said, the gleam in his eyes made it clear that he wasn't just talking about cards and for a reason she couldn't explain, the understanding sent her body into a panic.

"I don't need help."

"Yes, you do," Sebastian said.

Trying to ignore the flames that were now licking her face, she turned her attention to Edmund who for some reason was dealing. He, too, had a different gleam in his eyes. It wasn't dangerous or predatory as the one she'd glimpsed earlier. It was almost what she'd classify as knowing. Good gracious. Was it possible that he could see that Sebastian unsettled her? She frowned. No, Sebastian didn't unsettle her. His closeness did. There *was* a difference.

Edmund finished dealing the cards and she reached to pick hers up at the same time as Sebastian.

He pulled his hand back and allowed her to pick up her cards.

Fanning them in front of herself, she was painfully aware that Sebastian was leaning even closer to her than he had been before. She moved her hand to the left so he could see her cards better and quit moving so close.

He encircled her wrist with his strong fingers and pushed her hand back squarely in her direct line of vision.

"Fours," he whispered in her ear.

Isabelle looked at her four cards, two of which were fours. "What do I do with them?"

"Collect them." He put his right arm along the back of her chair, bringing him that much closer to her.

She resisted the urge to elbow him and picked up a card from the deck: a five.

"Discard it," he whispered.

She was about to carelessly fling it onto the table when suddenly something brushed her ankle. Sebastian's foot if she had to guess. She tossed the card down and immediately pulled her foot away, making the dratted man smile—and seemingly move closer. Something she didn't think was possible.

Looking for a distraction, she caught sight of Simon's face. Whether his lips were pursed because Giles was in the room or because Sebastian was on the edge of mauling her, she'd never know, but she did have her suspicions.

She played her next round. Barely. Sebastian was so close and his masculine scent of pine and leather so strong, she could barely read the number on her card. Actually, she was so shaken she was fairly certain that her last card hadn't had a number at all, but she couldn't say for sure. Sebastian's thigh pressing against hers was too much of a distraction.

She closed her eyes and willed herself not to sigh in vexation. A moment later it was her turn to draw again. Bracing herself for whatever bold move Sebastian might make when she took her card, she reached forward. As expected, Sebastian did something, but not at all what she'd expected. He'd somehow managed to get his dratted foot under the hem of her skirt and was pressing the side of his foot against her calf, slowly moving it up and down.

Even through her silk stockings, her calf burned. Burned? No, it was scorching! Flustered, she dropped her card and tried to clear her thoughts.

No such luck. Her attention was fully stolen by the strange, tingly sensation in her calf. She clenched her jaw and would have yanked her leg away from him if she didn't think it'd draw attention.

A delicate cough jarred her from her thoughts. She flushed and tried her best to meet Edmund's eyes.

"Your turn, Isabelle," he said with a quick wink.

A wink? Isabelle wanted nothing more than to bury her head in her hands and pray for the chaos to stop. She picked up her card and quickly dropped it.

"See the difference?" Sebastian whispered in her ear, his lips were so close she could almost feel them on her skin.

"The difference?"

He trailed his foot up her calf with a deliberate slowness that made her entire body feel like it was about to combust. Oh, there was definitely a difference!

Swallowing, she nodded. How was it possible someone's foot —especially *his*—could have such an affect on her?

"That's what you need to do," he said, withdrawing his foot. To the room his words were merely a confirmation that she knew how to play the game now, but she took his meaning. He was suggesting she do the same foot-on-leg action to Simon.

Isabelle stared down at her cards, at a loss. How could she possibly touch Simon the same way? She certainly didn't want to.

Sebastian straightened in his chair, presumably to give her more room to...to... Well, she knew what he expected her to do even if she couldn't form the thought without feeling a wee bit nauseous.

Tentatively, she kicked off her slipper and choked down the bubble of unease—or was that a surge of bile—that was lodged in her throat, suffocating her. She took a deep breath and extended her foot forward. *Oh, blast, what am I doing? I cannot possibly touch him.*

Edmund picked up a card and carelessly threw it down almost as if he hadn't even looked at it. Likely he hadn't, he seemed to be fixated on Isabelle in the most odd way. Isabelle pushed Edmund from her mind and focused her attention on Simon. He reached forward to snag his card and she moved her foot...

Oh, please save me! She couldn't do this. She pulled her foot back and grabbed her card, not sure if it was even her turn or not. She held her cards in front of her and leaned closer to Sebastian as if she were trying to show him her hand and ask for advice.

He leaned forward. "What are you doing?" he whispered.

She put the fan of cards directly in front of her lips and turned her head to whisper in his ear. "I can't."

"Try."

"No." She pulled the cards as close to her mouth as possible. "Perhaps you should since you're so skilled."

***

Skilled? Sebastian almost snorted. He wasn't skilled. There was no skill involved in touching someone with your foot. Sighing, he crossed his arms and leaned back. Tonight, he vowed. Tonight he'd go to her room again and show her exactly how to touch a man if need be. *If need be?* There clearly was a need. Who knew the brazen young girl he'd once known was so innocent and naïve?

Chapter Twenty-Four

Isabelle brought her hands up in front of her eyes to observe her fingers. They had more wrinkles than a prune. It was time to get out of the bath. Oh, but she didn't want to. After she'd scrubbed her foot until the skin turned a violent red, she'd relaxed enough to enjoy the warm water, but now it was cold and time to emerge.

She stood and quickly wrapped herself in a towel.

Tap. Tap. Tap.

Isabelle's heart stopped when she saw Sebastian's shadow against the closed drapes. *What was he doing here again?* Perhaps if she ignored him, he'd go away.

Tap. Tap. Tap. Tap. Tap. "I know you're in there." *Tap. Tap. Tap.*

Scowling, she marched over to the window and opened it just an inch or two. "Would you be quiet before someone hears you?"

"Let me in and I'll be quiet."

"No. I'm not decent."

Something flickered over his face, but it was hard to determine what it was in the moonlight. "Put on your robe."

"No."

"Fine, then remain indecent. I don't mind." Sebastian gripped the bottom of the windowpane and lifted it.

Panic built in her chest. He was coming in whether she wanted him to or not. She could try to fight him, of course, but that'd mean having to let her towel drop so she could grab hold of the window to keep him from opening it. Which was useless. He'd easily overpower her. Instead, she scampered backward, holding her towel even tighter. "Do you have no decency?" she asked when he'd let himself in.

An unapologetic, wolfish grin took his lips. "None."

"Well, at least have the courtesy to turn around while I put on

154

my robe."

Sebastian made himself comfortable atop her bed. Not giving him the benefit of seeing her irritated—or naked—she scampered behind her dressing screen and quickly threw on her dressing robe. Good thing she'd decided not to wash her hair tonight. That was one less thing she had to contend with.

"Why did you come here again?" she demanded, tightening the red silk sash of her dressing robe once more for good measure as she came out from behind the screen.

"To help you."

Why was his voice so thick? She pushed off the thought and crossed her arms. "I don't need any help."

"Yes, you do."

"No. I don't think I do."

"You do if you think *I'm* skilled."

Embarrassment flooded her. She'd wondered if he'd take her earlier words wrong. "I meant eager."

"No, you didn't," he said with a chuckle. "You think I'm skilled—which is a problem."

Indeed it was. He was the last gentleman she wanted to be attracted to in any way. "You know what I meant."

"Regardless." He shed his blue coat and stood. "You're going to learn how to touch a man."

"Excuse me?" Had she just *squeaked*? She cleared her throat. "I think not."

"Belle, if you're to catch his attention, then you need to learn how to get it in the first place and so far your efforts have been unsatisfactory."

"Perhaps that's because he's not interested in me that way." She hated the brutal truth in that statement, but it was the truth. Simon, for all of his previous attention he'd showered on her, had never tried to get her alone. Ever. He'd never asked to take her to the balcony or the gardens. He'd never held her closer to him than was appropriate when they'd danced. Sure, he'd been kind to her, and had admitted that he'd like to marry her, but his actions seemed to heavily contradict his words.

"Then you need to do something to get him interested."

"And how am I to do that?"

"Touch him."

"I cannot. It's indecent."

"And when have you ever cared about what's decent?"

She pursed her lips. Since it meant she'd have to make a fool of herself to get the attention of a gentleman she didn't really want. A wave of sadness came over her. *A gentleman she didn't really want.* That was an adequate description, sadly. But who else was there? Edmund? That man didn't know what he wanted. Seeing as how things played out today, he seemed to have some sort of strange interest in both her *and* Lady Vessey. If his game was to play with both of their affections until one chose him, then Lady Vessey could have him all to herself. That was a cruel game to play and she had no wish to marry a man who'd make a fool of her.

"Are you sure this is even necessary? Once we get back to London he—"

"Will magically be more interested in you than he is now?" Sebastian cut in doubtfully. He shook his head. "No. I don't think he will be. He's clearly bothered by Giles' presence for whatever reason, and I doubt that will go away once he gets back to London." He pursed his lips, then shrugged as if to cast off whatever thought had just formed in his mind. "So now it shall be up to you to remind him of your presence."

"By touching him?"

He rolled up his cuffs. "If done the right way, a woman's touch can completely captivate a man."

"And you'd know this because..."

"I'm a man."

"And apparently one who has denied himself nothing in the world of debauchery."

"You'd be surpris—" His lips formed a thin line. "Say, I think you'd be the one far more knowledgeable about such matters since you claim to have been sharing yourself with Lord Kenton for some time now. Perhaps it should be you teaching me something."

Her face burned with mortification. "You know as well as I do that I've never gone to bed with Lord Kenton—or anyone else."

He arched his left brow. "Then why did you claim to?"

To make you jealous. She froze. No, that's not why, was it? She'd just wanted him to leave, hadn't she? He shouldn't and likely *wouldn't* care who she'd bedded. "I thought it'd make you leave if you knew he'd be coming in there at any moment."

***

That's what he'd thought, but for a reason he couldn't place, he was relieved to hear her say it. He closed his eyes for an extended blink. He had to stop this nonsense. She might be his wife in a legal sense, but she needed a good husband. Simon would be that for her. *Then why did you come here?* He exhaled sharply and balled his hands into fists. Once she married, they could both move forward. That was the goal, wasn't it?

"All right. The first thing you need to do is find a way to make it look like an accident when you touch him."

She smiled in disbelief. "An accident? I don't think he'd find it an accident if I start to touch him."

"Well, no, he won't really think it's an accident—but it needs to look like one."

"Which is exactly what I tried to do today," she pointed out.

"But stomping his toe while playing a game of cards?"

"I didn't stomp."

"Are you sure because he nearly leapt out of his chair when your heeled slipper came down on his foot."

She waved him off. "That's just Simon. I assure you, I didn't stomp."

"Very well," he muttered, trying not to let it rankle him the way she'd said her suitor's name so informally, as if they'd known each other their whole lives. "Next time be less obvious."

"And how is touching his *calf* as opposed to his foot less obvious?"

"As I said, it just needs to appear an accident. He'll know it's not."

She buried her head in her hands. "Sebastian, I don't think this is a good plan."

"Why not?"

"I think he might desire a marriage of convenience."

"Is that not what you want?" He stunned himself with that question, but for some reason, he needed to know.

"Not particularly. I—I'd like to have children one day."

He nodded slowly, disappointment he didn't understand settling over him. "Then you most certainly will need to find ways to capture his attention."

"What if he doesn't see me that way?"

"Nonsense. Only a fool wouldn't see you that way." The truth of his statement turned him numb. He was the fool. He'd had his chance with Belle and had destroyed it. "Isabelle, is there any chance—" He broke off with a curse. There was no reason to ask. It was hard enough to know that it'd been because of his own stupidity that he'd lost her. There was no reason to completely devastate himself by having her confirm this. Or worse, accept his suit only because one Mr. Simon Appleton wouldn't give her children. Swallowing the bile that burned the back of his throat he walked closer to her. "Tomorrow, when he takes you to go shoot at the targets—"

"There's going to be archery?" Her eyes lit up the same way they always did when he'd allow her to use his bow and arrow during the summers when he was home from Harrow.

"Yes. I asked Giles if he'd get targets set up. I thought it would provide the best opportunity for you to accidentally touch Mr. Appleton with a purpose." He grimaced at the very thought of her touching him. "Tomorrow, it's important for you to pretend that you don't know how to shoot."

She groaned. "But then it won't be any fun."

"You can have fun after you're married. For now, you need to work on making sure he still plans to offer."

"He does."

"Are you sure?"

"I believe so." She studied the floorboards. "I don't think that was ever in question—just if we could suit."

"As lovers?"

Was it just him or did she shudder when he said that? "In general," she said, looking up at him. "I told him I'd consider his suit, but that I wanted time to make sure we actually suited."

"And you don't," Sebastian said flatly, refusing to let any sort of excitement build.

"I don't know. One minute it seems things are going well, then he just loses interest." She shrugged. "I know you don't think it'll improve in London, but I think it will once Giles isn't around so much."

Sebastian doubted that. "When did you promise to give him an answer?"

"I haven't."

Sebastian tamped down the hope her answer had sparked. He had no right to be excited about her revelation. She wasn't his anymore. "It doesn't matter. Once you get back to London, you won't have the same opportunity to use your wiles on him that you have now." He moved to stand behind her. "As I was saying, tomorrow, you'll need to pretend that you've never shot an arrow before so he'll come help."

"Like he helped me with bowls?" she asked with a shaky laugh.

He snorted. "That was wretched. I was embarrassed for the man just watching."

"Yes, I think that was obvious by the way you acted when you stalked off."

Grinning, he shook his head in disbelief. "He needed to come up behind you, like this." He stepped forward, bringing his body flush behind hers. All laughter and thoughts of her suitor fled at the feel of her warm body against his. The smell of lavender filling his nose. "A gentleman can be far more persuasive when standing behind his lady, wouldn't you say?"

She nodded.

Wordlessly he wrapped his arms around her, chastising himself for enjoying it so much. She wasn't his to enjoy, he reminded himself. "Put your arms up like you're about to shoot an arrow."

***

She would if she could. Unfortunately, her body had gone boneless in the past thirty seconds. No thanks to Sebastian. She licked her lips and steeled her spine. He wasn't hers. He didn't want her. If he hadn't been clear enough about that six years ago when he so coldly rejected her, he certainly wasn't disproving it now by trying to help her seduce another man.

That bitter thought steeled her resolve, giving her the strength she needed to put her hands into position.

Sebastian's big hands found hers and covered them. "This will be your best opportunity."

She swallowed, feeling suddenly unsteady.

"That's it," he murmured.

"What's it?"

"You just pushed your hair closer to me."

"I did?"

The low rumble of his chuckle reverberated in his chest. "Yes. It's one of your best features."

"My hair?" How absurd.

"Mmmhmm." He inhaled. "It smells like lavender—a natural aphrodisiac."

"A what?"

"An aphrodisiac. Something that compels men—or women—to want to explore their baser needs."

"Baser needs?" she burst out. "I just want to have children, Sebastian. I don't need a...a...lover."

"I think that you do," he murmured, his lips brushed the sensitive skin behind her ear, sending fire straight through her veins. "See?"

She dropped her arms and pulled out of his hold. "If you intend to mock me and humiliate me, you may go."

"No." He swallowed and reached for her hand. "I was just— *Ahem*, never mind." He glided her back around and repositioned her hands. "Whether you know it or not, gentlemen like hair. Yours is very attractive with your current style. It looks nice, but isn't pulled so tight that it looks painful or coarse. And of course, the soft curls that you had hanging by your face today only made it more attractive."

"You're saying I need to shove my hair in his face?" she jested to diffuse the heat that had once again filled the room when he'd taken her back into his arms.

"That might be exactly what's necessary for your Mr. Appleton to take notice, yes."

Her Mr. Appleton. She shuddered. Then sighed. He was still better than Lord Kenton. "All right. What else?"

"Move your shoulders. Press them back."

She leaned back, hitting him square in the chest with her shoulder.

"Not so much. Just a little. Just brush my chest with your shoulder. Good. Now, he'll help bring your right hand back to take the arrow back. When he does, that's your chance to nestle more firmly against him." He guided her hand back slowly and she did her best to put her back against his chest.

"Like this?"

"Exactly," he said in a broken whisper.

"Now what?" she breathed, closing her eyes to savor the moment that she knew she shouldn't be enjoying as much as she was. It would only take a single second to end her bliss and send her once again back to the bottom of the deep pit of despair. Though she knew this, she was powerless to be the one to end it and save her dignity. Or her heart.

"Hold the position and let him help you shoot." The thickness in his voice sent a measure of pride through her. Not a lot, but just enough to assure her she wouldn't fall to pieces when he let go.

Which she didn't a moment later when he did let go.

"Shall we try it again?"

***

What had he just said? Did he intend to torture himself?

"A-all right."

Sebastian regained his former position behind her, praying she wouldn't notice the bulge in his trousers and ask questions. "Put your hands up."

She did and waited for him to cover hers with his before leaning her left shoulder toward him. She cocked her head as if she were looking down the end of her arrow which put the creamy expanse of her neck within an inch of his lips. He forced his eyes away from her skin before he gave into the temptation to kiss her neck again. He had no idea what he'd been thinking before when he'd kissed her, but he couldn't do so again.

"Sebastian?"

He started. "Sorry." He moved their hands back. A task not so easily done by a man with an overwhelming desire for his own wife. His desire doubled a moment later when she not only pressed her shoulders against him, but moved in a way that pressed her bottom against his groin. He didn't think it was possible to get any harder, but he did. "Too much."

"Hmmm?"

He'd have wondered how innocent her action was if he'd had any ability to think. Knowing her and her horrible attempts at flirting today, it was a completely innocent gesture with a not-so-innocent consequence. "Don't lean so much."

"Does it matter?"

"Well, do you want to interest him in what's to come or have him ravish you on the lawn?"

She gasped and jerked her entire body forward.

He tightened his hold on her to keep her there. "You don't need to move that far forward." He lowered his left hand and guided her to lean back against him. "There. That's perfect."

"No. It's not." She pulled away from his embrace again and rubbed her hands over her face. "I don't think I should do this."

"Why not?"

"I didn't intend to move so far back."

"I know."

"You don't understand." She sank onto the edge of her bed. "I'm not good at this, Sebastian."

If only she knew just how good she was. He crossed one leg in front of the other to conceal his erection. "You just need to practice."

She shook her head. "It won't help. I'm hopeless."

"No, you're not. Now, come back over here and we'll keep practicing until you're just as good at pretending you don't know how to shoot an arrow as you are at actually shooting one." Even if that meant he'd have to suffer the whole time.

Chapter Twenty-Five

It wasn't until the following afternoon that Sebastian learned what real suffering was. No, it hadn't been overly enjoyable to have his wife in his arms and unable to do anything about it except help her practice for how to charm another man, but that paled in comparison to the suffering that came with watching his wife use her newfound skill.

He knew he should go back home to London. He'd decided that'd be for the best the night before, but something had compelled him to go see Belle one final time before leaving, no matter how painful the experience might be.

Being an official guest as of yesterday, he could have just walked out to the archery field and pretended to shoot arrows while he observed. But he didn't want to risk anyone seeing him and decided instead to hang back and observe from a safe distance.

At first glance, he didn't see either Belle or Simon. Odd. He moved further down the wall, perhaps they were further down.

A door no more than three feet away swung open and a couple emerged: Belle and Simon. He didn't know whether to sigh with relief or beat the sense out of the man who was courting his wife. He settled for clenching his fists, pressing his back against the wall and praying they didn't see him.

That was an unfounded fear. He had no idea what the man had just said, but the peals of laughter that came from Belle filled the air. It was forced, he could tell, but as long as Simon couldn't tell the difference she'd done her job.

She grinned up at the man—a little too wide, but that was all right, she still looked beautiful, gesturing toward the archery equipment.

Simon must have hesitated because she cocked her head to the side and batted her lashes. Good girl. Once again, Sebastian could see through her ploy, but if Simon gave in and took her shooting,

SECRETS OF A VISCOUNT

she'd be well on her way to securing his proposal.

Sebastian closed his eyes for a moment and released a deep breath. It was for the best. She deserved a husband who'd always treat her right. He opened his eyes and watched them stroll over to collect a bow and quiver full of arrows, then walk to a platform in line with a vacant target.

Fortunately, they were close enough that Sebastian didn't have to move. Unfortunately, they were close enough that he could see everything they did perfectly clear. He scowled and shoved his fists into his pockets, clenching them tighter.

Belle took her stance and just as they'd discussed she'd do, she purposely fumbled with the arrow, pretending to be unable to know what to do. At first Simon didn't appear to be interested, but she must have said something about requiring help because he set his bow down, pressed his lips together and went to help her. *Pressed his lips together?* What the devil for? What man didn't enjoy an invitation to drape himself all over an attractive woman?

Simon walked up behind her and stood back at a distance.

As Sebastian had instructed her to, Belle leaned her shoulders back against his chest in just a simple gesture.

Simon almost lost his grip on the arrow. Recovering it, he stepped awkwardly to the side so he wasn't squarely behind Belle.

Sebastian stared in disbelief, his pulse racing. Was the man that inept?

Belle said something Sebastian couldn't hear and Simon moved closer to her. Together, they pulled their right hands back that took the arrow back, but instead of leaning into him more like Sebastian had told her to do, she kept her position and let him help her shoot the arrow.

It flew two feet above the target and came down somewhere in the grass.

Belle made a show of being disappointed they didn't hit the target—which didn't require too much theatrics on her part, she'd always hated missing—and somehow convinced Simon to help her again.

Nodding, the man came to help her, sliding into place behind her as if it were a punishment worse than death.

Belle paid him no mind and went about her flirtations. A hard knot formed in Sebastian's throat and grew until it filled his chest and stomach, too. He wasn't any better of a friend to her now than he had been six years ago. It might be true that his intentions had been good, but that's where it stopped. He'd encouraged her to make a total fool of herself by flirting with a man who wasn't just disinterested, he was completely undeserving.

If he was calm enough he'd march over there right now and put an end to this idiocy, but he wasn't. Likely if he went over there, he'd tear Simon's head from his shoulders or do something equally horrifying and only embarrass Belle more.

He jerked his eyes away. He couldn't take another second of it. Not that what his gaze fixed on was any better: Lord Kenton.

The two exchanged a look.

"If I were your age, Belgrave. I'd do something about it."

Perhaps it was time he did just that.

***

Isabelle squeezed her eyes shut and imagined it was Sebastian who was wrapped around her and helping her shoot the arrow. She knew it was sinful and wicked to do such a thing, not to mention the worst thing for her sanity, and most definitely not the safest thing for her heart. But she couldn't help it. Simon was so stiff and mechanical, the opposite of Sebastian's warm and fluid motion. She suppressed her sigh and leaned in a little more against the body behind her. He was broad and solid, but not the same solid that had been holding her the night before.

She let out a deep breath and briefly considered pushing things too far and "accidentally" brushing against his groin the way she had with Sebastian. Somehow she doubted that Simon would be very appreciative of such a gesture.

Sending up a silent prayer that she could feign a dislike for archery soon and spare them both such an uncomfortable situation, she allowed him to help her release the arrow and watched it fly.

Whooosh! Bfft.

Inwardly sighing with relief, Isabelle clapped and bounced

around, grinning like a simpleton. "We hit the target!" Never mind that it was the white edging that went around the bullseye. They'd hit something and she'd gladly use it as a reprieve. "Why don't you shoot for a while and I'll watch you?"

"Are you sure?"

Isabelle waved her hand in the air. "Of course."

Simon loaded his arrow and sent it down the lane. It hit just outside the center. He actually wasn't bad—just horrible at teaching.

He shot another. It hit close to the other.

Isabelle's hands itched to try it alone. Perhaps once she hit the center, she could claim it was a fluke. Better not.

"You're quite skilled," she said.

"Thank you." Simon reached for another arrow then halted. "This probably isn't any fun for you, is it?"

She shrugged. "It's all right. I don't mind."

He slipped the arrow back into the quiver and set down his bow. "How about a walk?"

Isabelle placed her hand in the crook of his proffered arm. She wondered if she should give him an encouraging squeeze, but the truth was, she'd encouraged him enough today and he seemed just as disinterested as he had been before. "Do you not like me?" She couldn't believe she'd just blurted that, but as soon as it was out, she found it humorous that she had no real regrets.

"Of course I do." He flashed her a slim smile. "I know I haven't been showing it as of late, but you must know that I'm interested in you."

"I see..."

He came to a stop and turned to face her, his green eyes full of concern. "Isabelle, is something troubling you?"

She twisted her lips. There was something they'd never spoken about and perhaps it was time. "The day you came to see me in London, you'd practically proposed in the drawing room—it was me who'd wanted more time. Then we come here and you're as distant as the moon and more distracted than a puppy."

He sighed and reached for her hand, leading her to a nearby

bench. "You're right. I've just been distracted. I know that's no excuse, but I—" He broke off; a distant, wide-eyed expression came over his face. "Everything I've ever been told has been nothing but a lie."

"You mean about Giles?"

Simon nodded slowly. "My mother had once mentioned that I'd had a brother who'd been born with something wrong." He shook his head. "I never asked what that meant. I just assumed by her rarely mentioning his birth and saying that things didn't go right that he was dead. I had no idea he'd been sent off."

"Do you think knowing all of this time would have made much difference to you?"

Silence hung between them for a while. "I—I don't know."

"Do you think this is even about Giles, but rather your mother and you feeling betrayed?"

He flinched at her words, telling her all she needed to know. "She's the one behind this blasted party," he muttered; then scoffed. "Apparently she thought it best to offer him a bride as a way to mend the separation between them. She's just using Lord and Lady Cosgrove as a means to manipulate the situation." He shook his head. "Giles is just too naïve to know the difference between genuine concern for his well-being and manipulations."

Isabelle sucked in a harsh breath. That almost seemed cruel. Almost. She wouldn't claim to be overly familiar with either Simon's mother or Giles, but considering Giles' somewhat off-putting mannerism, she could understand why his mother would think she was helping him as a means to mend a rift between them. She could also understand why that might be the worst thing she could do. "Does Giles want help?"

"How am I to know? Your friend Lord Belgrave knows more about the man than I do."

Isabelle didn't know if the edge to his voice was frustration at the whole situation or if it was irritation specifically aimed at Sebastian for any of his plethora of faults. "Simon, have you considered just talking to Giles?"

Simon's head snapped around so he could face her, a dubious

expression on his face. "Whatever for?"

"Well, the two of you do share a mother and—" She closed her mouth with a snap.

"I noticed the resemblance, too," Simon muttered. "I'd always wondered if the rumors about my mother were true since I resembled Father so much, but had convinced myself I was just an early baby. Now..." He twisted his lips. "It seems there is nothing left untainted by this."

Isabelle had the strangest sensation to wrap him in a hug. Not one that would hopefully lead to more, just a sign of comfort between friends. "Simon, I really think it'd help you both if you talked to him. I know you don't want to, but I don't think you'll be able to make better sense of anything until you at least speak to him."

"You're right." Simon's lips formed a tight line and he nodded once then removed his pocket watch. "Dinner will be served in an hour."

"Which is just enough time for you to go seek him out and speak to him." She offered him a smile. "If I'm not mistaken, I imagine he might enjoy some male companionship about now."

Chapter Twenty-Six

Giles Goddard silently contemplated the possibility that someone would literally 'stuff' anything, if told to stuff it, the very phrase he heard resounding in his head at the moment.

He clenched his hands into fists and filled his cheeks with air to keep from putting voice to his words.

"Are you all right, dear?" Lady Norcourt, or more respectfully known as his mother, asked.

He nodded his head vigorously, but didn't dare open his mouth. Over the past four days, his "mother" had become somewhat of an annoyance. She meant well, he knew, but she was dratted annoying with her constant questions—as if she were suddenly very interested in what he'd done in the twenty years that had passed since he'd been sent to Ireland after she and the old baron had learned of Simon's impending birth.

He'd give anything short of his right arm to be in almost anyone else's company at the moment and nearly shouted for joy when he heard the click of the brass doorknob.

A moment later, he was ready to scream again. Simon Appleton.

The two locked gazes and either their mother quit speaking or his ears had finally stopped hearing her.

"Simon," his mother greeted. "Do come in and join us."

Mr. Appleton came into the room and quietly closed the door behind him. "Mother." He turned to look at Giles. "Lord Norcourt."

"What brings you about?" his mother asked.

Simon's face took an expression that Giles couldn't determine. "I've come to speak to Lord Norcourt." When a broad smile took his mother's lips, Simon added, "Alone."

Lady Norcourt's smile faded and she shot a glance to Giles. "I don't know if that's a good idea."

Irritation bubbled inside of Giles. As much as everyone liked to pretend he was, he wasn't a child incapable of having thoughts for himself. They might not always come to him quickly or make sense, but he was capable of some things. He scowled at them. "I do."

"You do what?" Lady Norcourt asked, her eyebrows drawn together.

"We'll talk alone."

Lady Norcourt's lips thinned. "I don't think—"

"We'll be fine, Mother. I don't plan to eat him," Simon said, opening the door to the library for his mother.

She cast one last glance toward Giles, then gathered her skirts and made her exit. Giles was a hint jealous that it was her and not him who was escaping.

After she'd crossed the threshold, Simon closed the door. "Have you and my mother become bosom friends yet?"

"She's my mother, too," Giles said quietly.

"Indeed." Simon walked to a high backed chair and gripped the wooden frame of the back until his knuckles turned white.

***

If it weren't for his grip on the chair and his own stubborn pride, Simon would have left the room right behind his mother. Talking to Giles wasn't going to accomplish anything, he knew that now.

The infuriating man sat in his chair, tapping his foot. "Come to talk?"

Simon tightened his hold on the back of the chair as a sudden wave of irritation for the man formed inside of him. "You do know why you were invited here, do you not?" The words were out before he could think better of it, but Giles didn't seem the least bit disturbed.

"Yes."

"Because Mother thinks to right her wrong by finding you a bride?"

If his words had any effect on Giles, he didn't show it. "You're a fortunate man, then."

"Me?" Simon jabbed a finger at his chest. "She didn't invite those young ladies here for me to peruse, they're here for you."

Giles appeared indifferent. "Not interested. Have your pick."

"My pick?" He shook his head. "I don't need a swarm of ladies to choose from. I've already found my bride."

"She's taken."

Simon frowned. "Yes, by me."

"No. She's Sebastian's wife."

"*Was*, Lord Belgrave's wife," Simon explained as a small pang of sympathy built in his chest. His mother had once briefly explained that Giles had been born with his life's cord wrapped around his neck. She'd mentioned that babies born that way either didn't live long or would face a lifetime of difficulties at the expense of their minds not working right. Giles clearly fell into the second category.

"Still is," Giles said flatly.

"No, they had their marriage annulled. That means they were married, but they're not any longer."

"No, they're still married." Giles' tone would suggest he was just rambling off some random fact that everyone should know.

Simon narrowed his eyes on his brother. "Did Lord Belgrave tell you this?"

Giles nodded, sending a new round of emotions swirling through Simon that made his earlier irritation seem like bliss. Anger, rage, disgust and worst of all betrayal hit him like blow after blow to the gut. Isabelle was still married and she was carrying on a flirtation with him? Why? And worst of all, why would she have given him the promise of marriage? To make a fool of him? That would certainly explain her sudden eagerness to be close to him and touch him.

Bile surged up his throat and filled his mouth. First his mother had lied to him and now Isabelle? Was his entire life a fallacy built on one lie after another?

His vision blurred and a string of vile words sounded in his head, and perhaps even escaped his lips. Not that he cared one way or another. This was too much. He needed to get away from every liar here and sort this out.

Chapter Twenty-Seven

"Is your chicken dry?"

Isabelle started, then blushed. She turned to Giles, her dinner companion and blushed all over again. He obviously noticed she'd been distracted. And if he'd noticed, then she'd been quite obvious.

She flickered a glance down to him and would have blushed again if it were possible. He was staring right back at her with an intensity in his eyes she'd never seen before.

"He's quite smitten."

"Who?" She prayed he wouldn't say Simon because after today, she didn't know if she'd be able to feign interest much longer. At least not without more motivation from Sebastian. Perhaps he'd kiss her tonight...

Giles' harrumph of amusement jarred Isabelle to present.

"I'm sorry, what did you say?"

"You're smitten, too."

Her eyes widened and she looked at the couple across the table, hoping they hadn't heard him. For there seemed to be only one volume with Giles. He didn't whisper, and she doubted he'd yell. But his voice was always audible. "And who else do you think is smitten?" she asked more to get his attention off her.

"Sebastian."

Isabelle wanted to laugh. The last thing she'd consider Sebastian to be is smitten. But at least he hadn't suggested Simon.

"Tell me, how are you faring with your new relations?" Isabelle asked, taking a sip of her drink. Not that she tasted it. Her mind was far too occupied with Sebastian and the wicked desire to have him kiss her.

"They're pleasant."

Isabelle offered him a slight smile. "I don't know them well, I'm afraid, but I've known your mother long enough to know that she's quite genuine. Even if she goes about things in the wrong way. Her motives—and her heart—are good."

Giles nodded once. "And Simon?"

"He means well, too." She paused and bit her lower lip. "He's just not sure how to react."

Giles appeared as if he didn't care about her explanation. His expression was blank and he idly tapped his index finger against the edge of his plate, looking just beyond her left shoulder. But she knew he did care; he, too, didn't know how to show it.

"Have the two of you talked?" she asked as she looked down the table to see if she could catch Simon's eye. She hadn't spotted him in the drawing room before dinner and strangely enough, he wasn't here, either. "I take it that you have and it didn't go well."

He nodded.

"Perhaps you should try again tomorrow?"

Giles shrugged and turned his attention back to his plate as if the designs on the china he was uncovering with each bite were the most entertaining thing he'd ever seen—which was just fine with Isabelle. She'd rather return to her own thoughts, too. Specifically the ones about Sebastian kissing her...

***

Sebastian's dinner was bland, just as he'd assume the company would be for the gentleman's port that followed dinner. Therefore, he decided not to go.

Not that it was that much better pacing the floor of his room until he was certain everyone had gone to bed and he could slip into Belle's room unnoticed. Desire tightened within him at the thought alone and he checked his pocket watch. It was time.

A few minutes later, he was standing in his shirtsleeves on her balcony. He peered in the window and his breath caught. She lay on her bed with her belly pressing the mattress and the tops of her luscious breasts spilling out the top of her blue silk nightrail. Her head was propped up on her hands, with her elbows digging into the mattress and her bare feet up behind her with her ankles crossed.

It was all he could do to open the window without breaking the glass in frustration.

"Evening, Sebastian," Belle said when he was inside.

Sebastian closed the window with a hard swallow. "I take it you were expecting me."

"Of course. Who else is willing to give me another flirting lesson?"

He let his eyes do a slow, thorough sweep of her, fastening for a moment longer than was proper when he'd reached her breasts. "I don't think you need another."

Something akin to disappointment flickered across her face. "Oh?" She dropped her arms and rolled out of bed. "Then if that's the case, I suppose you'd better go back to your room." She walked across the room and positioned herself between himself and the window, so close she was just barely touching him, and yet, intensifying his desire for her until he couldn't stop himself and pulled her to him.

She felt good, no, not good, *perfect*, with her full breasts pressed against his chest and her soft belly surrounding his growing erection. "Isabelle," he breathed, his nostrils filling with her heady scent.

"Sebastian?" she said on a broken whisper. She licked her plump, red lips, a gesture that only served to excite him more. "A —are you going to kiss me?"

That was his undoing. He lowered his head and covered her soft lips with his. Sebastian lifted his free hand to cover her cheek, running the pad of his thumb along the delicate edge of her jawline. He parted his lips and ran his tongue along her bottom lip. She gasped and he deepened their kiss.

She tasted of ginger. Never before had he thought he'd enjoy the flavor of ginger so much, but he certainly did now. He swept the inside of her cheek, then brushed her tongue with his before he pulled back, panting.

He stared down at her kiss-swollen lips and immediately closed the gap between them again, capturing her lips in another kiss. This one more passionate that the last. He groaned in satisfaction when she mirrored his actions with her tongue and wound her arms around his neck, digging her fingers into the back of his hair.

"Sebastian," she gasped.

He murmured her name in response, taking his lips from hers and kissed her cheek then down her neck. She lolled her head back, allowing him greater access. But it wasn't enough. With his lips still on the warm skin of her neck, he lifted her up and carried her to the bed, laying her gently atop the mattress.

Her emerald eyes fluttered open, telling him everything he needed to know: she wanted the same thing.

***

What had started out as a quest for a kiss was quickly becoming so much more as Sebastian positioned himself above her and brought his lips back to hers. His kiss was so much more than she'd ever imagined. She knew it'd be extraordinary and had hoped his one kiss would be enough to sustain her, but she'd never imagined kissing him would be so intoxicating.

She returned his kiss, praying that her boldness wouldn't drive him off. His hands covered her shoulders and squeezed them affectionately. She twined her fingers in his silky hair, never wanting this moment to end.

Sebastian slid his right hand from her shoulder down to her breast. Isabelle gasped. His large hand covered her perfectly, making her breast swell against his palm. He squeezed ever-so-gently and rubbed his thumb on the undercurve. Moving his lips to kiss along her jaw and behind her ear, he dragged his thumb over the hardened crest of her breast. She involuntarily jerked and the wretch did it again, with more pressure this time.

Sebastian inched his fingers up to grip the thin strap of her nightrail and slowly slipped it off her shoulder. His warm lips followed the same trail, building an excitement in her she didn't understand. He pressed hot, open mouth kisses across her collarbone and down the valley of her chest, his fingers taking the top of her nightrail down as he went until suddenly her breasts were exposed. Her breath hitched. He'd seen them before, she knew, but this time it was different.

A small measure of female pride shot through her at the way

he swallowed audibly at the sight of her bare breasts.

"I thought breasts were breasts," she teased, pushing a lock of his brown hair away from his eyes.

"Not when they're yours," he rasped. He released his grip on her nightrail and brought both of his hands up to cup and caress her breasts.

She arched her back and he gave them both a gentle squeeze. Her erect nipples pushed against the calluses on his palms. Not taking his hands from her chest, he scattered kisses across the plane of her chest and down her sternum. He slid his left hand down to rest on her ribs with his thumb tucked under her breast and his mouth now moving over her breast. A jolt of excitement passed through her, then another more immediate and powerful when he closed his lips over her nipple. "Sebastian," she gasped.

His only response was to flick his tongue over her sensitive peak—making her gasp his name again, a little louder this time.

He moved to deliver the same delicious torture to her other breast. This time he brought his teeth against her nipple with just a hint of pressure, then soothed it with his tongue. He pulled back. "No, yours are definitely not ordinary."

She smiled as best she could and slid her hands down to grasp his shirt. She shouldn't be the only one half naked, should she? She'd barely pulled his shirttails from his trousers when Sebastian gripped the fabric of his shirt and yanked the offending article off his body, then leaned forward to resume the position he'd once held.

She playfully pushed at his shoulders. "I think it's my turn."

He groaned, making her grin.

"Roll over."

With a muttered statement she'd never heard before, he obliged.

Isabelle moved to sit up on her knees and reached for the straps of her nightrail to cover herself.

Sebastian's hand caught her wrist. "If I'm to play your game, you can play mine. Leave it."

She swallowed and dropped the edge of her nightrail, leaving it to pool around her waist. At his urging, she straddled him about the hips and began her exploration of his chest, noting how his intense gaze on her bare breasts made her skin burn as if there were a small fire in her blood.

She ran her fingertips over the broad expanse of his chest, tracing each of the lines and contours. She moved to the ridges of his hard abdomen. Under her fingers, his muscles leapt and the further down she moved, the more his breathing grew labored. Something hard pressed her intimate area and she shifted to get more comfortable, eliciting a groan from Sebastian.

"Did I hurt you?"

"Not yet," he choked. "But if you don't unfasten my trousers, I'll burst out of them."

She lifted a brow then came up on her knees again and walked backward until she'd exposed the placket of his trousers. Biting her lower lip, she traced the hard bulge in his trousers with her index finger until he groaned in frustration and reached down to unfasten his trousers and pull them open.

A myriad of emotions overcame her, and she reached tentative hands toward his erection. Closing her hand around it, she marveled at the contradiction that one body part seemed to be. Both hard and yet, soft. She tightened her hold and slid her hand down to the base, then back to the tip.

Sebastian closed his eyes, his face contorted as if he were in pain.

She immediately let go.

His eyes snapped open. "What's wrong?"

"I didn't mean to hurt you."

"You didn't," he rasped. "You're killing me...but in a good way."

"Then I should continue?"

He nodded and reached for her hand, bringing it back to his erection, then guided her hand up and down his shaft.

After a minute he loosened his grasp, then let go, letting her move at her pace. She watched as a bead of liquid formed along the slit in his tip. He encircled her wrist, stopping her.

"You'd better stop." Then in one swift motion, he had her on her back and was dragging his hands and mouth all over her naked flesh—caressing here, squeezing there and kissing and licking everywhere in between, making her blood simmer all over again.

He took hold of the nightrail she wore around her waist and bunched the fabric up around her stomach, exposing her most intimate area to his gaze if he were to look. And he did. Of course.

He trailed a slow finger down the middle of her curly nest of hair and into the delicate folds underneath. She sucked in a harsh breath. Nobody had ever touched her there. Ever. Nor had she ever imagined anyone would, but he did and it felt...felt... She couldn't explain it. Not when his strong fingers were touching her thus.

Sebastian brought his mouth to her breast and moved his finger to her opening, making her jump and let out a little squeal.

"Shhh," he crooned, tracing his finger around the edge of her channel. "When we get home you can be as noisy as you want, but this time—"

Whatever it was he said, was lost to Isabelle over the blood roaring in her ears. *When we get home?* Was that his proposal? Or did he just mean to make her his mistress until she found a husband? Uncertainty warred with waning desire. "Sebastian?"

"Hmmm," he said as he swirled his tongue around her nipple and mimicked the action below.

"Sebastian," she repeated. She closed her legs together, trapping his hand where it was and keeping him from pressing inside her.

He didn't seem to notice and just moved to the other breast as easy as you please.

Isabelle brought her hands to his shoulders and gave him a slight shove. "Sebastian, stop."

He pulled away, his wide brown eyes, dark and full of heated desire. "Is something wrong?"

"What did you mean?"

He blinked. "When?"

"Just a moment ago when you mentioned when we get home, what did you mean?"

"Just that. When we get back to London and you're in my bed, you can make as much noise as you'd like. But it'd be best if we didn't bring attention to ourselves here or we'll have a scandal."

"Your bed," she repeated, a thrill of excitement shooting through her. "A-are you proposing?"

He chuckled and leaned forward to drop a single kiss between her breasts. "No."

A hostile wave of understanding came over her, bringing a sense of shame and coldness she'd never experienced before. She suddenly was mortified to be lying half naked in front of him and covered her breasts as best she could with her hands.

"Don't cover yourself," he murmured, reaching for her hand.

She recoiled. "You may go."

"Pardon?"

"I won't be your mistress."

"I didn't ask you to."

"No, you just assumed that I would. Which is worse."

He shook his head. "I never said that, either."

"You didn't have to. You said you weren't proposing. That can only leave one option: you expected me to be your mistress." She inclined her chin. "And I will not."

"Are you saying you would say yes if I were to propose marriage?"

She blushed. "I might."

"I see." Sebastian nodded slowly and idly ran his fingertips over the skin of her abdomen. "And what would you say if I told you that we were still married?"

Chapter Twenty-Eight

"Wh-what did you just say?" Isabelle asked, attempting to move away from him. The edge of her nightrail was pinned to the bed under his elbow, but that didn't deter her long, she slipped free and scampered up to the pillows. She grabbed the counterpane and crawled underneath it, holding it to her chin.

Sebastian sat up and ran his hand through his hair. "I never signed the annulment papers."

"Why not?"

"Guilt."

She winced at his words and a bitter taste filled her mouth. "So we've been married this entire time?" she asked in disbelief.

He nodded sending a flood of betrayal through her very marrow. Her vision blurred and she wanted nothing more than to throw him out of the room, but now that she knew this much, she needed more answers.

"Is that why your mother left me that money? Because I was her daughter-in-law?"

"No. That was a ploy by our fathers to get me to return and sign the papers."

Isabelle squeezed the counterpane until her fingers went numb and blinked back the tears that stung the back of her eyes. She was nothing but a pawn. "When exactly did you think you'd tell me this? When I was walking down the aisle to Simon?"

His face grew dark. "You won't be walking down the aisle to Mr. Appleton, Belle."

"And just who do you think you are to make such a declaration?"

"Your husband," he said with a quick grin.

She wasn't so amused and if she wasn't naked, she'd take the pillow in her hands and beat him senseless with it. "I want that annulment."

He shook his head. "I don't see why. You've already admitted to having the same feelings for me that I have for you."

"Well, I don't have them now," she said ignoring the hot tears that slipped from the corners of her eyes.

Sebastian lifted a brow. "You've changed your mind in the last thirty seconds, then?"

Mortification burned in her cheeks. "It's time for you to leave."

"No." He crossed his arms. "I want to know what's changed your mind. Two minutes ago you were gasping my name and letting me make love to you and now you want nothing to do with me. Why?"

"First, I was not letting you make love to me—"

"No? I seem to remember you lying underneath me naked with your breast in my mouth and my hand—"

"That's enough," she burst out in a tone that bordered on hysteria.

"I don't think it is," he countered. "Why are you so upset? I'd have thought you'd be relieved to know you were about to give your virtue to your own husband."

"You conceited, arrogant man!"

"I'll admit, I'm at least one of those, but not both," he said, presumably in an attempt to defuse the tension.

It did not.

"Get out!"

"No, I want to know why you are suddenly having an attack of morals."

"I'm not suddenly having an attack of morals," she fired back.

"I suppose you're right. You did seem far more willing to share your bed with me before you knew I was your husband."

Isabelle gasped at his cold words and sharp tone. "I did no such thing! I would have stopped."

"When? Just as I put my—"

"Need you be so filthy?" Scorching flames of embarrassment licked her face.

He shrugged. "I didn't say anything that isn't true. You might not like to hear the words, but that doesn't make them any less true."

No, it didn't. The truth was, what had started out as a quest to get him to kiss her had turned into far more. "Sebastian, I didn't intend to let things go so far."

"Then what did you intend to have happen when you greeted me in a seductive nightrail and rubbed your body against mine?"

She swallowed. Hard. She couldn't deny it, as much as she might want to. "To kiss."

"I don't believe you."

"Believe what you want, but you're the one who's the proven liar around here."

Fire flashed in his brown eyes. "And you're not? I seem to remember it being your lie that started this whole disaster between us."

She nearly flinched at his word choice. But the truth was, he was right. Everything between them had turned into one disaster after another. "You won't mind signing the annulment papers, then."

"The devil I will. I don't want an annulment any more than you do."

"What makes you think I don't?" She'd willingly brave the scandal that was likely to form when all of this came to light rather than be chained to Lord Deceitful for the rest of her life.

"Because your other marital choices are the philanderer Lord Kenton or the awkward Mr. Appleton."

A new round of tears stung the back of her eyes. "Those are not my only choices. I could marry Sir Michael or Giles. I understand he's in want of a wife."

"You can't marry any of them. You're still my wife." The triumphant gleam in his eyes made her heart fill with dread. What if he didn't give her an annulment?

"Fine, I won't marry any of them. I'll just take a lover. Would you prefer that? Then when all of this breaks, it can be known that not only did I fraudulently trap you into marriage, but I cuckolded you, too."

A hard, impassive look came over his face. "How do I know that you haven't already? You seemed quite the seductress tonight."

"You'd be the one to know."

He crossed his arms. "What's that to mean?"

She scoffed. "You're the one offering lessons on how to get a man's attention. Surely you don't expect me to believe you are some sort of mastermind who just naturally knows of such things."

"I've enjoyed the flirtations of a number of women while on the continent, yes," he said, pursing his lips. "But that's where it ended. They could drag their foot all over my body for all I cared. It changed nothing. I was married and despite what anyone else might believe of me, I might not have made my vows in good faith, but I did keep them."

She stared at him through her watery eyes. "You—you didn't?"

"No, I didn't," he snapped as if taking her meaning. "When I make promises, I don't break them easily. Even if it's a promise I never meant to make." He twisted his lips in displeasure, whether at her or himself, she'd never know. "I suppose I cannot hold you to the same standard since you didn't know we were married all this time."

She forced a smile and a stiff, lopsided shrug. "You'll never really know, will you?"

Something fierce lit his eyes then suddenly it was gone.

***

Sebastian didn't believe for one second she'd already lost her virtue. Not only had she admitted to him that she hadn't actually shared a bed with Lord Kenton, she was too inept at the art of flirtations to catch the attention of someone as lovesick as Simon.

Even so, he couldn't understand why the devil she was so upset. He wasn't some lecher out to steal her virtue, he was her husband and he loved her, damn it all. He froze. Love?

His heart squeezed. Yes, love. He didn't know when or how or even why, but he was undeniably in love with his own wife! What a tangle.

"Belle, can we talk about this please?"

"We already did, and now it's time for you to leave." The hurt in her voice hit him like a punch to the stomach.

"I'm sorry," he said softly. "I said some very cruel things and I didn't mean them. Can we please start again?"

Belle let out a shaky laugh. "That's what you said when you came to my townhouse a few weeks ago. You wanted for us to be friends and start over, then you..." She trailed off and swallowed convulsively.

"Then I?"

"Then you encouraged me to act a fool!" she burst out unevenly; those once unshed tears that filled her eyes, flowed out of her eyes in rivulets.

"Belle, I didn't mean to make you look a fool."

"Yes, you did," she said on a sob.

"How?" He had a feeling he already knew the answer.

"With Simon," she said through her tears. "You—you made me flirt with him and encourage his suit all the while knowing that I couldn't marry him."

"I think that'd be a relief considering his interest in you seems to be trumped by Giles." He felt guilt for his blunt words as soon as he'd said them, but it didn't make them any less true.

She swiped at the tears coursing down her cheeks with the back of her delicate hands and Sebastian clenched his fists. That was his job as her husband. He was the one who was supposed to dry her tears, not make them form. "I understand his interest in me is fleeting and temperamental, but the fact is, you encouraged me to humiliate myself by throwing myself at him and all along you knew I wouldn't marry him."

"That's not true. I didn't plan for things to work out this way. I intended to sign the papers when I knew you'd make a good match." Not to mention he never would have imagined Simon would have acted so disinterested.

"But until I found a match you just thought to keep lying to me?"

Her question brought him up short. "Is that what this is all about?"

"Yes, 'this', as you so casually refer to it is because you're a liar."

He pursed his lips to keep himself from once again reminding her of her own lie in all of this. "Would you have preferred then that it was your former husband you were about to share intimacies with? Would that have been better?"

"I wasn't about to share intimacies with you," she said through gritted teeth. "I would have stopped."

He resisted his urge to laugh. "Oh, really? I had no intention of stopping. Is that your way, then, to tease a man until it's almost too late?"

She blinked her glistening eyes. "No. I already admitted that things went further than they should have, but the fact remains that you lied to me."

"I don't see why this is a problem, Belle," he said in frustration.

"You wouldn't. Everything was just fine for you. You knew all the pieces to the mystery. Why don't you try thinking about it from my position, Sebastian? I woke up from my accident without a friend in the world, then I spent the next five years trying to start over with a modest life in the country when suddenly a windfall comes my way and changes everything." Her voice wavered and tears gushed from her eyes. "Only the fortune really wasn't mine, and neither was the opportunity to marry."

"You don't need to marry one of them, Belle." He reached for her hand. "You already have me."

She pulled her hand away. "And what a pity that is. I made a simple mistake of not revealing my identity to a stranger who entered my bedchamber when I was sixteen and I ended up with a man who despises me enough to abandon me after my accident, then lies to me and encourages me to make a fool of myself in front of the whole *ton*."

"Are you finished recounting my sins?"

"I don't know if I am or not. I'm sure you have more that I don't know about...just like our marriage."

"That's the only thing I lied to you about."

She didn't look like she believed him, but there wasn't anything else he could say. She was right. He was a liar. His reasons for not annulling their marriage might have seemed honorable at the time, but his lack of explanation wasn't.

He forced himself to stand and right his clothing. "Belle, can I ask you something?" He took her sniffle as an affirmative and took a deep breath. "Had we not been married this whole time, would you have considered my proposal had I made one?"

She closed her eyes and rested her head on her drawn up knees for a moment, then lifted her head and met his eyes with her bloodshot pair and said, "I don't know."

He'd take that. It wasn't the 'yes' he was hoping for, but it wasn't a 'no', either. With one last, long look in her direction, he took his leave.

Chapter Twenty-Nine

Isabelle wasn't sure when the last time she'd cried herself to sleep had been—naked no less.

She rubbed her fingers over her swollen eyes and wanted nothing more than to go right back to sleep. But she couldn't. Now that Sebastian had made his announcement that they were still married, she had no choice but to end things with Simon. Not that she minded so much. Sebastian was right, his interest in her wasn't very strong if Giles just being in the same vicinity could distract him so much. But it still didn't make it any easier. Especially if Simon decided to start asking questions.

With a grimace she got out of bed, threw on her chemise, rang for her maid and stared at that offending blue nightrail until Tilde came to help her dress. She never wanted to see that scrap of fabric again and would have tossed it straight into the fire if she were sure it'd burn to ashes before Tilde arrived.

An hour and a half later she was dressed in a pink morning gown that had white lace around the cuffs and hem and she was gliding down the stairs, choking down her growing discomfort with each step.

"There you are, dear," Mrs. Finch greeted, sailing out of the breakfast room. Her face fell. "Isabelle, is something wrong?"

Isabelle wanted to say no, but she couldn't. Instead, she tried to force a wobbly smile. Unfortunately it didn't stay.

"Come, let's go talk."

That was the last thing Isabelle wanted to do, but it looked like she might not have much choice.

"Isabelle," Edmund called from down the hall—both relieving her and setting her on edge.

Beside her, Mrs. Finch went rigid. "We were just on our way to have a chat. Privately."

Edmund came toward them. "I'd like to talk to Isabelle, it

won't take but a moment."

Isabelle didn't know if this was a good thing or not, and the hard expression on Mrs. Finch's face only made her more unsure. What did they already know?

"Please," Edmund said quietly.

"All right," Mrs. Finch allowed. "Shall we go to the small library?"

Edmund nodded and opened the door on the opposite side of the hall.

Isabelle tamped down her irritation that neither had actually addressed her specifically about wanting to hear what Edmund had to say and walked into the room. She blinked. Had she not been told this was the library she'd have never known it. There were shelves that lined the walls of course, but not a single book on any of them. Instead, there was a whole array of unusual trinkets and baubles. Vases of different sizes and mediums. A small collection of miniatures that were in lopsided stacks or fallen piles. Stray or broken items here and there: an ivory chess queen, an embroidery hoop, a broken hand mirror, a two-string violin, a ripped painter's canvass with a brush that appeared to be stuck to the front, a partially shredded notebook, an earscoop, a torn playing card, a horribly neglected and trampled wig, an iron, a few loose matches and keys, a bent spoon, a slipper... The items were endless.

"This must be Lord and Lady Cosgrove's collective," Edmund remarked. He bent down and picked up a half smoked cigar. "This could still be used." He sniffed it then suddenly stopped when he locked gazes with Isabelle. He tossed the cigar down and ran his hands along the fabric of his breeches. "Isabelle, can we talk a moment?"

Did she have a choice? "I suppose."

"I'll just be over here...looking at things," Mrs. Finch said, giving Edmund a hard look.

He nodded to her once, then smiled at Isabelle. "How about we sit over here on these chairs?"

Isabelle threw a glance behind her to the chairs he'd indicated. They were threadbare in places and literally ripping at the seams in other places. Under each of the feet were the books that should have been on the shelves of the library—all of which were of a different thickness.

"I think I'll stand."

Edmund waved her off and went over to the closest chair. He gripped the back and gave it a little shake. "It's sturdy."

Just then, a small rodent scampered out from the hole in the side of the chair! Isabelle would have shrieked had she not been stunned into silence.

"Was that?" she asked breathlessly, her toes curled up inside her slippers almost to the point of pain.

"A baby mouse," Edmund confirmed. "Best we not sit."

"Perhaps we should go to another room," Isabelle suggested.

"No, I think he's gone now." Edmund rubbed his hands together. "I suppose the mystery surrounding the identity of Giles Goddard has been solved," he said quietly.

"Yes, it has." Was it just her or was there a palpable tension in the air? Why? She'd spent a considerable amount of time in Edmund's company over the past few years. Why did it seem so awkward just now? A memory from the other day when he'd tried to flirt with her under the table came to her mind and she shuddered.

"Isabelle, I wanted to talk to you about something."

"Yes, I'd surmised as much when you said you wanted to talk." She sent up a silent prayer he'd find her statement slightly rude and decide not to propose they marry again. She knew without any uncertainty now she couldn't marry him.

Edmund smiled. "That's the Isabelle I know." He sighed. "My aunt reminded me again this morning at breakfast that I haven't been as honest with you as perhaps I should have been."

She almost choked on her own laughter. "That makes two of us." She shook her head. It wasn't her fault she'd been dishonest, it was *his*. Sebastian's, to be clear.

"I don't consider your flirtation with Simon Appleton to be dishonest, Isabelle," he said softly. He flashed her a quick smile. "Nor your feelings for Lord Belgrave."

She felt her eyes widen and her chest squeeze. He knew?

Edmund raked a hand through his hair. "I think he's the better match for you."

"You mean instead of Simon?" she asked.

He nodded. "And instead of me."

Not that Isabelle had been entertaining such a thought, she felt the need to try to offer him at least a little compassion to make him feel better. Unfortunately, she couldn't think of what to say.

"As it would happen," he continued a moment later. "My heart belongs to another." A light blush stole over his cheeks. "And while I cannot marry her, I also cannot *not* continue to see her."

"Cannot not continue to see her?" Isabelle repeated slowly, trying to make sense of his unusual statement. She reached forward with intent to pat his arm to assure him it was all right, but before she could, she retracted her arm and offered him a weak smile. "I'm not asking you to."

"You're not?" His voice held an edge of excitement, then his face fell and he shook his head. "I can't ask you to do that."

"Do what?"

"Turn a blind eye to me and Lady Vessey."

Isabelle blinked. What was he talking about this time? Only a blind person could have missed the flirtation between the two over these past few days. "I'm not sure what you're talking about, Edmund. I have no intention of turning a blind eye to anything so obvious."

"But you have no interest in joining?"

"Joining?"

He flushed. "I assumed by your lack of response to my flirtations while playing Whist that you weren't interested in a relationship with the both of us."

"The both of you?" she asked, aghast.

He nodded. "I can't give her up, Isabelle. It'd just be easier if you embraced what I'm suggesting. Then I won't have to choose."

She absolutely would not! Besides that it was indecent, she had no such feelings for either Edmund or Lady Vessey. "Edmund, you're not talking any sense." Then again, he'd talked a little out of her range of comprehension on many occasions.

He sighed. "Don't you understand, Isabelle? I cannot marry her. I need an heir and she is too old. But I cannot give her up."

"And you don't have to," Isabelle said pointedly. "I know you've offered marriage to me before, but I'm not holding you to it."

"Then who will you marry?" His tone dripped with disbelief.

"Apparently, I'm still legally married to Sebastian."

His expression hardened, then softened, then turned to one that said he was torn between shock and outright confusion. "I take it you just learned of this last night."

"Is it that obvious?" she asked, trying to keep her forced smile in place.

"It is now." He twisted his lips and drummed his fingers along the top of the backrest of the chair recently vacated by the mouse. "I assumed by your face that there had been some sort of trouble between you and at least one of your suitors. I also found it very odd that they both left the party early this morning. Now, I know why."

"Excuse me, they both left the party?"

Edmund nodded. Lord Belgrave left before the sun came up and I saw Mr. Appleton's coach pulling away while I was in the breakfast room."

Isabelle's mind spun until she was almost so dizzy she needed to sit. Almost. There wasn't anything in this world that would make her want to sit *anywhere* in this room. She should have been the one to inform Simon. Not that she was positive he knew, he might have left following another disagreement with Giles. "It was because they both left that you decided to approach me about this..." She waved her hand through the air, words failing her. "Development. You thought both of my potential suitors had abandoned me—" she tried not to snort at the idea of referring to Sebastian as a suitor, he was the furthest thing from it, especially now— "and you thought to explain the circumstances of what a marriage to you would entail?"

"Something like that." He picked at the cracked leather on the chair with his thumbnail. "My aunt thought you needed to know of my feelings for Lady Vessey and let you decide if you could live with the arrangement. But now I don't think it'll matter to you."

"No," she agreed numbly. There was still so much to take in: both Simon and Sebastian had left without a word to her of explanation. Not to mention whatever unusual relationship Edmund had just suggested to her. She covered her face with her hands and tried to make sense of it all.

"If it helps, I think Lord Belgrave will make you a fine husband."

Isabelle dropped her hands and straightened. "He's a liar."

"Well, that's true," Edmund conceded. "Did he say why he lied?"

She shook her head.

"Did you ask?" he pressed.

She shook her head again. "Why should I? He lied and if that wasn't bad enough, encouraged me to act a fool."

"By flirting with Mr. Appleton?"

"Yes."

Edmund lifted his right hand to his chin and idly tapped his finger against his lips. "I'm probably not going to say this right, so please assume the best." At her nod, he continued. "Your flirtations were wasted on Mr. Appleton. Not to say you're not desirable, because you are," he rushed to add. "But he's not the one to see it."

"Yes, I know. He's far too distracted with Giles."

He blinked. "No, I don't think there's anything between those two."

"Except that they're brothers," Isabelle clarified while trying not to laugh. She'd quite forgotten that it might not be public knowledge about Giles and Simon's relation—especially if very few even knew of Giles' existence until a few weeks ago. Besides, now that she knew what kind of relationships Edmund was interested in she should have been more clear.

"That explains more, but not everything." Edmund swiped his hand through the air. "Isabelle, if he'd truly been interested in you, his brother's presence wouldn't have kept him from responding to you. And it certainly wouldn't have made him seemingly unaware of what was going on between you and Lord Belgrave at the card table. He'd have been jealous and might have even called the man out for what he was doing." He shrugged. "But he didn't."

"Then why would he have acted so interested in me while we were in London?"

"Maybe he was then."

"And then suddenly he wasn't?"

"He might have just realized it was only a passing infatuation and been willing to accept that."

"Accept that?"

Edmund lifted his hands in a casual show of defeat or indifference. "Very few marry for love, Isabelle. You know that. When his infatuation faded, perhaps he realized that while his feelings for you weren't that strong, he valued your friendship and thought that was a good enough reason to marry."

She nodded her understanding. That's all she was looking for in a marriage to him: friendship.

Edmund crossed his arms and continued, "While some might marry for friendship, it wouldn't make him take exception to Sebastian's closeness nor make him take notice of your flirtations." He offered her a wide smile. "Just like you didn't seem to mind my relationship with Lady Vessey."

He was right on that score. "And Sebastian? What was his plan?"

"I wouldn't begin to know. Did he tell you anything?"

"If he did, I don't remember it," she admitted, racking her brain for any snippet of conversation she could dredge up from last night. The truth was there wasn't much she could remember after he informed her that they were still married. Between the blood pounding in her ears and the disbelief and humiliation swallowing her whole there was more that she didn't remember than what she did.

"Then you should ask him."

She frowned. "I don't think I want to."

"Why not?"

"I don't know what to say to him."

"I think the words, 'I love you', might help."

She sputtered with laughter. "Now, that's wasted breath. Sebastian doesn't care if I love him or not. The only reason he even told me the truth last night was because—" She broke off as a violent blush came over her.

"All the more reason to tell him how you feel," Edmund said with a chuckle.

"Sebastian doesn't want my love, only my body." She almost couldn't believe she'd said that, but considering everything else they'd just discussed, there wasn't a reason not to. She craned her neck around to catch a glimpse of Mrs. Finch. She was sitting on a green velvet chaise in front of the far window, reading a book.

"The gentleman I saw creeping around the estate observing you didn't look to just be in lust."

"Then why did he leave without saying anything to me?" she demanded, not sure why she was suddenly so hurt by his leaving.

"I didn't ask him. You'll have to do that."

"I don't think I can."

"Are you afraid that he'll tell you he only lusts after you?"

She bit her lip and nodded.

"Then you *must* ask."

Chapter Thirty

It had been two days since Isabelle had convinced Mrs. Finch to go back to London and she was still numb.

Just as the sun was setting the coach came to a stop in front of Mrs. Finch's rented townhouse.

Warily, Isabelle climbed out and went straight up to her bedchamber where Tilde helped her change and she fell asleep from pure exhaustion.

The next morning, she was no closer to resolving her feelings than she'd been since Sebastian had informed her they were still married.

But Edmund was right, there were so many things she didn't know and the only way she ever would have definite answers was to go to see Sebastian, because she doubted he'd be coming to see her after the way he'd left her room that night then disappeared from the house party.

"Tilde, I'd like you to follow me on a walk this morning," she said to her maid who stood at the door.

"Yes, miss."

Mrs. Finch gave her a knowing look, and instead of saying anything, waggled her eyebrows.

"Thank you," she murmured to Mrs. Finch, kissing her cheek.

Mrs. Finch reached for her arm to stay her while she was still so close. "Just to be clear, I wouldn't be letting you go if I wasn't so sure he'd act a gentleman while alone with you."

Flames crawled up Isabelle's face as memories of her last time alone with Sebastian came to mind. "Yes, ma'am," she croaked; then ignoring Mrs. Finch's cackle, she left the room and went to the front door.

She waited for Tilde to finish tying on her bonnet, then taking a deep, determined, breath, she opened the door and with heavy feet, descended the stairs.

Halfway to his bachelor lodgings, she spotted a bench and sat to rest. What would he say? Would he care that she came? She shook off the thought. It didn't matter if he was pleased or annoyed that she came. She wanted answers. So why then, if she wanted them so bad, no matter what they were, did her entire inside feel as if it were being crushed beneath a team of four?

She jumped up from the bench as best that crushing weight would allow and continued in the direction toward his townhouse.

He lived close enough that in only ten painfully long minutes, she had arrived and found herself clenching the handrail on the side of the stairs.

Tilde cleared her throat.

"I'm paying a call," Isabelle said with more confidence than she felt.

Tilde looked skeptical, but didn't question her.

Inclining her chin and willing away the imaginary weights that held her captive, Isabelle climbed the stairs. Extending her hand forward, she debated whether she should bother to knock or just go in. She was Lady Belgrave, after all.

She decided to knock. Best to not scandalize the butler on her first visit.

After giving two swift bangs she clasped her hands together and waited.

"May I help you?" a stoic, aging butler with thin lips asked.

"I'm here to see Lord Belgrave."

He pierced her with his gaze. "This isn't the hour to be entertaining your sort."

"And what sort is that?" Isabelle challenged.

Wordlessly, he began to slam the door in her face, but she stopped him—barely—by reaching forward and pressing her hand against the door.

"I'd be careful were I you, sir. Your job depends upon your treatment of the lady of the house."

His facial expression didn't change and Isabelle just wiggled her way into the house. "Madam, I don't know who you are—"

"Yes, that is quite clear." She flashed him a smile and prayed he wouldn't be able to see how nervous she was. "Allow me to introduce myself. My name is Isabelle Gentry, Lady Belgrave, the mistress of this house."

The butler crossed his arms. "His lordship is unmarried."

"Yes, that's what many believe, but the truth is, he is married. To me. So if you'd like to keep your post you'll take me to see him post haste and make sure my maid is made comfortable."

The man's nostrils flared, the only sign that he was anything but impassive. "Madam, I might be a score past forty, but I am not too old and frail to put you out on your ear myself."

Isabelle pursed her lips. "Touch me and you'll be sacked without a reference."

White lines appeared around the butler's mouth. "John, Daniel," he clipped.

Irritation built in Isabelle's chest. She wasn't about to be tossed out of her husband's townhouse by two ruffians. She spun around and headed down the hall at a half-walk, half-run, almost like a trot.

"Come back here, madam!" the aging butler demanded, hobbling after her.

Isabelle picked up her pace. "My name is Lady Belgrave, not madam."

As soon as the words were past her lips a door ten feet down the hall swung open and a tall form emerged: Lord Clearcreek.

Isabelle skidded to a halt and two seconds later the butler was at her side.

"My apologies, my lord," the older man said, gasping for air. "She pushed her way inside." His face grew bright red and Isabelle would wager it had nothing to do with his recent bout of exercise. "I'll have her removed right away."

"That's not necessary, Goosey," Lord Clearcreek said tonelessly from where he stood in the hall just past the threshold of the room he'd been occupying. He flickered a glance to Isabelle. "She is who she says she is. For now."

Ignoring her father-in-law's stiff posture, she waited for the butler to offer his apologies and scurry back to the door where Tilde was waiting for him.

"I'm here to see Sebastian," she said by way of explanation as she let herself into Sebastian's study.

"He's not here," Lord Clearcreek barked, coming into the room behind her.

Isabelle studied the room. She'd never actually been in a study before and wasn't sure what to expect. There were two large windows that filled two-thirds of the back wall, parquet floors, a large mahogany desk in the center of the room with a stack of papers on each of the two far corners. There were two wing-backed chairs positioned in front of the desk and another two chairs opposite a red settee on the far end of the room. There were a few side tables here and there and a fireplace near the settee and chair arrangement. It wasn't the most inviting room she'd ever been in, but it was still comfortable in a masculine sort of way.

"When shall I expect him to return?"

"Perhaps you'll see him again in another six years." The bitterness in Lord Clearcreek's tone was unmistakable.

"Pardon me?"

Lord Clearcreek leaned his hip against the side of Sebastian's desk and crossed his arms. "He signed the annulment papers, Miss Knight."

Her breath left her lungs in one swift *whoosh*. "Pardon?" she choked, unable to know why his simple statement had the power to grind her heart to dust.

"He signed the papers. You are welcome to marry whoever you want."

"Why?"

"It's what you wanted," he said, his tone and expression full of annoyance. "As I said, you may go and marry another."

No, she couldn't. Not when her knees were about to buckle. She collapsed in one of the armchairs in front of Sebastian's desk in an undignified manner.

"Is there something about my words you don't understand, Miss Knight?" Sebastian's father snapped.

"There's a great deal I don't understand, Lord Clearcreek," she said, matching his tone. "Why didn't he just sign them in the first place?"

"Does it matter?"

"Yes, actually, it matters a great deal."

Lord Clearcreek's cold stare sent chills down her spine. "If I answer your question, will you agree to leave?"

Isabelle didn't really think she had a choice, but at least if she agreed to leave after he answered, she'd get at least one answer. That was better than nothing. "Yes, my lord." She dropped her eyes to wait for whatever cold response he'd offer her and her eyes caught on a folded piece of parchment addressed to the head of parliament on the top of the stack of papers closest to her.

"He wanted to thwart your father, and me," the last was more of a mumbled afterthought.

She looked up and gave him a cold stare. "I don't doubt it irritated you significantly that Sebastian didn't sign the papers, seeing as how you wanted him to have a more noble bride befitting his title. My father, however, might not have been pleased that there was a scandal surrounding my marriage to Sebastian, but I doubt he'd press for an annulment which would only cause a larger scandal."

Lord Clearcreek twisted his lips into a sneer. "All right. The truth is, when Sebastian was made to leave, you were not doing so well, but the physician was hopeful that you'd make some sort of recovery—even if not completely well enough. I think perhaps he felt guilty that he'd not only made you unmarriageable because of the scandal, but also felt enough pity for you and your circumstance that if something happened to him while he was on Tour, at least you'd receive a jointure upon his death—even if it was undeserved."

The disdain that filled his unkind words barely registered to her and for as much as she hated to admit how much Lord Clearcreek disliked her, she recognized his words as the truth. Sebastian might have been angry with her for deceiving him, but he'd have never been so heartless as to have completely abandoned her. She still didn't know why he'd left the country for five years, of course. However, his wanting to make sure she was cared for in one way or another was a trait he'd always possessed—just like the time when she was eight and he was eleven and he'd told her if she fell in the frigid pond she'd have to shiver home naked because he wasn't gentleman enough, nor was she lady enough, for him to strip off his clothes for her to wear home; then when she really did fall in, he'd found her a blanket in the stable to bundle up in while he gave her a ride on his horse back to her house.

Even then, he'd had a soft heart and had wanted to make sure she was taken care of in some way.

Her heart clenched. Why hadn't she seen this earlier? Was she that hurt and angry that she'd been blinded to his real motives? Her questions and understanding quickly gave way to panic: he'd signed the papers. Did he no longer care for her at all? Tears filled her eyes, blurring her vision.

"I must go." She stood and quickly swiped the stack of papers on the edge of Sebastian's desk. "I'll bring these to the butler on my way out to be put in the post."

Chapter Thirty-One

One week later

Isabelle sat in the drawing room unable to thread her needle, much less work on her embroidery. The house party had officially ended three days ago and today would be the first full day anyone who'd attended would be back in London and ready to receive guests. Would Sebastian come to see her?

Tingles ran up her spine and she cast a quick glance to her reticule. Every day since she'd been back in London she'd considered going to see him again and decided against it. Mrs. Finch had gently reminded her that she'd been fortunate to escape scandal the first time she'd gone to his house and it would be best to wait either for him to come to her or to see him at a social event. Because it'd be absolutely scandalous if it became known Lady Belgrave was visiting Lord Belgrave's house! Actually, it would, but only because hardly anyone knew they were still married.

She'd admit that she'd been a little disappointed that he hadn't come to see her yet, but if she were honest with herself, she doubted he knew she was even in town—Lord Clearcreek surely wouldn't tell him. And the other reason, the one that nearly paralyzed her, was the possibility that he didn't want to see her again.

Tears clogged her throat and she swallowed them down. He was going to see her again whether he wanted to or not, he still owed her answers and she had no desire to let him go without hearing them.

"Lady Townson is holding a ball tonight," Mrs. Finch said as she absentmindedly flipped through a stack of invitations. "We were invited a few weeks ago but with the excitement of the sudden house party, I nearly forgot. We could go if you'd like."

Yes, she would. "I think that sounds like the perfect form of entertainment."

***

Sebastian buttoned his blue waistcoat then smoothed his hands over where it lay on top of his white shirt and fell below the waist of his buff trousers. He turned to Fowler, his valet, and took his cravat and tied it around his neck. The man could shave him, for all Sebastian cared, but he didn't like the man to tie his cravat. He always had a secret fear of being strangled to death that way, and the hulking size of Fowler didn't help.

After making the perfect mathematical knot, he pushed his onyx stickpin squarely in the middle. He turned his back to Fowler and allowed his man to help him put on his freshly pressed coat. He declined the polished walking stick Fowler extended his way and looked in the mirror. He didn't know what most young ladies would consider dashing, but he hoped the adjective fit him. Or at least in Belle's opinion.

He clenched his fist and took a deep breath. Likely no other husband in the country was this nervous about seeing his wife. He swallowed. Hard. No, she wasn't his wife any longer. He'd signed the papers. They might not have been received and recorded yet, but that was as good as promised. He took his felt hat from his valet and put it on his head. Confident he looked his best for the first time since he'd seen Belle in a little over a week, he went into the hall.

"Out to search for a wife tonight, Belgrave?" his father asked from down the hall.

"As it would happen, I am." He flashed his father a genuine smile. Ever since he'd returned from Lady Cosgrove's party, his father had become a bur in his side. Sebastian had casually mentioned that he was signing the annulment papers and conveniently left off that he planned to one day wed her again. But first, he had to woo her. Which was why he was hoping she would be in attendance at tonight's ball.

"I'm glad to hear it," his father said. "I'm quite pleased this whole annulment situation is now behind us."

"As am I," Mr. Knight added from where he stood beside Father. If Sebastian didn't know any better, he'd think the man's tone held a hint of disappointment. Though what he had to be disappointed about, Sebastian didn't know. He'd had the loudest voice in insisting that Sebastian sign the papers—even attempting to blackmail him about smuggling whisky to get his way.

"I'm sure you are," Sebastian said before he could think better of it. "Now that it's been annulled, you can collect your money."

"Money?" Mr. Knight demanded. He narrowed his eyes on Sebastian. "What money?"

Sebastian pursed his lips. Why did the man try to hide the truth? "Whatever money it was my father promised to pay you to push me to sign the annulment papers after I told him that I wouldn't, even if he disinherited me of everything but the title that's mine by birth."

"And what a lot of good that did," Father burst out with a huff. "You still managed to go cavort around the continent."

"I'm not sure I'd call it cavorting," Sebastian countered, recalling the days he'd spent trying to sell one of Giles' paintings so they'd both be able to eat and sleep for the month. "But yes, despite not having your help, I managed just fine."

"And so did I," Mr. Knight said, obviously still affronted that Sebastian would accuse him of accepting such a bribe from Sebastian's father.

"I'm sorry, sir," Sebastian said. "I meant no disrespect."

"Yes, you did, which is exactly why I wanted you to annul this marriage in the first place," Mr. Knight said with a twist of his lips. "I knew you'd be a poor choice of a husband for my daughter even then. That's why I wanted you to annul it. You have no respect for anyone, young man, and I knew with certainty by the things Isabelle said in her sleep about you, that you had no respect for her when you married her and wouldn't respect her as a wife."

What had Isabelle said about him in her sleep? No matter. He really didn't want to know. He remembered their wedding day well enough and could well guess what she might have said. He swallowed past the hot shame that consumed him. What a foolish boy he'd been.

"When you said you were helping Isabelle find a husband, I

thought you might have changed," Mr. Knight continued, cutting into Sebastian's thoughts. "But I can see that I was wrong and now I agree with your father it's best you granted her the annulment."

"It'll be better for them both," Father commented.

Sebastian had a suspicion Father's glee over the annulment wasn't for the same reason as Mr. Knight's. Father would have never considered Isabelle a suitable bride for him. But Sebastian did.

"If you two will excuse me, I am off to the Mart to find a marriageable young miss."

"Perhaps this marriage will be a touch more successful than your last," Father added sarcastically.

"It should," Sebastian retorted, brushing past the two men and heading for the door. Now, he just had to convince Belle she was destined to be his wife. And not just for six years this time, for eternity.

***

Isabelle contemplated what might happen if her dance card were to somehow go missing. Not that she'd purposely drop it in the side of a potted plant or anything. But under a pillow on the settee in the ladies' retiring room... No, she couldn't. She'd hoped to see Sebastian early in the evening and he'd claim at least one of her waltzes, if not two. But she hadn't seen him at all.

Well, that wasn't true. She'd seen him, but he hadn't seen her. Or if he had, he hadn't given any indication of it.

Instead, he'd spun one young lady after the next around the room while she stood off to the side and had all of her dances claimed by fortune hunters or other unsuitable gentleman. She glanced down at her dance card. This particular dance was one of the only two she didn't have claimed. The next dance was a waltz and her last unclaimed dance.

She bit her lip and tried to play the rest of the dance out in her head so she'd know where she should be standing when it ended so she could get his attention. She stopped herself. What was the use? If she had to guess by the way the young ladies had been fawning over him since she'd first seen him this evening, she could almost guarantee that he already had a partner for the next dance.

And as if only to prove her point, she watched as not ten feet away, Sebastian returned his dance partner to her chaperone and turned toward the former Edwina Banks, now Lady Benedict. He said something to her that made her smile then led her to the dance floor.

Isabelle considered going over to stand by Sir Wallace and expressing her sympathy for her incorrigible husband stealing his wife away, but decided against it.

Of course if she just went to stand near him Sebastian would be forced to see her. But what was the point? He seemed rather content without having seen her. It was almost as if he was made for this life: flirting and charming. Emotion clogged her throat and she glanced back to where Sir Wallace was now walking through the crowd with his new brother-in-law, Lord Watson.

That's what Isabelle needed to do: leave. Not with Lord Watson, mind you. But she needed to leave. It was quite evident that there wouldn't be a chance to talk to Sebastian here and she had no desire to dance another set.

***

Sebastian felt a small dose of relief that Edwina, Lady Benedict was content to just dance without asking him questions that he was expected to answer. How unfortunate that some of the other ladies hadn't offered him the same courtesy.

She was a good partner, he'd grant her and he was able to use that to his advantage as they danced around the room without giving it much thought. He peered over her head to once again look for Belle.

He knew she was there, he could feel it. The air was charged and his skin tingled in the way it only did when she was near. But he didn't see her. Not now and not earlier.

The waltz ended and at her direction, he escorted Lady Benedict to the edge of the ballroom, then went in search of Belle again.

She was nowhere to be found.

But Lady Mary was and since he'd claimed one of her dances

earlier, he'd better go collect before she made a scene.

After Lady Mary, he danced a set with Ladies Hellen, Elizabeth and Watson.

After them, he wasn't even sure who he'd danced with all he knew was it wasn't who he'd wanted in his arms, but he couldn't find Belle anywhere.

By one o'clock, he was ready to go home.

If he hadn't seen her yet, she wasn't there. He sagged against the wall as he waited in the hall for his coachman to bring around his carriage. Had he truly lost her, then? Was she so hurt and closed off to him because of his lie that she'd rather not even attend one of the biggest balls of the Season just to avoid him?

His carriage arrived and without giving it much thought, he climbed inside and rode home as not for the first time, memories of his last conversation with Belle played out in his head. By the time he arrived back at his bachelor's lodgings, he was convinced now more than before that he had made a mistake. He should have stayed at the house party at least another day and tried to talk to Belle. Now a week had passed, which was undoubtedly enough time for her to have hardened her heart toward him. Or grown more angry.

Fowler met him just inside the door and Sebastian waved him off.

"My lord—"

"Go to bed, Fowler. I think I can remove my own clothes," Sebastian said as he slipped the knot of his cravat.

Fowler looked like he was about to say something else but before he could, Sebastian gave him his hardest stare and the insolent man closed his mouth with a snap.

Relieved Fowler had decided not to be a pain in the arse who Sebastian would have to threaten to sack, Sebastian shrugged out of his coat and started unfastening the buttons of his waistcoat and shirt as he walked up the stairs and down the hall to his room.

By the time he reached his chamber, he was half undressed and ready to climb into bed and berate himself until he fell asleep. Closing the door behind him with his right hand, he used his left to yank the shirttails from his trousers, then pulled off his cravat, followed by his waistcoat and shirt and threw them all into a pile on the green chair by the door.

He padded across the darkened room to his bed and sat down on the edge of the mattress, then with a sigh brought his elbows to his knees and dropped his head into his hands.

With another sigh he straightened and dropped his hands to his knees, staring aimlessly into the fire blazing in the hearth. He might have been unsuccessful at talking to her at this ball, but there'd be at least one other later in the week. He could woo her then. His heart clenched. What if she didn't want him to woo her? What if she'd seen him tonight and left because of him? He released a breath. He'd determined he wouldn't force her to see him by going to her townhouse—either by fair means or foul—he wanted the chance to do things right, which meant he'd just have to wait for the opportunity.

Just then, a sharp *click* rent the air from the direction of his bedchamber door.

Sebastian jumped to his feet. *What the devil?* A low orange glow filled the space of the partially opened door and grew as the door creaked halfway open. Sebastian blinked. "Belle?"

Chapter Thirty-Two

Isabelle swallowed her nerves and nodded. "Yes."

A bare-chested Sebastian came toward her and took the single candle she carried from her fingertips. "Is something wrong? Why are you here? Is everything all right?"

"Everything is fine," she said, allowing him to lead her to the edge of his bed. She sat. "I need answers, Sebastian."

"Answers," he repeated.

She nodded again. She'd gone home and had been unable to sleep as images of Sebastian grinning and dancing with all of those other young ladies kept filling her mind. While all of this must not have mattered one jot to him, it did to her, and seeing him act so *joyous* only a week after he'd nearly made love to her, only hurt worse. She needed answers and there was no way she'd be able to wait to get them.

"Apparently you needed them quite desperately or you wouldn't have come in the dead of night," he said with a wide grin.

She'd love nothing more than to slap the arrogance right off his face. "Yes, well, I learned the technique from you—the lord and master of appearing in someone's bedchamber late at night."

He *tsk, tsked.* "I always used the window, not a door."

"I'd have broken my neck trying to scale the side of your house—and while you might have enjoyed such a fate to befall me, I'd rather spare myself another six months abed. If I even survived, that is."

He sobered. "Belle, I don't want anything to happen to you. Why would you think that I do?"

Isabelle blinked back her tears. This wasn't going at all how she'd planned. All she wanted was answers, and instead she sat beside him on his bed, barely able to move, much less speak, all because of the horrible crushing sensation in her chest. She jumped to her feet. "I need to go."

SECRETS OF A VISCOUNT

Sebastian reached for her. "No, not yet."

She tried to pull away from his searing grasp, but he wouldn't let her. "No, I really must go. Your man already knows I was here, but if Mrs. Finch or someone else finds out—" She shook her head. "This was a bad idea. I need to—"

"Shh," he crooned, standing. "You're not going home like this. I'll take you home." He pushed a fallen lock of her red hair behind her ear. "But not until you tell me why you came."

"Why did you do it?" she burst out.

"Why did I do what?" His soft voice did nothing to calm the storm of emotions roiling inside of her.

"Lie to me about our marriage?" she blurted on a sob. Then, before he could have any time to answer her, she continued. "Leave me—both at the house party and when I was injured after the carriage accident? Sign the annulment papers?" Each question was punctuated with another, harder sob until finally she couldn't speak.

Sebastian murmured something in her ear that she couldn't hear over her own heartbeat. A moment later, he pulled her onto his lap and wrapped his strong arms around her, holding her to him.

She so very much wanted to give into his embrace and let him hold her for eternity, but she *needed* answers. No matter how painful they were. She pressed her cold palm to his strong chest. "Sebastian, answer."

He exhaled, his breath slightly blowing her hair. "All right, I'll start at the beginning."

She moved to get off his lap, but he didn't let her.

"After our accident, I took one of the horses and went for help. It wasn't far, but they had nothing to offer except a rickety carriage." He swallowed. "I knew you weren't doing well when I left you, but I thought it was more important that I go for help. Belle, you have to understand—" his voice cracked— "I was the only one who could. Abrams, the coachman, was in worse condition than you were. Neither of you had a chance if I didn't leave. Once the Fosters—the family I found—had you loaded into their carriage and I gave them directions, I rode to find a physician

211

who could attend to you at your father's house. Somehow, I found the physician and made it to your father's house before you did.

"That wasn't very well received and I had to go track down where you were. When we returned, your father—and mine—were waiting. Your father yanked open the door and turned into a madman. He yelled and ordered everyone about and thundered at me how it was all my fault. I shouldn't have taken you to Scotland, shouldn't have married you, and shouldn't have left you when you were hurt. Everything he could think of.

"Being only nineteen, I was young and foolish and I let his words bother me and left when he demanded it. I thought I'd come back to check on you after he had time to calm down. But he never did. When I tried to see you again, he refused, saying that if I'd truly been concerned I'd have stayed when we'd first arrived." He gave her an affectionate squeeze. "I did care, Belle, I cared very much; but I was a coward and let my father convince me it was better to leave and let him calm down." He paused, swallowing convulsively. "I returned every day for two months and was turned away. The only way I knew anything about your condition was by paying the housekeeper and once your father found out I'd been doing that, he threatened to sack her if she spoke to me again.

"After another month, your father approached me and told me I wasn't welcome to darken his door again. He said that you weren't my concern, even as your husband, since I'd admitted to him initially that I was supposed to take Rachel to Scotland and got confused. He then handed me the annulment papers—he'd had them drawn up on your behalf because you weren't of age, nor conscious."

"Could he do that?" Isabelle asked around the lump of emotion in her throat.

Sebastian shrugged. "I imagine my father helped him bend a few rules."

That made sense. Lord Clearcreek had never seemed too fond of her and had been especially pleased the other day when he'd informed her that Sebastian had finally signed the papers. "So you took the papers and left?"

"Not exactly. I took the papers and came back the next day."
A small smile took his lips. "Your father was none-too-pleased that
I hadn't brought with me signed papers. When I asked to see you
again, he told me in no uncertain terms that if I ever came back and
I didn't have those papers signed, he'd tell the magistrate that I
was smuggling whisky."

"Were you?" She clapped her hand over her mouth. "Pardon
me."

"No need." He waved her off. "Actually, I had. My father had
stills that nobody knew about and every now and then, I'd sell
barrels to smugglers. I didn't know anyone knew that I'd actually
had any part in selling it, but either your father knew or he was a
great bluffer because it put enough fear in me not to go back for a
while."

"I imagine it did." Even if Lord Clearcreek was an earl and
Sebastian a viscount, the charges they'd face for having the stills
and selling whisky were too high, not to mention adding more
scandals on their family.

"That's when I decided to leave. I'd tracked down the
physician in the village who'd been attending to you and paid him
for details. He was stingy with them but I knew all I needed: you'd
live." He closed his eyes for an extended blink. "Unfortunately, I
couldn't get out of the man if you'd have a very satisfying
existence or not—"

"Which is why you left without signing the papers," she
finished. His father had been right. He'd wanted to make sure
she'd been taken care of—even if it irritated both of their families
he did so.

"I wanted to make sure you were taken care of," he explained,
paying her no mind.

"If you didn't make it back," she supplied.

"There's that, but I was more concerned if—" He swallowed
hard. "If your recovery left you an invalid. I-I was never told the
extent of your injury, Belle. I could only assume the worst because
of all that blood and the way your body was contorted."

He took a deep breath, but when he spoke again, his voice was harsh and raspy. "I wanted to do the right thing. Even if I couldn't be there. Had word reached me that you were left a cripple or in some other way unmarriageable, I would have petitioned the courts to demand my husbandly rights and taken you home and made sure everyone knew you were Lady Belgrave, a viscountess. I—I didn't want you to be cast out or shunned because of me. That was never my intention."

Her heart ached at the raw emotion in his voice and the power of his words, but she still didn't fully understand. "Then why did you stay away so long?"

"Because I wasn't ready to face you yet." He lowered his lashes. "I know, that's the cowardly answer, but it's the only one I have. I wanted so badly to spare you being a pariah if the results of your injuries would have left you disfigured, but when I was informed you'd recovered better than anyone had expected and were more beautiful than before, I didn't think I could face you. I don't know what memories you're able to recall from that day, but I hadn't been a very good friend, let alone a good husband. I'd been so irritated with you for withholding the truth from me until it was too late that I'd snapped at you each time I spoke and had agreed with Abrams not to stop for lunch when you requested it. I was just trying to be an ass and because of that, you got hurt." A faraway look filled his eyes. "I'm so sorry, Belle, I never meant any of what I said, I—"

She pressed her fingers to his lips. "Shhh. My memory isn't quite as clear, but if I remember my part correctly, I wasn't acting a very good wife—or friend—either. I can't remember exactly what I'd said, but I do remember that I was so excited that I'd been right about the marriage registry or something like that that I was purposely trying to provoke you." She blushed. "If the roles were reversed, I wouldn't have been too keen on granting any of my wishes, either."

He didn't look too convinced. "I should have. And I'll forever feel guilty about not."

She froze. Guilt. That's it. That's what all of his actions had been about. *Guilt.* All of his kindnesses toward her had been because he felt bad for his role in her injuries, not because he was her friend. He just wanted to assuage his guilt. He'd even said something about it that last night at the house party, she'd just been too shocked by his announcement that they were still married she hadn't been able to really put everything into perspective. She swallowed the bile that burned the back of her throat.

"That's why you came to visit me, isn't it? Because you felt guilty for the accident," she asked for clarification, inwardly congratulating herself on holding a straight tone that belied the new round of angry emotions that were overtaking her.

"Yes. I wanted—"

"And that's why you never signed the papers," she cut in, pushing at his hold and moving to stand.

"Yes, I—"

"And, it was also why you wanted to help me find a husband. Because you felt guilty for making me a social pariah."

He nodded.

Isabelle suddenly felt very cold and instinctively wrapped her arms around herself. There was one final question. Though she already knew the answer, she had to ask. Then she could leave and never think of him again. "Is that why you signed the papers, Sebastian?"

"No."

"No?" she echoed. Had she heard him right?

"No." He reached for her and she pulled back. He reached for her again, this time, standing and taking a step toward her. "I signed the papers because I realized I had no right to hold you back from your own happiness. I might love you to a distraction, and I might hope that you feel the same for me, but it wasn't fair of me to use our existing marriage as a means to keep you as my wife. I wanted one last chance to do things the right way to make things right between us."

She knit her brows. "I—I don't understand."

He chafed her hand between his larger ones, a hint of a nervous, boyish smile took his lips. "I know you were angry with me last week when I told you that we were still married, but I hope you won't stay that way, for I'd like the chance to court you."

All of her blood drained to her toes. "Court me?"

"Yes. If you're agreeable, that is. I'd like to court you." His smile grew a fraction, melting the remaining ice that she'd encased her heart with to keep it safe. "I'd like to claim your first—and last waltz at every ball, race you on Rotten Row, send you a bouquet or two, call upon you and fawn over you in the drawing room with poetry and trinkets. Everything. I want to marry you proper this time."

"Y—you want to marry me? Forever, this time?"

He chuckled. "Yes, I want to marry you again. But first, I need to court you."

"No, you don't." She reached her trembling hand into the inside pocket of her hooded frock and withdrew a folded stack of papers. She flashed him the direction on the front of the papers and tried not to laugh at his look of astonishment.

"Where did you get those?" he breathed.

"I came to see you last week, but you weren't here. Your father met me—"

"My father," he said in a hard tone.

Isabelle nodded. "He met me and told me you were out for the day, but that I could be on my way, you'd signed the papers."

Sebastian's eyebrows knit. "And then he gave them to you?"

"No." Isabelle's mouth went dry. "I stole them."

Sebastian's face went blank, then suddenly his lips started to twitch. "You stole the annulment papers. Why?"

"Because I love you. I—I know I was angry when I first learned the truth, but the real truth is that I love you and I don't want an annulment."

"I love you, too," he whispered, closing the space between them. "I signed those papers because I loved you and wanted to do things right this time."

He'd already said that and apparently he was bent on it. Impulsively, she flicked her wrist in the direction of the low-burning fire and sent the papers sailing into the hearth. "I don't want you to court me, Sebastian. I want you to claim me."

Chapter Thirty-Three

"Claim you?" Sebastian winced at the raggedness of his own voice, forgetting all about how she'd gotten those papers.

She nodded. "I don't need any of that other nonsense, Sebastian. Just you."

"Hopefully you don't think *I'm* nonsense," he teased, lowering his lashes. "Are you sure this is what you want? Once we..." He cleared his throat, his blood turning to fire in his veins at the very thought. "I won't let you go again. Are you certain this is what you want?"

"Are you certain this is what you want?" she countered, taking a step back. A seductive smile played on her lips as she idly reached for the sash of her hooded frock. She quickly slipped the knot free and let it fall open, exposing another of those silk nightrails she had—except this one was red. "Because if you aren't, I might need to return home." She moved to close her frock and he reached his hand out to stop her.

"The devil you will," he growled, gripping both sides of her frock and pulling it open further. He swallowed, then cast a glance to the fire that had just consumed their annulment papers. "I suppose it's plenty warm in here now that six years of our past has burned."

"Indeed," she agreed, shrugging out of her frock.

He released his hold and let the garment fall to her feet. He didn't know whether to drool over the luscious sight that presented itself in front of him or be furious she'd traveled to his house wearing something so enticing.

As if she'd read his mind, she said, "I couldn't sleep until I had my answers, but I didn't think it'd be considered appropriate to wake my maid and ask her to help me dress so I could go sneak into my husband's bedchamber in the black of night."

He nodded. "Do you always sleep in—" he gestured to her

delectable form— "this?"

"No." She tucked a tendril of her hair behind her ear. "Only when I think my husband might see."

He took a step toward her, cocking his head to the side, "Oh, so you came here tonight bent on seduction."

"No. I came for answers." She narrowed her eyes a little above his left shoulder. "You have something in your hair."

He blinked. What the devil did that matter? He mindlessly swatted at his hair. Did she find it repulsive that there was a little fuzz or powder in his hair? Why would she even bother to bring up such an inconsequential matter at a time such as this?

"Allow me," she said; her pink tongue poked out between her lips, moistening them.

He froze and watched her lips as she closed the gap between them, bringing her barely covered breasts flush against his bare chest, then came up on her toes, dragging her plump breasts up his chest as she went. Instinctively, he put his arms around her and held her there, then bent his head down and captured her lips with his.

***

Her plan had worked. Partially. She'd hoped to spark his desire a little by pressing herself close to him. She'd never imagined he'd kiss her in response.

His tongue traced the seam of her mouth and she parted her lips for him, gasping when his tongue brushed past her teeth and touched her tongue. He lifted one strong hand to cup the side of her face and she wrapped her arms around his neck, sinking her fingers into his soft, brown hair.

He murmured her name against her lips then pulled back.

"Did you get it?" he said hoarsely; his eyes dark and intense in a way that set her blood to simmering.

"I'm not sure." Rotating her body just so that she'd brush his groin with her hip, she moved her fingers to the side of his hair and removed an imaginary piece of string, then slowly returned her heels to the floor, going slow enough to drag her body along the rigid bulge in the front of his trousers. "It's out now."

"No, it's not, but it will be," he muttered, tightening his hold and pressing her against his solid erection. He'd clearly caught onto her game.

Not that she minded. She certainly didn't, especially if that meant he was about to play the game with her. He released his gentle hold on her face and trailed his fingers down her cheek and jaw, then to her neck and finally to her shoulder. He traced her collarbone with the fingertip of his index finger. His lashes were lowered and his eyes appeared to be fixed on her breasts. A thrill shot through her. She never would have thought she'd have this affect on Sebastian, nor him have this strong of affect on her.

He slowly skimmed his callused fingertips along her skin, taking the strap of her nightrail with it. He reached the end of her shoulder and lowered his warm lips to kiss his way across the path his fingers had just made. When he reached the tip of her shoulder, he planted one last kiss, then pressed open-mouthed kisses back across her shoulder and to the plane of her chest. He stopped when he reached that dip at the bottom of her throat and flicked his tongue in the hollow. She shivered.

Seeming encouraged by her reaction, he slid the other strap of her nightrail to the edge of her shoulder, this time following it with parted lips and the barest hint of his tongue.

When he reached the ball of her shoulder, he lifted his head and kissed her lips, then let go of the fabric, letting it make a silk and lace puddle at her feet. He brought his hands to her sides, his palms covering her ribs and his thumbs resting just below her breasts. He held her close to him and deepened their kiss. Her hardened nipples pressed into the warm, smooth skin of his chest, her breasts swelling in response.

He skimmed his hands down her sides, then back up, brushing his palms over the sides of her breasts. Her breath caught. He'd touched her thus last week, but tonight it felt different. The only way she could think to explain it was his touch then was charged with lust and desire, as was her response. Tonight though, all she could feel between them—his touch, his kiss, his gaze—was love.

He pulled back, ending their kiss; his breathing labored. With a swallow, he let his gaze travel from her eyes to her lips then down to where their chests were still pressed together. He swallowed again and took a step backward, separating them.

"You're breathtaking, Belle," he whispered, giving her breasts a gentle squeeze from the side. He reached both of his thumbs up to sweep across the hardened tips.

Isabelle bit her lip to keep from gasping and the insufferable man made another pass, pressing harder this time. Twin sparks flew through her and she was unsuccessful in holding back her gasp, which seemed to please Sebastian greatly, if his hooded gaze was any indication.

Regaining her wits only momentarily, Isabelle reached between them and ran the edge of her knuckle along his erection until she reached the tip that rested just under the fastenings of his trousers. She inched her fingers up to the buttons and began to unfasten his placket. On the second button, his erection sprang free and into her waiting hands. He stilled instantly, his hands still cupping her breasts.

She wrapped her fingers around his length in a firm grip and chanced a quick peek up at his face. His eyes met hers. They were dark and full of a heated promise. She shivered and slid her hand down to the base of his erection. He groaned and moved to cover her breasts with his hands, giving them a firm, yet gentle, squeeze that made her entire body tingle.

She glided her hand back up his shaft and brushed her thumb over the swollen tip, eliciting a groan from him. Which of course spurred her on to repeat the gesture. His Adam's apple bobbed once, then suddenly he slid his hands down her body to her hips and lifted her and carried her to the bed.

Isabelle lost her hold on his erection and gripped his shoulders for support as he set her on the mattress. He murmured something about giving him a moment then he straightened and removed the remainder of his clothing. Isabelle's mouth went dry. She'd never seen a naked gentleman before for comparison, but no matter what any other looked like, Sebastian was magnificent. His chiseled chest and abdomen full of edges and rounded muscles tapered off to a lean, trim waist. His muscular legs were covered in a thin sheet of black hair that grew thicker near his groin where a dense patch surrounded his thick erection.

Paying her no heed, he climbed onto the bed and came up on his hands and knees, surrounding her. He dropped his head down to her chest and used his mouth to explore every inch of her. Kissing here and licking there. She sank her fingers into his hair to hold him in place as pleasure zinged through her and her body arched and bucked on its own accord.

His hand found her left thigh and without pausing in his exploration of her, he guided her legs apart. She was powerless to stop him from doing so. Not that she'd want to stop him. Ever.

A moment later his palm was sliding down her and toward her nest of feminine curls. She sucked in a breath. She remembered this and the delicious feelings it evoked.

"Sebastian," she murmured when he reached the apex of her legs and brushed his fingers over her delicate flesh.

Sebastian said her name against the sensitive skin just under her left breast and moved his fingers to her opening. She gripped his shoulders a fraction tighter in anticipation. Would it hurt? Would it feel good? Would it feel at all?

She had her answer less than a second later as he eased his finger inside. It felt...different. Almost as if she were being stretched. He nearly withdrew, then pushed in again, this time bringing her a little shock of pleasure. He did it again. Then again; and again. Each time another arrow of heated pleasure shot through her while simultaneously the tension in her abdomen tightened. He sped his pace, his thrusts coming harder and faster than she could keep up with as her entire body filled with an intoxicating pleasure.

Then suddenly he stopped.

Isabelle choked on a sob. The tension just above her waist was too tight, too demanding for him to stop. "Sebastian—" Her words died on her tongue when she felt something else at her entrance. His erection was much thicker than his finger had been and she winced in pain as he slid inside. After the initial sting subsided, she lay still for a moment to get used to his body inside of hers. It didn't hurt, necessarily, but it didn't feel quite the same as earlier. Was that it, then? Was this the part where he found fulfillment and she tried not to disrupt that?

"Relax," he murmured as he brushed a kiss on the edge of her ear. He moved his lips to her jaw then to the back of her ear before going to her neck. She sighed and lolled her head to the side to give him more access—which he took. He dragged his slightly parted lips along her neck and slowly started moving on top of, and inside of, her. Though some of the tension in her midsection had eased, there was still some there that was coiling much faster and tighter than it had before. The friction between their bodies lessened and he sped his movements, stoking some sort of inner fire in her abdomen and sending sprays of hot sparks through her. Pressure and excitement built higher and higher with each thrust until it threatened to consume her.

Her breathing grew labored and ragged as the inner excitement in her took hold and she forced herself to look up at Sebastian's dark eyes. They were heated, so much so that if they got any more heated, he'd combust. And so would she.

And then she did.

With one powerful stroke, he hit something deep inside her and it was as if a dam broke, flooding her body with waves of hot and cold as her muscles tightened and released and her mind went completely blank. Gasping for breath, she met Sebastian's eyes again, just in time to see him squeeze them shut and to feel his muscles tense beneath her hands as a savage growl rent the air and he slowed to a stop.

The following seconds stretched out between them to what felt like minutes until Sebastian lowered himself to lie on top of her with his upper body supported by his forearms that were planted on either side of her.

"What are you thinking, Belle?" he asked.

She blushed. Had she been so obvious? "Nothing, just a little woolgathering."

"Woolgathering?" he burst out, blinking.

She nodded and traced the edge of his clenched jaw with her index finger. "I was just thinking that while I enjoyed your attentions last week, and likely would have enjoyed this particular activity then, too, I think it was all far more enjoyable this week—knowing you're my husband." She closed her eyes; she wasn't explaining this right. "I know you were my husband then, but—"

He kissed her lips, silencing her. "I know what you meant." He kissed her again. "And I quite agree," he said between kisses. "I knew I was quite taken with you that night, but—" he kissed her once more— "it wasn't until I left your room that I realized that I loved you. I think that's the part that made it that much better tonight."

She couldn't help but smile at his words. "Indeed. Oh, but Sebastian, just because I agreed to become your wife in truth without all the courting, doesn't mean that I won't still expect you to lavish me with attention."

Sebastian moved his hands up to cup her face. "I'll shower it on you like a rain in June," he murmured between kisses. Then proceeded to show her once again just how much he loved her now and always would.

Epilogue

The Next Morning

Isabelle's eyes snapped open. There was a hand cupping her breast. A big hand. Her husband's hand. A smile pulled at her lips and she turned to face him.

Sebastian lay as naked as she with his left elbow digging into his pillow, propping his head up while he lay on his side and ran his right hand over her bare body.

"You're just as beautiful today as you were last night."

She choked on a giggle. "Did you expect me to look different?"

"No." He feathered kisses on her shoulder. "No regrets?"

"None." She swallowed. "You?"

"Never." Then as if to prove his point, he showed her once again what she meant to him without uttering a single word.

An hour later, a soft scratch at the door woke them both from their sated slumber.

Isabelle froze as a slight sense of panic swept her. "Do you think your man has informed your father that I'm here?"

Sebastian's brows knit. "Does it matter?"

"He doesn't like me," Isabelle pointed out. "He won't be happy about this."

"I suppose that makes us even since your father doesn't like me, either," Sebastian countered, grinning. He reached over and wound a tendril of her auburn hair around his finger. "But I don't give a hang about either of them and who they like. I love you and that's all that matters to me."

Isabelle opened her mouth to ask another question, but closed it when the unmistakeable sound of paper sliding against a hardwood floor drew her attention.

Isabelle and Sebastian exchanged looks, then he climbed out

of bed and retrieved the unsealed missive that had just been pushed under his door.

He read it to himself, a small smile curving his lips.

"We should respond post haste," Sebastian murmured, handing the note to her.

Isabelle took it from his fingers and paid him no mind as he went over to the crude desk in the corner.

Dear Lord Belgrave,

I am assuming due to her lack of return that my dearest companion Isabelle Gentry, Lady Belgrave has either been abducted—in which case you must inform the authorities (and me) immediately, or she's now been made your wife in every way—in which case you'd do well to come collect her clothes and bring her by this afternoon to bid me farewell.

Yrs,

Suellen Finch

Isabelle shook her head. It was notes like these that made it most clear that Edmund and Mrs. Finch were of a close relation. She set the note down and padded over to where Sebastian sat naked at his desk and peeked over his shoulder.

Dear Mrs. Finch,

I'm pleased to inform you that Lady Belgrave is safely with me and if last night was any indication, she should be entering her confinement shortly—

Isabelle squeaked. "You can't write that."

"Yes, I can," Sebastian said, turning his head just enough to brush a kiss on her cheek.

However, as you likely already know, her increasing state will not take effect immediately and she shall need some clothes. If you'd be so kind as to have Belle's—

Isabelle blinked as an odd memory of a conversation with Edmund over how Sebastian might spell his nickname for her came to mind. "You spell it B-E-L-L-E," she murmured without thinking.

Sebastian looked up at her with an expression that might suggest she was cracked. "How did you think I spelled it? B-E-L-L?"

She flushed, making him chuckle.

He shifted in his chair and pulled her to his lap. "I won't lie to you—"

"That's good, because it didn't turn out very good the last time you did," Isabelle interjected.

Sebastian grinned. "Not at first, but it did in the end." He gave her an affectionate squeeze to emphasize his meaning. "I can't remember when I first came up with the nickname for you, but I have no doubt it was when we were playing some such game and I thought you were being annoying—like a bell. Which might have made it an appropriate name to my eleven year-old mind, but to my twenty-five year-old mind, I think B-E-L-L-E, like the most desirable woman in the room suits you far better." He tucked a tendril of her red hair behind her ear and kissed her neck. "There is no denying it, my love, you are my Belle."

If you enjoyed *Secrets of a Viscount*, I would appreciate it if you would help others enjoy this book, too.

Lend it. This e-book is lending-enabled, so please, share it with a friend.

Recommend it. Please help other readers find this book by recommending it to friends, readers' groups and discussion boards.

Review it. Please tell other readers why you liked this book by reviewing it at one of the following websites: Amazon, Barnes and Noble, or Goodreads.

Coming Soon by Rose Gordon

Gentlemen of Honor Series
Regency set series that is coming in 2014!

Secrets of a Viscount—One summer night, Sebastian Gentry, Lord Belgrave hauled the wrong young lady to Gretna Green. When her identity is exposed, the only obvious solution is to get an annulment. Only, just like his elopement plans, things didn't go as planned and while she has reason to believe they are no longer married, he knows better. Wanting to make things right for her, he offers to help her find a husband —what neither counts on is it just might be the one she's still secretly married to.

Desires of a Baron—Giles Goddard, Lord Norcourt is odd. Odder still, he has suddenly taken a fancy to his brother's love interest, the fallen Lucy Whitaker. Lucy was once thrown over by a lord and she has little desire to let it happen again, but she's about to learn that his desires just might be enough for the both of them.

Passions of a Gentleman—Having been thrown over twice already, Simon Appleton has given up his pursuit for a wife—especially if his only choice is the elusive Miss Henrietta Hughes. But when he discovers a secret about her, he's not above helping to protect her...

If you'd like to stay current on Rose's releases, please visit her website at www.rosegordon.net to sign up for her new release newsletter.

While you wait for the next Regency, why not take a trip to Fort Gibson where three handsome Army Officers are about to find love where they least expect it!

Fort Gibson Officers Series

American-set historical romance series that takes place in Indian Territory in the mid-1840s.

The Officer and the Bostoner—While on her way to meet her intended, Allison Pearson was abandoned by her traveling party at a desolate Army fort in the middle of Indian Territory. It's a good thing there is a handsome, smooth talking officer named Captain Wes Tucker will temporarily marry her until her intended can reclaim her.

The Officer and the Southerner—Lieutenant Jack Walker sent off for a mail-order bride. Ella Davis answered the ad. Jack forgot to mention a few living details, and Ella's about to let him know it!

The Officer and the Traveler—Captain Grayson Montgomery's mouth has landed him in trouble again! And this time it's not something a cleverly worded sentence and a handsome smile can fix. Having been informed he'll either have to marry or be demoted and sentenced to hard labor for the remainder of his tour, he proposes, only to discover those years of hard labor may have been the easier choice for his heart.

And the series that started it all...

Scandalous Sisters Series

Three American sisters have arrived in England for a brief visit, but they're about to all find something they never bargained for: love.

Intentions of the Earl—Faced with never-ending poverty, a gentleman is offered a handsome sum if he'll ruin a certain young lady's future—only she has other plans, and it might entail her ruining *his.*

Liberty for Paul—There's only one thing Liberty Banks hates worse than impropriety: one Mr. Paul Grimes, and unfortunately for her, it's her own impropriety that just got her married to him!

To Win His Wayward Wife—Not to be outdone by her sisters' scandalous marriages, Madison Banks is about to have her own marriage-producing scandal to a man who, unbeknownst to her has loved her all along.

Groom Series

Four decided bachelors are about to have their freedom ripped right from their clutches with nothing to show for it but love.

Her Sudden Groom—When informed he must marry within the month or be forced to marry the worst harpy ever to set foot on English shores, the overly scientific, always logical Alex Banks decides to conduct his courtship like a science experiment!

Her Reluctant Groom—Emma Green has loved Marcus, Lord Sinclair for as long as she can remember, so when he slips up and says he loves her, too, it should all be so simple. But it's never that simple when the man in question was once been engaged to and jilted by Emma's older sister.

Her Secondhand Groom—What Patrick Ramsey, Lord Drakely AKA Lord Presumptuous wanted was an ordinary village girl to be a "motherness" to his daughters and stay out of his bedroom; what he's about to get is something so much more.

Her Imperfect Groom— Sir Wallace Benedict is a thrice-jilted baronet who is about to finally have his happily-ever-after, if only the family of his one-true-love, would stop being so darn meddlesome!

Banks Brothers' Brides

The first two are prequels to the previous series and the second two are follow ups.

His Contract Bride—Since just a lad, Edward Banks, Lord Watson knew Regina Harris would one day be his bride, he'd seen the paper to prove it many times; only someone forgot to inform Regina...

His Yankee Bride—John Banks wants *nothing* to do with the scandalous, sweet talking, ever-present, American beauty named Carolina, or so that's what he keeps saying...

His Jilted Bride—Amelia Brice has a secret...and so does Elijah Banks. Hers is big...but his is bigger!

His Brother's Bride—Presented with a marriage contract his twin brother has signed but cannot fulfill, Henry Banks has to form a plan to save the Banks name, even if it means pretending he's his brother, or worse yet, marrying a lady who holds a grudge against his family.

About the Author

USA Today Bestselling and Award Winning Author Rose Gordon writes unusually unusual historical romances that have been known to include scarred heroes, feisty heroines, marriage-producing scandals, far too much scheming, naughty literature and always a sweet happily-ever-after. When not escaping to another world via reading or writing a book, she spends her time chasing two young boys around the house, being hunted by wild animals, or sitting on the swing in the backyard where she has to use her arms as shields to deflect projectiles AKA: balls, water balloons, sticks, pinecones, and anything else one of her boys picks up to hurl at his brother who just happens to be hiding behind her.

She can be found somewhere in cyberspace at:

http://www.rosegordon.net

or blogging about *something* inappropriate at:

http://rosesromanceramblings.wordpress.com

Rose would love to hear from her readers and you can e-mail her at rose.gordon@hotmail.com

You can also find her on Facebook, Goodreads, and Twitter.

If you never want to miss a new release, click here to subscribe to her New Release list or visit her website to subscribe and you'll be notified each time a new book becomes available.